D1708567

Miracle in the Ozarks

Miracle in the Ozarks

The inspiring story of Faith, Hope, and *Hard Work U.*

Jerry C. Davis

Copyright © 2007 College of the Ozarks®

All rights reserved.
Printed in the United States of America.
First Printing April 2007
Second Printing April 2008
Third Printing October 2009
Fourth Printing August 2014
Fifth Printing May 2018
Sixth Printing December 2021

For additional copies of this book,
or for information about College of the Ozarks, contact:
Office of the President
College of the Ozarks
P. O. Box 17
Point Lookout, Missouri 65726
417-690-2470
www.cofo.edu

To Shirley,
my wife of many years,
whose shared commitments and
companionship have been indispensable
in my life's unlikely journey--from a broken
home to an impossible dream.

All proceeds from this book will go toward the operation of Camp Lookout--a camp for deserving youngsters where students at College of the Ozarks serve as counselors, thereby helping themselves by helping others.

Contents

Foreword

This book tells the story of a uniquely American college. I am proud to be a first reader of this magnificent journey from its creation through its development and the bringing to maturity of a place so unusual as to be classified as one of a kind and one of the best. I have known the author, Dr. Jerry Davis, for over thirty years, and as an ardent admirer, I regard him also as one of a kind and one of the best.

The story of the College of the Ozarks, or *Hard Work U.* as it is known, and how it came to be is inspiring. The development of this school parallels much of the story of America during the 20th century. You will read about faith, humble roots, sacrifice, and hard work--the building blocks of our nation. The end product of this is reflected in the character of the College today. It is a place where visits from prominent leaders, including presidents and prime ministers, have become commonplace.

That the College of the Ozarks has appeared on the national scene late in the 20th century is no accident. It has taken its place as the result of unparalleled efforts on the part of committed people led by a president totally dedicated to its mission. Educated at a work school, he knows firsthand the meaning of the school he leads. He identifies with the students who attend the College. He was one of three small boys left to be raised by godly grandparents, and with strong ambition and hard work, he attained high success from modest beginnings.

During over fifty years of leadership in higher education, I have observed one thing most essential to institutional success: leadership. No institution is any better than its leadership nor can it thrive, by that I mean stay focused on its mission, without this ingredient. It is what determines success or failure, as well as excellence or mediocrity.

This school has been fortified by unusual leadership throughout its history. Those in its early years brought the enterprise into existence and were followed by persuasive and dedicated men, such as R. M. Good and M. Graham Clark, who led it through stages appropriate for its time. What they accomplished is simply amazing. The transition from Dr. Clark to Dr. Davis involved two short-term presidents seeking to adjust and adapt to the kind of forceful leadership essential to bringing the College out of a period of financial strain and setting it on its road to high acclaim.

I know of no other college or university president as capable of the strong leadership required at this time in the history of this college than Jerry Davis. He is as mission-driven as the College itself. He knows when to act and how to act. He never makes plans without action, nor does he take action without plans. He is a bull-by-the-horns kind of leader who is determined, confident, persevering and apt to prevail in staying the course as he strengthens the foundation on which this college is built. His faith is sure and his trust is beyond himself.

The author's capability as an outstanding educational leader is complemented by his reputation as a man of character, friendly disposition, warm personality, unpretentious style, and unyielding determination to maintain the historic mission of the College. He has not allowed the school to wander from its basic purposes as a small school with a big mission, even as it evolved into a highly respected college.

This story is told in a captivating manner balanced by a description equally as vivid for its early and mid-years as for the years of its author's leadership. Building upon these foundations from the past, the College has advanced to a new level of service and quality. An ardent salesman for his college, Dr. Davis's capacity at raising money has been the hallmark which has made possible the dramatic progress during his tenure.

It has been my good fortune to have visited scores of college and university campuses across this great land. In so doing, a few of them stand out as truly different. This is one of them. I can say with conviction that those who have been responsible for building the College to its current and respected level of quality and service in the one hundred years of its existence have pioneered an institution that reflects "The American Dream," where faith, opportunity, and hard work intersect.

During the time of turmoil on college campuses across the country, one of the students at this college was asked about burning down buildings. His response was, "If you help build the buildings, you are not interested in burning them down." This represents the results of an environment that has produced citizens of all dimensions, including, among many others, two Marine Corps generals, an Air Force general, a Missouri State Senator, and an ABC News national correspondent. Basic American values and character are the result of the work ethic of this truly American institution with its Christian commitment.

I have been on the campus of *Hard Work U.* many times. I enjoy being a part of and supporting a school that is focused on helping youngsters help themselves to a higher education and a better way of life. Not far from Branson, Missouri, it's in a beautiful part of our country. I encourage you to visit, and I know you will enjoy reading about its remarkable first one hundred years.

While many good men have led the school and ultimately the College over the years, history will credit Dr. Davis's strong and visionary leadership during the past twenty years for lifting the College to the national level and the high reputation it has attained at the publishing of this excellent story. He, along with the College, has risen high in the ranks of his compatriots in higher education and his contemporaries in the community of which he has been a part. Yet, his time to fade away has not yet come. He has promises to keep and miles to go before he sleeps.

Truly, the slogan historically interwoven in the fabric of its history, "No greater gift can man bestow, than giving of his life to help others grow," is appropriate for those who are described in this book as the movers and shakers of its progress over the years.

This book is an easy and interesting and inspiring read.

Dr. E. Bruce Heilman, Chancellor
University of Richmond

Introduction and Acknowledgements

Writing this book has been an arduous, though meaningful, experience.

It has been arduous in the sense that much of the material for the book was collected over a period of a dozen years while I was, at the same time, serving in the presidency of this unique institution. The College of the Ozarks has evolved into a focused but complex organization with expectations in every direction. Anyone who knows much about the demands of the contemporary college or university presidency understands the challenge of taking on a book-writing project simultaneously. Most such presidencies simply don't last long enough.

In the process, I have also found this task to be very meaningful. The heart of this book is reflected in the lives of those individuals who granted interviews, giving me a chance informally to discuss and record conversations about the College. I am deeply grateful to those who shared their personal stories which I have tried to weave into a narrative; they were both interesting and inspiring. There are obviously many, many others associated with this school who could equally have contributed to this project.

From those interviewed, I have extracted what seemed to be the essentials, enough to help tell the story of The

School of the Ozarks, now the College of the Ozarks. The goal has certainly not been to write a history of the institution. The *Flight of the Phoenix* by Helen and Townsend Godsey covers three-fourths of the school's history, and no doubt it will eventually be updated. Accordingly, not every building, event, or personality through one hundred years of existence is mentioned, as it is not within the scope of this book to do so. Many of the sources used are listed at the back of the book. Also, a general timeline has been provided.

An asset in the writing of this book has been the easy access to the College's archives, board minutes, old periodicals, publications, and correspondence, as well as my personal knowledge of some of the College's leaders and benefactors.

Photographs from the College's archives, public relations office, and friends were used and very much appreciated. Also, many of the photographs of recent prominent speakers on campus are the result of the excellent work of Larry Plumlee, Kevin White, and the Washington Speakers Bureau.

The following individuals, both living and deceased, provided firsthand accounts of much of what has been written: Mr. York Jackson, Tempe, Arizona; Mrs. Willa (Coulter) King, Owasso, Oklahoma; Mr. Douglas Mahnkey, Forsyth, Missouri; Dr. Roy Southard, Springfield, Missouri; Mrs. June (Keener) Moore, Rensselaer, Indiana; Mrs. Eula (Shelton) Shipman, Chadwick, Missouri; Mr. Ray Simkins and Mrs. Delphia (Phillips) Simkins, Blue Eye, Missouri; Dr. Harry Basore, Leawood, Kansas; Mrs. Annabelle McMaster, Forsyth, Missouri; Mr. J. Hugh

Wise, Springfield, Missouri; Lucille (Knight) Harp, Clark Fork, Idaho; Mrs. Margaret (Willbanks) Applegate, Holts Summit, Missouri; Mr. Roy Hopper, Albuquerque, New Mexico; Dr. M. Graham Clark, Point Lookout, Missouri; Mr. Stanley Dixon, Alpena, Arkansas; Dr. Beulah (Gutridge) Winfrey, Point Lookout, Missouri; Dr. G. Stanley Fry, Point Lookout, Missouri; Dr. Mayburn Davidson, Walnut Shade, Missouri; Mr. Jerry Brannan, Phoenix, Arizona; Dr. Howell Keeter, Point Lookout, Missouri; Mr. Gary Wortman, Springfield, Missouri; Mrs. Ruth (Cheek) Raley, Point Lookout, Missouri; Dr. Kenton Olson, Branson, Missouri; Mr. F. Lowell Hawkins, Chuluota, Florida; Mr. Earl Woodard, Kirkwood, Missouri; Mrs. Judy (Mackey) Morisset, Ozark, Missouri; Mr. Francisco "Frank" Moreno, Las Vegas, Nevada; Mr. James Keeter, Atlanta, Georgia; Dr. Courtney Furman, Branson, Missouri; and Miss Lynda Jesse, Point Lookout, Missouri. All deserve a hearty "Thank You."

Others who have been helpful with this project include Mrs. Linda Schmidt, reference librarian, Mrs. Ruth Raley, secretary to the Board of Trustees, Ms. Gwen Simmons, media specialist, and Mrs. Helen Youngblood, director of alumni affairs.

A few individuals took quite a bit of time to review the manuscript and make helpful suggestions: my wife, Shirley; former Distinguished Professor Dr. Bradford Crain; College Attorney Virginia Fry; Chancellor E. Bruce Heilman, and Professor Dr. Hayden Head.

My longtime secretary and assistant, Tamara Schneider, deserves much credit for the culmination of this book project. Keeping up with years of interviews, transcribing interviews, and arranging and searching for materials was a major undertaking in and of itself. She gladly accepted the extra work, while also managing the myriad activities of a president's office. No doubt, there were times when Tamara was unsure if the project would ever be finished or even if I would be around to finish it. Our goal was to finish the book for the Centennial Celebration, especially for the benefit of the alumni and supporters of the College.

The staff and students of the graphic arts department deserve credit for the creative jacket design. Craig Cogdill, along with Laura Lane and Don Codillo were especially helpful.

Near the end of this book you will read a letter written by a student at College of the Ozarks. Many of the struggles of this student have been experienced by others, including me.

Writing this book has given me an opportunity to reflect on so many things I have in common with that student, as well as with this institution.

My growing up in a broken home has forever influenced my life. But so did those who helped me along the way, as I went off to a little self-help work school. I never dreamed that one day I would be responsible for running one. It was at The Berry Schools that a "head, heart, and hands" philosophy of education opened to me the doors of the future, a future that led to the presidency of America's most distinctive self-help college. As a Berry student, I learned firsthand much about what was needed to succeed in life: faith, hope (even dreams), and hard work.

For some thirty years Shirley and I have tried to make a difference, during a presidency at Alice Lloyd College in

Kentucky and now, for two decades, at the College of the Ozarks. I am most grateful to those who saw potential in me so many years ago, to the individuals and institutions who contributed to who I am. The College of the Ozarks reflects my own life's journey. Its values are the same as mine: commitment to the Christian faith, the value of just plain hard work and perseverance, and a love of country which never goes out of style.

To have led *Hard Work U.* is one of God's richest blessings in my life. To tell its story is a privilege.

Jerry C. Davis

Chapter I
"We Must Give These People a Chance."

"This is a red-letter day...We have lived all these years hoping, praying for a chance to give our children a better education...We have a duty to perform...We are not an ungrateful people. Ingratitude is a crime. I believe we will do our duty and do it well...."

A sense of commitment was reflected in these words uttered on The School's opening day by a local citizen humbled by the occasion. Colonel A. S. Prather's remarks focused on values such as duty, loyalty, and especially trust. The depth of his feelings for unity of purpose was revealed by his choice of an illustration:

> Before the capstone was placed upon the vault, at the laying of the cornerstone, when it was asked if any person had anything further to deposit, two old veterans of the Civil War, without previous understanding, one of whom had worn the blue and the other the gray, each took from the lapel of his coat the badge of his respective order and placed them side by side in the cornerstone, where they rest in peace, typical of the union of hearts and hands, of a reunified country under one flag, and of the united efforts which will make of this School of the Ozarks all that its name implies. May the management prove as fraternal and as loyal to their trust as did these grizzled veterans to the cause each believed to be right.

The Colonel's gratitude for the inception of what was

first called The School of the Ozarks was clear to all who heard him. "Today is a glorious epoch in the history of Taney county. We rejoice in the fruition of our hopes. No words of mine can tell how thankful we are for this great blessing...."

Following Colonel Prather's remarks, the keynote address was given by prominent Presbyterian churchman E. C. Gordon. His address, covered by the *Taney County Republican,* focused on just exactly what the new school should represent. Dr. Gordon described the great good to be done "through the education of hand and brain and heart of the young men and women...."

The character of the education which was envisioned for what is now College of the Ozarks was clear from the start. It was to educate the "head, heart, and hands." Its overall goal, as stated by Helen and Townsend Godsey in their book *Flight of the Phoenix,* was equally as clear from the start: "to promote the cause of Jesus Christ through the avenue of education to any who were willing to work for it--to learn as they earned!"

But the idea for such an institution did not originate with either Colonel Prather or Dr. Gordon. Credit must be given to James F. Forsythe (Fig. 1). No doubt Colonel Prather, in his welcome, was signaling the grati-

Fig. 1
Reverend James Forsythe (far right) and relatives

tude, as well as the duty of the people, to honor the intentions of the Reverend Mr. James Forsythe, whose dream for such an institution was becoming a reality.

According to the late Mrs. James F. Forsythe, it had been the original intent of her husband to become a missionary to Africa. Apparently God had other plans for him as a missionary within his home state of Missouri--in what was the isolated, poor section of the country known as "the Ozarks."

Forsythe could not have been prepared for what awaited him in the Ozarks. Educated at Westminster in Missouri and Union Seminary in Virginia, the young evangelist of the Presbyterian Church must have been in culture shock the few years he spent in and around Taney County, Missouri. But his reaction to what he saw gave birth to a uniquely American institution--one built on faith, hard work, and intellect.

Reverend Forsythe, no doubt, became deeply bothered by what he saw in the Ozarks, especially the plight of youngsters who were bright but with little hope for a better future. High schools were scarce, school terms were erratic, and money was even more difficult to obtain for education.

Mrs. Forsythe (Fig. 2) later wrote in her notes that

from the beginning her husband said, "We must give these people a chance." Reverend James Forsythe had a real zeal

Fig. 2
Reverend and Mrs. James Forsythe, later years

for missions, and he saw in the Ozarks the potential to make a difference. But he needed help and turned again and again to his family, friends, and the Church.

Before long, young Forsythe was practically begging the Home Missions Committee of his church for help. His longtime friend Dr. E. C. Gordon was encouraging, and so was Dr. W. R. Dobyns. There were, of course, other sympathizers to the constant pleas coming from the "missionary in the Ozarks," but support was hard to come by. Very few "northerners" from upstate Missouri knew much about the Ozarks, and even fewer had seen the area.

Forsythe's pleas for help were so dire that some didn't believe things could be so bad "down there." Mrs. Forsythe remembered Dr. Charles Foreman. "He would say, 'I don't believe a word Jim Forsythe says about that field of his. Conditions such as he describes plainly do not exist in Missouri. I would have to see it before I would believe those things he tells us.' As a result Reverend Forsythe asked Dr. Foreman to visit him on the field...They walked miles. They climbed mountains. They crossed the streams by swimming and holding their clothes high above their heads." Apparently, Dr. Foreman's shoes were literally worn out on the trip. But his eyes were opened, and he joined others in believing something should be done.

The young home missionary, James Forsythe, never faltered in his zeal to attract attention of the Church to the people of the Ozark hill country. Mrs. Forsythe wrote that he "admired the mountain people. Many were uneducated and underprivileged, but to him they were people, and people for whom Christ died. He wanted better things for them--salvation, education, material blessings."

One of Reverend Forsythe's most publicized letters began, "Once again, I am petitioning the Synod for help to found a school here in the Ozarks. As I have pointed out previously, the need is present and it should be the mission of the Church to undertake the task of providing the boys and girls of the Ozarks with an education...."

But still not much help came, other than the Education Committee having recorded that such a school be considered. Young Forsythe, perhaps out of desperation or a sense of urgency, started taking matters into his own hands by conducting his own "summer school" in the area. This really stirred up local interest, but then things ebbed when Forsythe was called to another assignment. Probably, few understood the impact the young missionary had made. But he had lit a flame, and the budding interest in a Christian work school continued. The Church Synod made a bold decision to start The School, but finding funds was almost as difficult as finding those willing to listen to James Forsythe's early pleas for help.

The effort of Dr. William R. Dobyns (Fig. 3), Chairman of the Home Missions Committee, was critical in getting money to construct a building and start The School of the Ozarks. Local citizens cleared the very ground for the pro-

posed school atop Mt. Huggins, overlooking Swan Creek in the tiny village of Forsyth, Missouri. At the groundbreaking, Reverend A. Y. Beatie described in the *Taney County Republican* newspaper the nature of The School being established:

Fig. 3
Dr. William R. Dobyns

The Literary Department staffed with "experienced and successful teachers"; The Industrial Department with work "...to provide a way for those who have no means for securing an education...." And the Religious Department which was to be non-sectarian but where "The Bible will be taught as any other textbook, and the principles of Gospel truth essential to salvation will be kept before the mind of the student."

The year was 1906 and James Forsythe's dream was to become a reality. With minimal funds and maximum prayer, a cornerstone-laying was held for the first building, thanks to the herculean effort of church members and local residents. Reverend Forsythe was invited back for the event and spoke to those assembled. He was properly credited by the public and press with the idea for beginning such a school.

The Taney County Republican covered the cornerstone-laying in its October 18, 1906, edition reporting, "Intense Interest Shown." The following week's edition offered a synopsis of the ground-breaking program:

> Reverend James F. Forsythe briefly outlined the history of the inception of the undertaking, as was fitting, he having been under Providence chosen to take the first steps...his name is appropriately linked with the history of the institution.

Dr. E. C. Gordon's remarks concerning "The Importance of Training the Mind" were cited:

> It was his part to show that it [The School of the Ozarks] stood for the best intellectual training. There was no need to occupy much time in showing the importance of such training.

Next, Reverend A. Y. Beatie discussed "The Importance

of Industrial Training." The paper quoted Beatie:

> He showed its importance to the student in that it would
> enable him (the student) to secure the advantages of the
> mental training so purposefully set forth by Dr. Gordon.
> It would help solve the problem confronting many a boy
> and girl with ambition but without the means to secure
> an education.

A summary of Beatie's remarks included important values (self-respect, self-discipline, etc.) to be taught in this area.

Finally, Reverend L. E. McNair's comments on "The Importance of Religious Training" were explained:

> By way of introduction, he emphasized the point that
> though the money to equip and the men to manage the
> 'School of the Ozarks' had been furnished by the Presby-
> terian Church, the religious training in the school would
> in no sense be sectarian in character. The fundamental
> principles of the religion of Jesus Christ would be taught,
> and that in a way that would be agreeable to all evangeli-
> cal denominations.

McNair's final comment was carried in the paper: "all mental training and industrial development would come to naught unless the life was also trained in the religion of Jesus Christ."

By late fall the Articles of Incorporation were issued. The official seal of The School of the Ozarks was adopted, including the Latin inscription *"Menti Manui et Animo"* or "for the mind, for the hand, and for the soul." An operating philosophy of educating the head, hands and heart was breathed into the institution's creation.

Months later, the first day of school finally arrived on Tuesday, September 24, 1907. We know from Colonel Prather's remarks that opening day was a banner day. Few could have envisioned that what was beginning as a

Fig. 4
Willa (Coulter) King, later in life

small, self-help, Christian school with only the lower grades would one day touch the lives of so many and blossom into one of America's most admired institutions.

Willa (Coulter) King (Fig. 4) enrolled on opening day. Her story is typical of most students in the early years. "I was eight years old and in the third grade. I was a day student.

"There were six children in the family and I was the fourth one down. There were three boys and three girls. I walked to The School. It was just half a mile."

Mrs. King remembers well The School's environment. "Mr. Utterback was principal. I know the thing we enjoyed the most was our May Pole Drill. I was always in it. I was on the basketball team, as short as I am. I jumped center. I was five foot then, and I am four feet ten now!" The School apparently had uniforms, "bloomers and a midi."

Mrs. King remembers more than school activities; she recalls class expectations. "We went to chapel every day and we had Bible every day. I studied the Bible every day I was in school. And I know I memorized verses. I have a Scofield Bible that I won for memorizing the most verses a certain time. I think there were over 600 that I knew and could tell where they were in the Bible."

Evidently, learning took place in a disciplined environment as Mrs. King described. "It was no-nonsense. They didn't put up with any foolishness. They [teachers] took students out and made them sit in the corner when they'd whisper. That is what students were punished for more than anything else. I never took part. I wouldn't answer when they would talk to me." When asked if she would have gotten into more trouble at home if she'd caused a problem at school, she laughed, "Considerable more and I knew it. Mother and Daddy agreed with the teachers; they stood right behind them all the time."

From the earliest years students sensed a serious school. They had to work, study, behave, and worship together. Chapel was a thread running through the school year, but it was not denominational. Mrs. King remembers, "My mother was a Methodist, and my Daddy was a Baptist, but we all went to this Presbyterian school."

The little school was focused on its mission and, from the earliest years, didn't miss an opportunity to ask others to support it. In the third year of operation (1909), a little newsletter was sent out to friends for twenty-five cents per year. The first issue of *Our Visitor* got directly to the point:

> The aim and purpose of this monthly visitor to your home is to bring you information concerning our work, our plans, and our ideals, for we have ideals and with your assistance and the blessing of the All Wise we propose to realize them. Not all at once. 'Rome was not built in a day....' If you will show us your faith by YOUR CHECKS we will show you our faith by our works. It is an easy thing to say in public and in private 'Thy Kingdom Come.' It is an entirely different thing to offer that prayer by DOING SOMETHING to bring it...One of our needs is that we may have a printing press...God's work in the world is done by a few. Does He ask that THIS WORK be helped by YOU?

The little paper went on to ask for miracles: $10,000 for a girls dormitory, $10,000 for a boys dormitory, $5,000 for equipment, $100 for a scholarship (work) or $10 for a donation for a library book. Clearly, fund-raising was infused into the life of The School from its roots and has never diminished.

Even more than its public relations and fund-raising objectives, the newsletter in its very first issue explains to the reader THE BEST EDUCATION in an article by Trustee Chairman William R. Dobyns. "This is what The School of the Ozarks desires and is determined to furnish. Let us inquire, 'What is the best education?' In answering this I shall outline the purpose of this school."

Chairman Dobyns eloquently answers his own question:

1) Education of the heart--that is, the training of young men and women to know and to realize their relation to God and to their fellowmen. The Bible says, 'As a man thinketh in his heart, so is he.' Then it is all important that the heart be right to make the life right. We therefore make the Bible, which is the word of God, the foundation of our system of education; give it a place in the course of study of such prominence as it deserves, and require all students to study it every year of their course.

2) Education of the head--that is, the development of the mind, through study, for effective work in any subject that may ever come to it. We therefore have equipped The School with most competent teachers who are able to open up to the pupil the treasures of knowledge and to train young men and women to THINK.

3) Education of the hand--that is, the fitting of young people for the practical duties of home, and also of trades. To this end we require every pupil to do his or her share in the work about the house and farm. By this we mean just the things that any boy or girl would have to do at their homes....

Still, the editor of this little newsletter felt more needed to be said about the religious nature of the developing school:

> With the opening of The School of the Ozarks a systematic course in Bible study is entered upon. The purpose of this course is not merely to give our students an intelligent view of the contents of the Bible but primarily to win them to a saving knowledge of Christ and to build them up in Christian character.

Further, the Bible Department was reported to be successful in carrying out its mission:

> The first year of The School was marked by...the conversion of nearly every student in the boarding department.

> The second year (last year) several students openly confessed Christ...two young men and one young woman are preparing themselves for work in the foreign field.

> This department is sorely in need of good missionary literature such as an Encyclopedia of Missions, Atlas and Geography of Missions, readable biographies of missionaries, good stories and tracts bearing on missions.

By its third year of operation, it is obvious that the little school desired to play a role in carrying out, as well as reflecting, the Great Commission.

To carry out its grand vision, The School attracted dedicated teachers from the very start. Mrs. Willa King fondly recalls just a few: "Miss Craig, Miss Grace taught the Bible, Miss Pogue, J. F. Oliver, Lyta Davis--she was a friend to everybody."

The teachers that joined in pioneering The School were hardworking and dedicated. They faced hardships that would have deterred the fainthearted. For example, The School was big in heart but minimal in facilities. The main building that constituted the campus was Mitchell

Fig. 5 Mitchell Hall, Forsyth, Missouri

Hall (Fig. 5), a large stone structure built by the contributions and sweat labor of citizens and school people alike. It sat atop a hill near the small Ozark town of Forsyth, with a commanding view of Swan Creek and the White River below.

Mitchell Hall was used to house students and provide classroom and work areas. From the time The School opened in September of 1907 until it was moved in 1915, Mitchell Hall was the only major building The School enjoyed. Other nearby wooden structures were ancillary.

Mitchell Hall was the physical heart of The School as remembered by all who lived and studied there. But it was not to survive. On a cold, wintry night a few days after

Christmas (1914), The School's building went up in flames, shortly before Mrs. Willa King was to have graduated.

One who vividly remembers this dreadful occasion was a young man by the name of York Jackson (Fig. 6), who was born in nearby Bradleyville, just a few miles from the fledgling school.

Fig. 6
York Jackson,
later in life

"I have walked a many a time from Bradleyville to The School," he recalls. "My father owned a little farm at Bradleyville and had a general store. I have been told he was a very industrious fellow. And, he was also postmaster at two or three different times. I think he was the oldest member of a family of about twelve."

York Jackson was only four when his father died and six when his mother died. He sadly remembers, "Both of them had tuberculosis. Just worked too hard. I know there was no cure at the time."

Most of the earliest students came from poor backgrounds, at least materially. In that sense, York Jackson was typical. But, losing his parents at an early age placed a greater burden on him (and his two brothers), and home was never a stable location. "My father's brother was my guardian, you see. He had a family of seven children--six boys and a girl. He sorta took me under his wing. I was shuffled around from one place to the other...finally landed with a distant relative of mine who had three daughters! I was there until I went to The School."

When York Jackson showed up on the doorstep of The School of the Ozarks in 1914, he was impressed with what he saw. Mitchell Hall certainly impressed him. "I was surprised at the enormity of it," he laughed. "It was a big building."

Through the eyes of young York Jackson, his prayers were being answered. "The School rescued me in the summer of 1914...and was my home for five years, with no cost to me. I am still amazed and deeply grateful."

York Jackson worked hard at this new school, in and out of class. "I think one of the first things I did was harness up old Beck and go out into the field and do some plowing." The work ethic was no stranger to York Jackson.

Mr. Jackson remembers his academic record as "not outstanding" and President John Crockett as "a father-like fellow. He did his best to get me to go into the ministry, but I was just not prepared."

Actually, Reverend Crockett was the acting president. His predecessor had resigned during the summer that Mr. Jackson showed up for school. The Board turned to Reverend Crockett, belovedly called the Bishop of the Ozarks, and agreed to pay him $300 for the school year and to support Crockett and his mother.

No doubt most of the activities of the little school centered around Mitchell Hall. Other than nearby Independence Hall, a small wooden structure, not much of a campus existed on the few surrounding acres.

According to York Jackson, Mitchell Hall served as kitchen, dining hall, classroom, men's dormitory (second floor), women's dormitory (third floor), and some offices. This was pretty much what schools would have housed in separate buildings, all crammed into one! And so this is the way it was. That is, until Tuesday, January 12, 1915. On this date, remembers York Jackson, a big fire virtually destroyed The School of the Ozarks, and with it the hopes and dreams of many.

"It was right after the Christmas holidays," Mr. Jackson sadly recalled. "Back then we didn't consider New Year's a holiday...I was in this ward at about one or two o'clock in the morning. Well, I had a dream that night that some big animal had gotten in the girls department, and I heard some girls screaming--that woke me up, and they were hollering, 'Fire! Fire!' I woke the boys up. I threw the trunk--we had all we owned in our trunk--out the window. We were on the second floor. We began to get out of the building."

Evidently the students, staff, and community tried as hard as they knew how to save the building. But it was too late. Mr. Jackson still remembers their efforts. "I was scared. Most of us boys got our trunks and threw them out the window. Down on the second floor, one of the boys, Roy Parkey, and I got a piano down the first steps. I recall that after that I tried to lift my end of that piano, and I couldn't. But Roy and I finally got it down."

The cause of the big fire was debated. But Mr. Jackson remembers, "We found out later that one of the girls had taken a wax candle in one of the dressing rooms looking for some clothes, and it caught afire. She went to sleep. The fire got started and I guess it got under the floor. When it got out on the floor it scorched her feet--it was so hot. But that's how the fire got started."

Regardless of how the fire got started, the results were devastating (Fig. 7). The main building was gone. Much of what little the students had was up in flames, even meager Christmas gifts.

Fig. 7
Mitchell Hall, smouldering ruins (early 1915)

"Several of the students didn't come back after the fire," according to York Jackson. "I didn't have anywhere to go. That was my home for five years."

Property loss was great, but no lives were lost, and there were just a few injuries. "Other than those girls that scorched their feet, those were the only injuries I ever heard of," explained Mr. Jackson.

The surrounding community reacted to the disaster with open arms. Many of the students were taken in by nearby families. Meetings were held in the community to see what could be done to help the little school that had been reduced to a pile of rubble. A makeshift dining hall was even constructed. But a certain uneasiness prevailed because the future of The School was now in question.

Exactly two weeks after The School had burned to the ground, the Board of Trustees met in Kansas City. The minutes from this critical meeting show a businesslike, don't-give-up approach to what must have seemed like insurmountable obstacles. A small group of trustees, led by the ever-present Chairman William R. Dobyns, had visited The School shortly after the fire and summed up for the Board what they had gleaned from their visit:

- The entire loss of Mitchell Hall

16

- The safety of every person in the building, with loss of much of their personal effects
- The saving of a small amount of property in the building, such as manual training equipment and some bedding
- The cordial hospitality of the citizens in caring for those made homeless
- The generous offer of the people of the community to provide a temporary kitchen and dining room
- The tender of the local board of education of the free use of certain rooms in their new school building for continuing our classes

The record shows that the Trustees methodically faced their problems. They launched into a thorough discussion about the future of The School and after "a most thorough discussion," adopted a resolution of their intent--"to continue the work of The School." In their actions that day, housing of students was temporarily discontinued, other than for those that could be crammed into the still-standing Independence Hall. They also decided to retain as many grades as possible, accepted the local school board's offer for temporary facilities, elected officers and appointed standing committees, and designated a committee of five (with Dr. Dobyns as chairman), "to formulate adequate plans for the future of The School."

This historic meeting, that signaled that The School of the Ozarks still had a future, closed with a board directive, "to have printed and immediately circulate an announcement of the action of the Board with reference to the fire and future of The School." By this time it was evident that Dr. Dobyns was the "glue" holding the Board together and his leadership was undoubtedly looking providential.

The meeting closed with prayer.

Chapter II
"God Had Sent Yet Another Blessing...."

The trustee committee charged with planning for the future of The School wasted no time in facing up to its challenge. Its efforts were obviously fueled more by faith than funds. It could count on only $15,000 it had received in insurance money for Mitchell Hall, now lying in smoldering ruins.

It must have been a shock when word leaked out that the Trustees were looking beyond The School's location on Swan Creek. No doubt, most locals simply expected Mitchell Hall to be rebuilt, and they were prepared to do their part in starting over. But the committee made an exhaustive report to its chairman, and Dr. Dobyns evidently moved quickly when he learned of the availability of a large facility already constructed and land to go with it.

The large structure that captured Dr. Dobyns' imagination was not located overlooking Swan Creek, but nearly twelve miles away overlooking the White River, near the tiny Ozarks town of Hollister, Missouri. And, unlike the native stone Mitchell Hall, the large building was made of logs!

After seeing such a large building, Dr. Dobyns checked with as many board members as he could reach and acted quickly, taking a thirty-day option on the property by putting up $500 of earnest money. The agreed-upon purchase price for the building and acreage was $15,000, ironically the same amount as available funds!

Thus, at the Spring 1915 Board Meeting, while the little school was holding classes in a few rooms made available by the struggling Forsyth school district, the Trustees voted to relocate The School of the Ozarks, and they approved of the deal worked out by Dr. Dobyns.

The big log building at the new location was quite distinctive (Fig. 8). For several years it had served as a hunting lodge and had been moved to its present site from the 1904 St. Louis World's Fair, where it was known as the State of Maine building. The Hunting Club operated the lodge but lost interest in it, and apparently no one wanted to purchase such a large structure, even though it had a commanding view from a high bluff overlooking the White River.

Fig. 8 State of Maine building (Dobyns Hall)

From overlooking this high bluff, or the lookout, The School of the Ozarks opened for classes in September 1915. Its president had resigned. Its principal, Miss Weld, was in charge when the Trustees came to "campus" for a dedication of the building, with a renewed commitment to keep the little self-help school going. The official program was for "dedicating the building and all the property for the purpose of Christian education...." After the program the audience adjourned to town for a barbecue, which had been prepared by the people of nearby Hollister.

The School not only got a new location and a new lease on life, but the large log building got a new name. The Board named the major part of the building Dobyns Hall, in honor of its ever-present and able leader, Dr. William R. Dobyns. They also called one end of the building Mitchell Chapel to recognize another trustee and the now burned-out Mitchell Hall some twelve miles away.

Those who attended the fledgling Ozarks school at its new location recall that Dobyns Hall housed practically all of The School's operations until other buildings could be added. Students assembled in a large room for chapel, teachers and students were first housed in it, and the library, classroom and dining hall were all inside.

Of course, The School could only handle a few dozen students. Those who got the opportunity to enroll quickly sensed the seriousness in purpose of The School of the Ozarks, but a few still recall less than academic experiences.

Doug Mahnkey (Fig. 9) and Roy Southard (Fig. 10) were roommates. They were typical of the earliest students--from humble roots and large families.

Fig. 9
Doug Mahnkey,
as a young lawyer

Fig. 10
Roy Southard

"I graduated from a one-room school at Mincy, Missouri," Doug Mahnkey recalls. "My mother insisted that we try to get an education; high schools were scarce. My father drove a wagon to The School with a team of mules--had a little trunk with my things in it...."

"I was living at Pine Top," remembers Roy Southard, who must have been thrilled to meet up with Doug Mahnkey. "We knew each other. I remember the first day. I was surprised when I got over there. There was Doug Mahnkey!"

Due to the generosity of Kansas City businessman, H. T. Abernathy, the second building, Abernathy Hall, was begun as soon as the little school was taking root at its new location.

The contract for the building was "approved for

$11,475.06" by the Trustees. Sensing the significance of the times, the Trustees ordered a box be put in the cornerstone of the building, a tiny box which was made by York Jackson, one of a few students who stuck with The School during its relocation. The box contained some very special articles--including a Bible. It was to be opened fifty years later.

"There were two buildings there," Doug Mahnkey remembers. "We all ate over at the Maine building [Dobyns Hall]." He says teachers and students lived, ate, worshiped and studied together. "They had a big bell on a pole. And, they would ring that bell for classes, for us to get up, for meals, and for time to retire at night."

With very few material comforts, Roy Southard and Doug Mahnkey became good friends. They almost died together. "Roy was so sick," according to Doug, "and I was sick. Roy was just coughing terribly. They separated us, and I don't know which one of us they thought was going to die. But we both pulled through."

Roy Southard remembers well that The School may have changed physical locations, but little else changed. Certainly not The School's operating philosophy.

"It was a very strict school," Roy says. Everybody had to work and Roy's assignment was simple enough, "to cut wood." Everybody had to work four hours a day. "If they didn't they could expect to be 'booted out,'" he remembers.

Roy says that girls made up about half of the student body. No exceptions were made for them. "They did housework and kitchen work. I think some of them helped pick green beans; we always had a green bean patch. We picked them and canned them for food. The girls were there, and the boys were glad of it!"

As Roy remembers, complaints about the food, or the quantity of it, were common. "We didn't have plentiful food like you have here now. These kids were coming from off farms around there and were pretty well fed. You know, they knew what good food was. We were short of food, good food, but surprisingly everybody seemed to gain weight while we were complaining about the food!"

It was not all work and no play in those days. Students such as Roy Southard still managed to have fun, usually at someone else's expense.

Fellow student Durward Mackey found out. Roy and some of his friends took young Durward "hunting." "He [Durward] came the same year and from around Bradleyville. So, we took him snipe hunting. Snipe hunting was a trick we played on most anybody. We took them out looking for snipes, but there really wasn't any such thing as snipes."

Roy's tale continues, "We went out there north of The School, which was all woods then. He wanted to know what snipes were. We gave him a big sack and told him we didn't know, but if he saw a big bird come by, just put him in the sack! We left Durward out there. He stayed out there until about midnight.

"Of course it was very strict then. The rules were such that you were supposed to be in bed at nine o'clock. So he was scared to death to come in."

When Durward came in, Roy and his friends made things even more difficult. "We stretched a rope across the hall between the doors. So, when he came in, he tripped on that and fell down! He was trying to slip in. I think the proctor caught him and docked him so many hours."

While students like Roy, Doug, and Durward kept themselves busy trying to meet the expectations of The School, the Trustees were busy trying to keep The School going and adding buildings, which were desperately needed. But aside from the never-wavering leadership of Board Chairman W. R. Dobyns, The School had not been able to sustain executive leadership.

It was a critical time. During and after relocating, The School had been served by more than one faithful principal and president. But the demands at the growing little school required a special person who could run The School, raise money, build the Board, and deal with the Church hierarchy.

It was the need for fund-raising that brought one of the earliest challenges to the stability of The School. Some early success, such as the generous gifts of Abernathy and Stevenson Halls (in honor of Abernathy's wife), showed that the unique school had a strong appeal. The Board believed that it needed a leader to match the nearly overwhelming financial needs.

The Trustees received an early request to join another Synod college in a special joint campaign with The School sharing one-third of the expenses and getting one-third of the proceeds. But some trustees thought such an arrangement unwise, voted it down, and proceeded with the idea of their own campaign. Once again, the Board was approached about a joint campaign.

Squabbling over whether or not to participate in a joint campaign was just one troublesome issue before the

Board. Now in its fifth year at the new location (1920), other contentious concerns seemed to arise.

The October 20, 1920, meeting puts conditions in perspective. Saddled with yet another acting president, the Board listened to problem after problem. One trustee objected "to the purchase of mules." Another recommended decreasing the size of The School and said he "was opposed to the idea of a junior college."

Obviously, some trustees were thinking big. Any thought of a junior college is astounding, given the fact The School had no president, only three buildings, fewer than one hundred students, no endowment, and relied mostly on prayerful gift income to survive. Most lacking was strong, sustained leadership. Also, the idea of an endowment campaign had not yet gotten very far.

So it must have been an act of near desperation when at the aforementioned meeting, a trustee motion ordered that a "Dr. Cook be elected president of The School at a salary of $2,700 per year for the services of himself and his wife, he to assume the duties of president, as outlined by the Board, and Mrs. Cook to take the position of matron...." The Board then expressed its desire for the Cooks to visit The School and render their decision.

Perhaps the next board meeting (March 1921) will always be viewed as one of the most critical. For at this time it was reported that "Mrs. Cook made a visit to The School, and later a letter was received from Dr. Cook, stating that both he and Mrs. Cook were impressed with the work of The School. But as it was different from the line of work they had been engaged in, they felt they must decline...."

Rejection must have discouraged the Board. Finally,

the meeting ended with evident determination to keep going and keep looking. "Several names were proposed, and it was directed that correspondence be conducted with them. Dr. Dobyns proposed R. M. Good of Lexington, Mississippi. Trustee Abbott [suggested] Mr. Tadlock of the Stuart Robinson School, Indian Bottom, Kentucky."

It was, however, at the fall meeting that two critical issues surfaced; the first one had to do with a trustee re-election dispute with the Church Synod, and the other had to do with the introduction of R. M. Good as president. The latter undoubtedly reflected God's Providence in the life of a noble endeavor.

It is obvious that the Trustees came close to revolt. For its entire existence, the Board had been dependent upon the Church for the election of its trustees. But there had never been anything in The School's charter requiring members of the Board to be members of the Synod. So when the Synod abruptly took action that precluded non-residents of the state from serving, the President of the Board, who was widely regarded as the pillar of the institution, was rejected for continued membership.

This forced exit of Dr. W. R. Dobyns from the Board must have been a heavy blow to the little school. Everyone associated with The School knew it had depended on the leadership of Dr. Dobyns who had been aboard from the earliest days, through struggle after struggle, including relocation after the Mitchell Hall fire. The Trustees were so dependent on him that they made a special unanimous petition, but it was rejected because Dr. Dobyns had moved out of state.

Therefore, Dr. Dobyns was not present at the fall meeting (1921). But his shadow was still around. Trustees passed lengthy resolutions extolling the unique contributions this man had made. They made clear their feelings to "express our great regret at the action which deprives us of the unusual services of this man of God, and our sorrow at the necessity which severs our association with him in the work which lies so close to his heart."

To register their disgust further, the Board recorded in its minutes a letter addressed to them by their beloved, now former, leader. In his letter Dr. Dobyns begs the Board not to desert The School, to "stand by The School," and reminds the Board that "the institution is greater, far greater, than any individual, and I want to know that you will do me the honor to continue management of the enterprise, which I helped found, and to which I have given sixteen years of faithful service as I was able...." Dr. Dobyns also goes on the record in his letter, saying that The School's squabbling over joining a fund-raising campaign had been the root cause of the Synod's changing the rules "to have the thorn in their side removed."

Obviously, Dobyns didn't go quietly! The Trustees seem to have accepted it, however bitterly, and instructed the secretary to write Dr. Dobyns and tell him that they agreed with everything he had written.

It is important to note that all of Dr. Dobyns' letter to the Board wasn't negative or directed at the Synod. He makes some insightful comments about the coming of a new president, one whom Dr. Dobyns himself had recommended, and on whose shoulders so much would be placed. As if to know that Divine Providence was looking over The School, Dr. Dobyns describes this new man, "Dr. Good, whose coming to the presidency marks the accession of the first man whose vision and ability are commensurate with the task and opportunity of the institution. He is really able to make The School what it desires to be, and to accomplish the design of its founders and friends...he will lead The School into its real sphere."

The historical record shows that Dr. William R. Dobyns rendered great service to The School of the Ozarks. His recommendation (and the subsequent election) of Robert M. Good (Fig. 11) to head the little school provides clear evidence that God had sent yet another blessing to the Ozarks and intended The School to flourish.

Fig. 11
Robert M. Good,
President of
The School of the Ozarks

Chapter III
"Why Come Ye Here?"

It couldn't have taken R. M. Good very long to familiarize himself with the little Ozarks school. Only three buildings of any stature existed--Dobyns Hall, Abernathy Hall, and Stevenson Hall. Except for a few small wooden structures, that was the extent of the campus.

Dobyns Hall literally became his home. The old log building housed his room, office, and faculty offices, along with church and social functions.

Abernathy Hall served basically as a boys dormitory. It also housed classrooms on the first floor, with dormitory rooms on the second.

Stevenson Hall was a girls dormitory but also housed the dining room, kitchen, and living room.

Dr. Good wasted no time in taking over. He was well qualified for the position, having graduated from a military academy and having earned both undergraduate and graduate degrees from the University of Mississippi. An experienced teacher of math, athletic director, and subsequently a superintendent of schools, R. M. Good was more than up to the challenge. But, as he no doubt quickly found out, being president of such an unusual school required skills far beyond academic.

Fortunately for The School, Good's skills matched him

for the job. As well as a first-rate academician and administrator, he was a strict disciplinarian. As a man of strong Christian faith, Dr. Good led by example, and the personal interest he took in students, as well as employees, gained him respect from the very start.

Of critical importance was that R. M. Good was gifted at fund-raising, a subject that constantly came before the Board at most meetings as an absolute necessity for survival.

In short, the president was in charge of, and responsible for, everything!

The man on whose shoulders so much depended must have been encouraged when Dr. W. R. Dobyns showed up, as a guest, at the first meeting of the Trustees after the new president took office. This provided a smooth transition from the leadership of Dr. Dobyns to the new leadership of R. M. Good.

After a few board meetings, the Trustees were certainly pleased with The School's new leader, in as much as "the Board voted to increase Dr. Good's salary to $3,600 a year...." It must have seemed like more and more was being asked of him, but Dr. Good worked long days (and nights). One of his earliest concerns was the roof on Dobyns Hall, so much so that the Trustees asked him to make an appeal for funds to roof Dobyns Hall or "borrow the money from the bank to take care of the expense."

The old log building wasn't the only thing that required Good's attention. He had to hire the teachers, run farm operations, serve as surrogate father to students and staff alike, as well as manage The School's critical financial situation. Eventually, he delegated many of his responsibilities, but he was still the one responsible for everything. One thing remained clear to him; the story must be told and the very survival of the little school depended on his fund-raising success.

R. M. Good wasn't so consumed with running The School of the Ozarks that he failed to notice Lyta Davis, one of his best teachers, and of math, at that! Within a couple of years of accepting his position, he acquired a helpmate. The two were married with very little fanfare. Their marriage was to The School itself, as well as with each other. And all associated with The School became their extended family.

Shortly after his marriage to Lyta Davis, the Board added to his "to do" list. Since The School was already turning away fifty percent of its applicants, the Trustees wanted to expand. They wanted a new administration building to go along with a "smaller" project, "to install heat in Dobyns Hall." Knowing they needed to do more for President Good, the Board decided to "erect a president's home and devise means for appealing for funds...approximately the sum of $2,500." In essence, Dr. Good was given the opportunity to raise funds to build his own house while doing everything else. The Trustees also wanted "sufficient endowment to take care of enlarged activities." Dr. Good accepted these challenges and embarked on an ambitious plan to enlarge The School and help more youngsters.

The almost superhuman effort of R. M. Good was noticed by everyone. Students admired and respected him. So did the faculty and staff. He managed to keep food on the table for all, while conducting a never-ending campaign for funds. That R. M. Good accomplished so much so fast is remarkable in and of itself, but even more so considering the tragedy that struck the Good household early in their marriage. Their little daughter, Catherine Virginia, died of pneumonia before reaching the age of two. The little girl had become the "daughter" of the campus, and for sure, the apple of her father's eye. Those who recall the earliest years of R. M. Good's presidency still remember the glow of his success and the pain of his loss.

"I was born in 1906," recalls Eula (Shelton) Shipman (Fig. 12). "I grew up in Highlandville...two brothers and

Fig. 12
Eula (Shelton)
Shipman

seven half brothers and sisters...went down there with some neighbors...my dad didn't have a car, so he got a neighbor to take us down there the day I went to stay. We got about halfway down there, and he said, 'You better be makin' up your mind whether you want to stay or not. You're a long way from home....' He was giving me a chance to back out 'cause it was far away from home, about twenty-five miles. I was determined to stay. I thought it was a wonderful place."

Mrs. Shipman distinctly recalls, "I can remember the first day. We didn't have any classes that day--just enrolled and visited." She also remembers things got serious pretty quickly. And Dr. Good made a permanent impression on her.

"I liked him. I think all the kids liked him. He was strict. He went by the rules. I know some students that got kicked out. Some got sent home for slipping out to have dates...."

Mrs. Shipman didn't spend all of her time studying

and working. "I played basketball. Everybody got along, except when Highlandville played us in basketball. I was from Highlandville, so I got to hollering for Highlandville 'cause they didn't have anybody to holler for them. The girls picked me up and dragged me to the dormitory and were going to put me in the tub with my clothes on. They didn't get to put me in the bathtub...a friend of mine came running out with the scissors and was going to jab them... made them put me down!"

Time management was important, even in the earliest years. "I worked in the kitchen and in the laundry. Everybody had to work. Everybody had to go to chapel...We had lots of preachers. We had lots of revivals when I was at The School." Mrs. Shipman remembers and adds, "I got in trouble in the dining room one time. You know back then they'd give demerits; you got so many demerits, and you got sent home. I got twenty-five at one time. That's the only time I ever got any."

One offense of Eula Shipman brings back smiles for her. "Back then they bought syrup in great big containers. We'd been home and heard they found a mouse in one of the syrup containers. Just to upset everybody, they wanted to tell it in the dining hall. So they picked me to make the announcement...peck on a glass, get up, and make the announcement. I pecked on a glass and got up and said, 'Beware of the zip'--that's what we called the syrup. Then I sat down.

"I got twenty-five demerits. It wasn't funny at all. I had to work twenty-five hours because I got docked twenty-five hours. I guess I learned my lesson." Eula Shipman remembers one event from her school days above all else.

"We had something that was sad happen. Dr. Good had a little girl to die while we were there. She lived to be about two. Evidently many students didn't know about pneumonia. The little girl's death took its toll on everyone.

"Girls had taken turns taking care of her while Mrs. Good taught school. I babysat while she was a little girl. She died just before I graduated.

"It doesn't seem like they [the Goods] talked about it much to us. They had a little boy, Bob, after that."

No doubt one way the Goods dealt with such a tragedy was to lose themselves in the life of The School. Dr. Good's load was ever present, and Mrs. Good was one of the best teachers the little school had.

In reporting to the Trustees, Dr. Good constantly brought up the needs of the struggling school. In one meeting, he mentioned the need for a canning factory while, at the same time, emphasizing the need for a better administration building. His plea for the administration building project must have been moving, for pledges were taken right on the spot. Each trustee pledged from $25 to $1,000 per year for a period of up to three years to get things going--even the secretary made a tiny pledge.

R. M. Good saw the potential for the fledgling school, and he was more than willing to meet the challenge. But finding big financial backers took time, so the administration building project moved slowly. So much so that the Trustees, after only twelve months, had to authorize a loan to "enclose the new building, and when that has been done, we do no further work on the building until the money is in hand or in sight."

Not to be deterred or discouraged, at the next meeting

Fig. 13

The Green Administration and Classroom Building, nearing completion

in the fall of 1927, R. M. Good delivered the first of many miracles. He had found someone to finish the entire administration building project--Mr. A. P. Green, a business executive from Mexico, Missouri. Not only did Mr. Green offer to finish the building (Fig. 13), he offered funds to replace those already expended on the project. His only stipulation was that student labor be used in finishing the building. Further, he told Dr. Good to go buy the needed acreage adjoining The School and to let him know how much was needed for that, and he would take care of that, too!

Clearly, R. M. Good had delivered, and the Board knew it. Trustees directed a special letter to Mr. Green and his wife, gratefully thanking them for "coming to the aid of The School at this time." The Board also recorded "a rising vote of thanks to Dr. Good for his excellent work during the past year...."

Securing A. P. Green's support was important. But within a year another potential benefactor accompanied

Dr. Good as a guest to a trustee meeting. No one could have known that this visiting businessman from St. Louis would become one of The School's greatest leaders and benefactors. Lewis Wilkins Hyer was with the J.C. Penney Company and had been interested in helping young people who were willing to work.

It didn't take long for all concerned to see that Mr. Hyer had not only the wherewithal but also the willingness to help. At his very first board meeting, Mr. Hyer must have caught the contagious spirit and dream of R. M. Good. He listened to Dr. Good speak about the absolute need of replacing Dobyns Hall, the old log structure still in use, "which is unfit for school purposes." Also at this meeting, the matter of creating a junior college came up, no doubt at the request of R. M. Good.

Before the meeting was over, Wilk Hyer let it be known he would take care of the canning factory. It was to be the first of his many gifts to The School.

Undoubtedly to no one's surprise, within six months, Wilk Hyer was elected to the Board of Trustees and named to the Executive Committee. A few months later, A. P. Green was elected.

In a board report written for the year in which Dr. Good's leadership was beginning to pay huge dividends (1928), the feelings of the Board are captured in the very first line: "The School has enjoyed, during the past year, the greatest period of development in all its history." Cited as evidence of this sterling assessment were a new canning plant, the A. P. Green Administration Building, and hundreds of students being turned away, but most of all that "Teachers at The School of the Ozarks are very earnest, sincere Christian men and women."

The newfound optimism about the future of the little Ozarks miracle school was probably premature. Like much of America, things were on a roll. That is, until "Black Tuesday" (October, 1929) ushered in the Great Depression. No doubt The School was brought further in touch with reality when Dobyns Hall burned to the ground early the very next year.

June (Keener) Moore (Fig. 14) remembers well her days at The School of the Ozarks in the heady years leading up to and into the Great Depression. It was a time of great excitement and great anxiety.

Fig. 14
June (Keener) Moore

Mrs. Moore, above all else, sensed that R. M. Good was carrying the little school on his back, that everything depended on him. "Dr. Good *was* The School," she believes. "It wouldn't have been anything without him. When I got there, he'd been there about six years, and he had done an awful lot. It's hard for me to describe R. M. Good. He was just the greatest person. Without his energy and without his forethought, The School might not be here. He made lots of travels, always raising money and working hard. Contributions were often small, but Dr. Good appreciated them all."

Apparently the Keener family felt equally as good about the Ozarks school and how Dr. Good ran it. Mrs. Moore's brother preceded her as a student. "My mother heard about it and she was determined that he would go there. I remember the day he left. I remember that he cried. He was fifteen, and he was going off to a new place he'd never heard of. Francis left on the train. He graduated in the spring before I went in September."

June's sisters, Edith and Joy, were also students. The Keeners were from Keener, Arkansas, "a little town," Mrs. Moore recalls, "named for my grandfather."

Mrs. Moore well remembers her first impressions of The School. "I could never forget," she says. Actually, the campus hadn't grown very much and was still dependent on a few old buildings, though the new Green Administration Building was opened during her time as a student, and the venerable Dobyns Hall burned shortly before she left. "I lived in Stevenson Hall," she said. Stevenson Hall was still housing the girls, Abernathy the boys. Mrs. Moore remembers Dr. Good's little house. She also recalls how crowded things seemed to be. But change was occurring!

"Well, when we got the Green Administration Building, oh, it was like heaven on earth. It had an auditorium; we now had a gym. A real gym. We had music rooms for practice...The auditorium was on the first floor, and across the hall was Dr. Good's office. Then new classrooms. The next floor was all classrooms. The basement was a gym and the music room. I suppose there were other maintenance rooms, I don't remember that. But it was really wonderful to have a gym."

More than the campus, classrooms, or new buildings, Mrs. Moore remembers her work assignment. To this day, her face lights up when she describes working for R. M. Good.

"Yes, I'm someone special. He picked me for his first office 'boy.' Now that's what he called me! And he called me 'freckles.' You can guess why he would call me 'freckles,' because I had an abundance of them." Her job description indicates what would be expected. "He would send me on errands...I just did odd jobs. I kept my job for four years."

Mrs. Moore remembers that her younger sister, Joy, also worked for Dr. Good. "I took her to his office, and she worked with me. After I left, Dr. Good called her 'little freckles.' She came the year I was a senior. We roomed together."

No doubt June (Keener) Moore shared a special bond with Dr. and Mrs. Good. June's sister, Joy (Fig. 15), died of influenza while a student, the year after June graduated.

Fig. 15
Joy Keener

"They had a flu epidemic. Joy wrote us letters when she was sick. They sent her back to the dorm, not to class. She went back to the hospital and died of pneumonia. She was barely fifteen. It was before penicillin...Joy wrote to us all, and all her brothers and sisters...the last thing she wrote, was, 'I finished my course, I fought the good fight, and I kept the faith.'"

Joy died in the isolation room of the little campus hospital. "She and Mrs. Good had the same birthday. On her last birthday my mother sent a cake and Mrs. Good came; we had cake and some friends over in our room."

Having a homemade cake must've been a special treat, at least in contrast to what was served in the dining room. Mrs. Moore charitably recalls, "The food wasn't very interesting. We all came from the country...Mondays and Sundays we always had dessert. And they always had syrup on the table, and bread. The boys would sit there and eat syrup and bread. But we didn't go hungry."

Going to work in Dr. Good's office, going to classes, some of which were in the new Green Administration Building, and going to chapel consumed much of a student's time. Mrs. Moore remembers more about the Green Auditorium than its size; special occasions there stand out. "Once in a great while, the girls were summoned all by themselves. Well, nobody knew what in the world for. We knew something terrible had to be in the wind or we wouldn't be called there. One particular Sunday afternoon we were. So, everybody filed in and Dr. Good was standing there with his back to the stage. The stage was raised about four feet above the floor. He was kind of leaning against the footlights and everybody was real quiet. You could have heard a pin drop. He could look real serious. I mean, he did almost all the time, though he had a sense of humor. Now, everybody was wondering 'what in the world?' So, he turned around and picked up something. It was the plaque that Trustee Hyer had given to be hung above the stage. And it said, 'Why Come Ye Here?' (Fig. 16). He showed it to us, but he didn't say a word. He just

Fig. 16 Green Building, stage

40

held that plaque up, 'Why Come Ye Here?' That has a lot of thought to it."

R. M. Good had Wilk Hyer's plaque hung above the stage where students were always looking up at it. Most students knew why they were in school. If they didn't, they didn't last long. As Mrs. Moore reflects, "They always let it be known if you didn't want to conform, if you didn't want to do your best, make your best grades, there's somebody else that wanted to be in your spot."

June (Keener) Moore and her classmates shared yet another sad event--the day Dobyns Hall burned.

"I must have had a period off. It was before lunch, and the first thing we knew, it was burning. So, of course, we all ran over there and it was gone. In about thirty minutes it was down, and you know what was left? This huge big fireplace that you found when you walked in on the right. And, on the left were two other fireplaces, not quite as large, but still standing up. That was all that was left of it. The logs were just consumed."

Perhaps the speed with which old Dobyns Hall burned surprised all who saw it. "You couldn't get close to it," Mrs. Moore recalls. "Everybody ran out of class and was standing around, but there just wasn't anything anybody could do. Not even Dr. Good could stop it, and he always was worried about something like this happening. He used to have nightmares, because he was always afraid that it would get on fire, and he couldn't get the girls out of the upstairs rooms."

Lucille (Knight) Harp (Fig. 17), also a stu-

Fig. 17 Lucille (Knight) Harp

dent when Dobyns Hall burned, remembers it even more vividly than June (Keener) Moore.

"I, a lowly freshman in Mr. Cave's algebra class, was sent to the blackboard to work on a problem. Not sure I could solve it correctly, I was 'milling' it over. The classroom door was yanked open and a student yelled that Dobyns Hall was on fire. Everybody ran!

"It was truly awesome that so huge a structure can be consumed so quickly, leaving everyone stunned. A girl totally unaware of the fire was taking a bath. A miracle that she got out in a bathrobe. The rest of us, including four teachers and our house mother, got out with only what we had on. To fight the fire was totally futile. We were all thankful it didn't happen at night--lives would have been lost.

"When the ashes cooled and excitement waned, we who roomed there began to realize we had not so much as a toothbrush, change of clothes, or an assigned place to sleep. But we were rapidly taken care of. Clothes were provided from the charity box and then those parents that could, helped out. Gifts poured in as news of the big fire spread. And, Stevenson Hall was very crowded the rest of the term.

"We all lost more than just clothes. My prize possession was a beautiful white, leather bound Bible my beloved stepfather had given me for Christmas. I was ten years old at the time. He never lived to see another Christmas. He was a wonderful man, and I am still thankful for the few years that I shared with him."

For other students in school during this period of time, memories are still fresh.

Ray Simkins (Fig. 18) and Delphia (Phillips) Simkins met at The School. Mrs. Simkins remembered why she came. "I came because there wasn't a high school at home. My sister came first, and then my brother, and then me." Ray remembers when he arrived. "In December [1929], the stock market had just crashed!"

Fig. 18 Ray Simkins

He lived in Abernathy Hall; she lived in Stevenson. They both revered R. M. Good and remembered how strict The School of the Ozarks was. "Very strict," she says. "You had to wear hose; you couldn't wear shorts. You got demerits. I remember one couple got a demerit for putting an arm around the other."

Mrs. Simkins did her required work in the dining room. "We waited tables. But sometimes I worked in the kitchen. And, one time I worked in the boys dorm, spraying for mattress bugs!" Ray was one grade ahead. His work experience he could never forget. "One of the first things they made us do was pick turkeys. You know, pluck feathers. They hang them by their legs, slit their throats, and then they bleed. That's the only way those heavy quills release. But, I really didn't know what I was doing!"

Although neither Ray nor Delphia Simkins lived in Dobyns Hall, they both remembered the fire. Ray stood in front of Stevenson Hall and watched Dobyns Hall burn to the ground. "I ran to see where the print shop was because I had been assigned there to work. Dr. Good was just running in all directions because he was afraid somebody was trapped in there; a student was in there taking a bath but got out." Delphia felt the aftereffect of the fire the next day. "They had to bring girls from Dobyns to live in Stevenson where I lived. Cots were brought in. I was in a room where there were six girls, so we couldn't take any more. I think some of them just had to double up in a twin bed."

Ray Simkins was always glad he didn't have to live in Stevenson Hall. "I must now confess that it was rodent-infested. We would see those big suckers running around, six to eight inches long!" Ray also had memories of going to the movies with Delphia. "We would have movies, yes. They put up a screen somehow. But the boys and girls had to sit far apart. And, every time during the show it looked like they were going to kiss, the projectionist had to put his hand over the projector."

Watching Dobyns Hall burn (Fig. 19) wasn't what impressed Ray Simkins the most, nor was plucking turkeys or even the big rats in Stevenson Hall. What really made the most lasting impression on young Ray Simkins were the chapel talks given by Dr. Good. The talks were not boring, according to Simkins. "I can still see Dr. Good. Most of the time he conducted chapel. He would give us a talk. One talk I'll never forget. It was about the Fleagle boys. They were bank robbers from out in Kansas. They had

Fig. 19
Dobyns Hall,
on fire

robbed numerous banks but eventually migrated down here in the Ozarks. One of them was killed at the Branson Railroad Station. One of them, Jake Fleagle, got on the train but the FBI was waiting. Fleagle's gun got hung up, and he couldn't fire back; they shot him right there. Dr. Good got our attention. But none of us had ever even thought about being a bank robber!"

The Trustees didn't have time to worry about bank robbers. They had to face up to the loss of a major building and its aftermath. Shortly after the big Dobyns Hall fire, a special meeting of the Board was called. The Trustees, far from being in a mood to give up, accepted what had happened and heard some encouraging reports from Dr. Good.

Dr. Good officially reported to the Board the total destruction of Dobyns Hall and that the origin of the fire was unknown. He also had to report that the adjoining print shop was destroyed, too. Most importantly, "There was no loss of life or injuries of any kind." Because the fire had caused crowded conditions in Stevenson Hall and because of a generous gift, the Board authorized Dr. Good to move ahead with "Thompson Dining Hall" and, upon its completion, the remodeling of Stevenson Hall to convert the old dining hall and kitchen into additional rooms for girls. A boost came from Trustee Wilk Hyer, who made a gift to provide a temporary print shop. The Trustees gratefully directed Dr. Good to "prepare a letter of thanks to be sent out to the Chamber of Commerce of Springfield and other organizations that had contributed to the needs of The School after the destruction of Dobyns Hall and the print shop by fire."

The mood of the Trustees belied what was happening to the country. It was as if what was going on around the country didn't exist. As the little school started into the decade of the Great Depression, very few seemed to sense the rising threat to America, both from a deepening recession from inside the country and eventually a world war from the outside. But R. M. Good had no doubt answered the question on the plaque hanging in the auditorium of the A. P. Green Administration Building--"Why Come Ye Here?" Surely, all knew why Providence had blessed The School with such a leader, one on whose shoulders rested so much responsibility as storm clouds gathered.

Chapter IV
"Even the Students Understood."

The years of the Great Depression tested the very existence of the tiny Ozarks school. Used to operating under austere conditions, President R. M. Good plowed ahead with great energy and commitment, as if no depression existed. The fact that the Trustees were extremely cautious didn't seem to dampen Dr. Good's enthusiasm.

Life was busy and productive on the little campus, its purpose too important to be deterred by circumstances. The School managed to occupy the new Thompson Dining Hall building and a few others during the earliest years of the Depression. The DAR (Daughters of the American Revolution) had shown interest in The School of the Ozarks, and all were no doubt amazed at the ability of R. M. Good to keep The School moving ahead, no matter

Fig. 20
Harry Basore

what. Students continued to line up for admission, but the Board could not enlarge The School because of space and financial limitations. But those fortunate enough to have gained admission were getting a good education, having a good time, and preparing for the future.

Harry Basore (Fig. 20), one such student, remains grateful for his chance during this

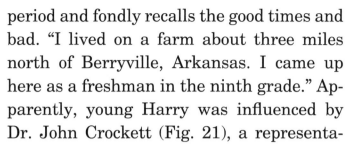
Fig. 21 Dr. John Crockett, Bishop of the Ozarks

period and fondly recalls the good times and bad. "I lived on a farm about three miles north of Berryville, Arkansas. I came up here as a freshman in the ninth grade." Apparently, young Harry was influenced by Dr. John Crockett (Fig. 21), a representative of The School that visited students who were making application. "My first contact was with Dr. John Crockett, who was known as the Bishop of the Ozarks. He was a Presbyterian minister that didn't have one particular church, but preached at all the small churches around the area and served as a sort of field man for The School. At one time he was acting president just before and during the time that The School burned down at Forsyth. He had told the people around Forsyth that The School would not move to another location--promised that it wouldn't be moved. But it was moved over here, because of an opportunity to buy this old log building [Dobyns Hall], which would serve ideally as school rooms and for places to live. So Crockett resigned when The School moved over here [Point Lookout] but still maintained his connection with The School."

Harry Basore proudly recalls that prior to his first classes he "came up and worked all summer." His earliest days as a student are unforgettable to him. "There were times when food was a bit scarce. I worked that summer on the farm." Harry took his farm work assignment in stride, but what he really wanted to do was work on things mechanical. Although he had done farm work at home for about ten cents a day, he felt as if his talent lay

Fig. 22 Clarence Parkey, work supervisor

elsewhere. So, says Harry, "I told the farm boss I didn't want to work on the farm--that I just preferred things mechanical." The farm boss told Harry, "You go ahead and work till school starts, and I'll see if I can get you on with Clarence Parkey (Fig. 22), the engineer who ran all the mechanical stuff."

Young Harry did what he was told and just before classes started "got assigned to Parkey's crew." It was a work assignment that probably made Harry yearn for the farm. "I had the 3 a.m. to 6 a.m. shift at the little power plant--for our heating, power, and lights. My biggest trouble was getting up and getting there at three in the morning. Whoever was on duty would come to the dormitory and wake you up." The work experience of young Harry Basore was anything but dull. One episode stands out in Harry's mind to this very day. "We had two boilers that were coal-fired, and the furnace was what was called a Dutch-oven type in that the furnace protruded out in front of the boilers. The coal was fed to the oven by hand. On one particularly chilly and early morning, the lad with the shift before me slept through his shift. Naturally, nobody woke me up. I was a hard sleeper, anyway. Fortunately, I did wake up at about, oh, it was probably around four o'clock. I bounced out of bed and tore off to the power plant. I knew something was wrong before I got there because I could hear the water pump pounding. What happened was the water in the boilers had gradually gone down below the soft plug." Harry had to go through detailed emergency procedures to keep the thing from being irreparably damaged.

He finished his shift, soaking wet. "I was just as wet as if I'd taken the hose and squirted it on me," he remembers. "The worst part faced me 'cause I had to walk over and wake Mr. Parkey up. It was almost six in the morning. I had to knock on his door and tell him that I blew a soft plug."

Harry expected the worst because he said Mr. Parkey had a volatile temper. "Surprisingly, he was very calm about it and said, 'Well, Basore, what happened?' So, I told him the story. He said, 'Well, looks like you handled it pretty well. You better go on back to the dormitory and get cleaned up.'" Harry's work assignment at the power plant was, understandably, short-lived. Evidently, Mr. Parkey had to modify Harry's work assignment to protect property and person! "That was the only time I worked in the power plant as a fireman. I worked in and out of there doing mechanical things but did not have a shift. That was my only time when I had a shift, 'cause I started playing basketball the next year. Parkey didn't like that much. He didn't think that much of basketball."

For Harry Basore there was a lot more to life at the tiny Ozark work school than working and going to class. But everything took place under the watchful eye of R. M. Good. "He was referred to behind his back as the 'big bear,'" Harry recalls. "He had a rather stern countenance; he could be stern at times." It must have been enough deterrence to keep the basketball players in line, as none of Harry's teammates got kicked out--at least as far as Harry remembers. "Easiest trouble to get into would be getting caught smoking or something. They'd get kicked out for smoking. They would get sent home." Behavior was viewed as a reflection of one's character and was to be taken seriously. The rules were designed to enforce that.

But more was expected in all aspects of a youngster's life as Harry recalls, even cultural things: "...back in those days, table manners for folks from out of the hills weren't... high society for sure." In order to improve manners as Harry remembers it, a concerted effort was required, but it was done with sensitivity. Harry explains, "For certain meals we were assigned tables with the faculty to help us with our table manners and whatever, and sort of to get people over that homesick period of being away from home. As high school students, we were just kids. I was only fourteen years old when I came up here; some kids were a lot younger than that.

"One student had a friend of his from home that came up this particular year, and this student told Mrs. Good, 'This boy comes from way back out in the hills, and he won't have any good table manners at all. For one thing, he'll be used to pouring his coffee in his saucer and blowing it, to cool it off. Of course we know that that's not good table manners. He'll be very sensitive, and I want to save his feelings...So breakfast tomorrow morning will be his first meal.' The student continued, 'I'll get him to sit with us at your table. I will pour my coffee in my saucer real quick and blow it; you can chew me out about it so he'll get the idea he is not supposed to do that!' So that's what they did. He [the older student] poured his coffee in the saucer and blew it, and Mrs. Good properly chewed him out about it and told him that wasn't right, etc. And apparently the new student got the hint!"

Teaching manners to Ozark hill kids was always a for-

Fig. 23

1936 Basketball Team and Coach "Shorty" Farrell, Harry Basore #11

midable challenge. Harry said, "Some of 'em, 'course, chewed tobacco and smoked, all that sort of stuff. It was kind of hard for them to quit. I heard about Dr. Good walking up to somebody with a chew of tobacco in their mouth, and they had to swallow it!"

Even during the Depression, things always seemed to brighten up during basketball (Fig. 23) season. The character expectations of the students extended to the court, as well. "I can tell you one thing we were very proud of," Harry Basore remembers. "We would nearly every year win the sportsmanship award at tournaments. We were more or less just projecting the teachings of The School...a very serious thing even with our coach, Shorty Farrell, who was an alum of The School. He knew the Christian background and purpose of The School, that a great deal of emphasis was placed on 'it's not that you win or lose, but how you play the game that counts.' That was, I guess, our team motto!"

From the classroom, to the

Fig. 24

Dr. Crockett and a student gospel team

52

workplace, to the gym, to chapel, students were exposed to virtuous living. Harry was quite fond of Dr. Crockett, who organized student gospel teams (Fig. 24). "Dr. Crockett was our, I guess, chaplain. He gave our Sunday services for quite a while. The only excuse for being out of chapel was if you had a job that had to be done." According to Harry, you had to go to everything. "Church on Sunday, Sunday School, and Christian Endeavor on Sunday evening. At certain times there would be sort of a revival service. I joined the church."

Fig. 25

Carl Cave, Principal

As described by Harry Basore, both faculty and students were required to attend services. Everybody went. The faculty were role models, but things weren't always so serious between students and staff. Harry remembers the fun times students had with Carl Cave (Fig. 25), head of the high school. "I don't have the faintest idea how old he was. Being an adult to us kids, he was just older! I guess he was a fairly young man--pretty young, younger than Dr. Good. He was a good sport. He'd get out and have snowball fights when we'd have our occasional snow, which wasn't very often. He'd get out and mix it up. He had a room in the boys dormitory...could take a joke."

It's a good thing, as illustrated by one of Harry's fondest stories about Carl Cave. "During the school year after church and after lunch, we had what was called quiet hour. Everybody had to be in their room and keep quiet. It was actually two hours. One of the purposes of that was that everybody should take that time to write letters home. But, I'm not sure that was the only purpose. It kept everybody out of mischief, I guess, when they didn't have an organized thing to do. One summer, right in the middle of summer, it was very hot. It seemed like we always had a herd of goats around. Somebody chased a half-grown goat, chased him until he was just exhausted, and caught him. Just before quiet hour they snuck up and put him in Carl Cave's bed, and put the covers up on it. The goat was totally exhausted. Their timing was absolutely perfect. It had to be perfect. Because, Mr. Cave's routine was that a short time after quiet hours started, you'd always hear Mr. Cave come in and go to his room. He was up on the second floor. I had a room right around the corner from his room. I heard everything that went on but didn't know about this. He walked into his room, and everything was pretty quiet. In two or three minutes, all of a sudden, there was this horrible racket. Something came out of there and tore down the hall, with Mr. Cave right behind it!"

Harry still laughs about it. "He came to his room to take his nap, turned the covers down, and this goat popped right out of there. Mr. Cave tried to catch him--got the door open; the goat ran down the hall with Mr. Cave right behind it, right down the hall. And, of course, since it was so hot, the window was open. That goat went right on out the window, got up on its feet, and ran off." No doubt, Mr. Cave had his sense of humor tested. "He came around checking rooms shortly after that. There wasn't much he could do but laugh. As far as I know, he never found out who did that. And, I don't know who did it. To this day, I don't know who did it."

Evidently, the summer session was filled with work intermingled with pranks. Although Harry's innocence with the goat episode is noteworthy, his involvement in another prank he now confesses to is instructive. Some now believe it to have been the very first episode of "streaking" on a school campus. Reluctantly, Harry Basore tells the story.

"This particular summer we were having problems with the water pump down on Lake Taneycomo; so it broke down. When it broke down, we were out of water. So, two lads were working out of the machine shop, and they were assigned to fix the pump. Working on the pump down there was a dirty, greasy job. You would be working almost waist deep in ole greasy, dirty water. Then, of course you'd strip, take all your clothes off, and just work in it--that's all." Time apparently meant nothing, as Harry continues. "It seems to me like the lights were turned out in the dormitory at about nine or nine-thirty at the latest. When you worked on a job like that, hours didn't mean anything; you just worked until you had to quit. I'm not sure whether the repairs were completed that particular night or not. Anyway, these two lads came up filthy and dirty from head to toe. And, they went from their room down to the showers in the basement with nothing but towels and their soap. They just got in the shower and got soaped down from head to foot real good, and the lights went out and the water went off. The water was turned off because of the pump. Well, there they were, soaped up from head to foot, wondering how in the world they were going to get rid of that soap with no water."

Harry now describes what happened. "Halfway between the boys dormitory and the girls dormitory was a walkway that went down to Point Lookout and also a lily pond, probably twenty to twenty-five feet in diameter--pretty fair sized. There were big water lilies growing in there, and they kept goldfish in there. One lad said, 'Well, I know where I'm going to get rid of this soap, so, come on.' So they went out a window in the basement--didn't even take their towels with them--streaked across campus, and got in the lily pond and washed the soap off. While they were doing this, both Dr. Good and Mr. Cave came strolling down the walkway discussing something; they were in deep conversation. They got right down to that intersection, and they walked back and forth--must've been something pretty serious. But they would amble back and forth and up and down the walkway right there where those two walks cross. A time or two they took a few steps down toward the big pond where the two boys were in that pond. You know what? They [two lads] were there underneath big ole lily pads and being just as quiet as they could be, until Mr. Cave and Dr. Good went on about their way. Of course, Dr. Good's house was just down from the other side of the dormitory. And, of course, Mr. Cave lived in the dormitory. So, they [lads] remained in the pond long enough to figure out when to get out, and then they took out for the dormitory. The moon gave a little bit of light. But, they didn't sneak; they just took out and ran, dived in through the window, grabbed their towels, and went up to their room."

According to Harry Basore, no one really saw the lads, at least not well enough to identify them. "There were some boys sitting on the front porch of the dormitory steps. All they could see were two figures; they had no idea what it was all about." No doubt, had the lads been apprehended, they would have been sent home. The only harm from the incident came to the pond's fish. "There was muddy water in the lily pond later, and the goldfish got kind of sick. But nobody could figure out what it was. Nobody told either," Harry recalls with pride. However, one would have to wonder how Harry could recall such a tale in such detail, were he not present. Finally, after almost three-quarters of a century, Harry Basore reluctantly admitted that he was, in fact, one of the two "streakers"!

Harry Basore was a good basketball player at the little school. But he modestly credits someone else with being better. "One of our best athletes during my time and for a long time thereafter was Eugene 'Peaches' Westover. He was a year ahead of me, but I did play with him one full year and part of the next. I understand the way he got his name. He swiped a can of peaches when he was a student. Dr. Good caught him and made him eat every one of them right there." "Peaches" Westover had come to The School from an orphanage, as did many others. Unfortunately, he was killed in one of the battles of World War II.

Another of Harry's classmates was Hugh Wise (Fig. 26). Like Harry, Hugh came to The School looking simply for an education. It was probably his only chance. Barely a teenager, Hugh has never forgotten the time he enrolled, the experiences he shared with Harry Basore and others, and certainly not the friends and influences which touched his life. He remembers well. "It's a funny thing...

Fig. 26 Hugh Wise

I typed a letter about admission, and Dr. John Crockett came to see me. I was in the cornfield when he arrived; Dr. Crockett had been president of The School."

As with Harry Basore, Dr. Crockett visited with Hugh Wise to interview him to determine his suitability for admission, to see if young Hugh was the type of lad The School could help. After Hugh showed up for summer work, no time was wasted. "The next day I was in the bean patch," Hugh recalls. He spent nine hours a day picking beans. "Then we'd go to the factory at night to string the beans," Hugh remembers. Hugh wanted to make the best of his opportunity, "My folks and granddad had a general merchandise store west of Blue Eye...we had so many droughts that all we had was livestock that was worthless. So my dad didn't have money to send me to school...." Hugh was just one of the many at The School who were given the only chance of an education they might ever get. "Many of them were worse off, because they didn't have a nickel to buy a lead pencil," Hugh reflects.

Times were hard and The School of the Ozarks was creative in staying afloat. Students were willing to do whatever was asked of them and were glad to do it. Hugh explains, "Harry Basore was here a year before me; his senior year and my junior year we lived up on the hill [near campus]. We roomed at Dr. Crockett's house, which was owned by The School. The reason we were up there was because the state of Missouri had a welfare program for the county of Taney, and they didn't have a place to can the beef that had been bought by the government. So, Dr. Good made arrangements with the state and the welfare program to let people on welfare work at the factory canning beef, but the requirement was that every student must work sixteen hours, too. So we worked with the students two eight-hour shifts on Monday; we got a check, but we never saw the amount. It was always turned over, and we just signed on the back. That went on from November to February. The dormitory was full, and that house had three students put in it. Harry and I slept on the back porch, and one of the students slept on the inside. We came down every morning at 6:25 for breakfast...."

Hugh Wise, with a twinkle in his eye, fondly remembers the good times. "There are a lot of things I should have gotten in trouble for, but I didn't get caught...I did get caught with another guy breaking a pillow...if you've ever tried to sweep up feathers you will find it impossible...charged me with five demerits and twenty-five hours. That's a pretty stiff penalty. Shorty Farrell docked me and kept me from getting a certificate for the year for being demerit-free."

Although Hugh got into a few more scrapes, he respected R. M. Good. "Dr. Good had a way of feeling you were doing something wrong, and he could just get you to confess without your ever knowing it." Hugh just rarely got caught. "I remember we made ice cream one time under Dr. Good's office in the Green Building. Dr. Good never caught us." One particular time sticks in Hugh's mind that he begrudgingly confesses. "I teamed up with three other boys; we went down to the power plant, took the power house boat across the river, and just loaded it with watermelons. The river was muddy and it got so dark we couldn't see. We were floating down the river intending to dock at the power plant...We tied the boat but then found out we were at an island in the middle of the river." Although Hugh and his buddies managed to get back, no one ever figured who had been taking the watermelons.

Other than pillow fighting, working, and stealing watermelons, Hugh remembers more important things about his time at the little school. "There were very capable teachers, longtime teachers. Mr. Cave taught geometry. Mrs. Good taught Algebra. The English teacher was good. All the teachers were very dedicated. They were fine teachers." Above all else, R. M. Good made an impression on Hugh Wise--just as he did on all students. "I remember that he demanded that people be truthful, that people be industrious, and that they maintain accountability for what they did--their conduct and their performance on whatever job they performed. He was a religious man, but not a minister. He was a school superintendent before he came here as a young man."

Hugh Wise knew the early leaders of The School of the Ozarks up close and personal. He even remembers the remarkable Trustee Wilk Hyer of J.C. Penney fame. "His chauffeur would stay in Abernathy Hall, the boys dormitory. That was the first black man most of us had ever talked with."

According to Hugh Wise, Mr. Hyer (Fig. 27) enjoyed

Fig. 27
R. M. Good and L. W. Hyer (right) with fish, not caught in campus pond

fishing in the campus pond, but it was a poorly kept secret that Mr. Hyer was wasting his time. "Mr. Hyer was always fishing in the pond down here; it didn't have any fish in it!...He wanted to fish in it, so we got some worms for him. We'd go out to the lumber yard, and under the lumber there would be some big worms. I wasn't about to tell him there were no fish in there." Needless to say, Hugh professes, "He didn't catch any!"

Hugh and other students knew they were to be careful in dealing with Trustee Hyer. "We were told not to do certain things. They told us if he ever offered us a nickel, don't take it. He never offered us a nickel either." Hugh Wise shared many good times with other students. But everybody in the little school knew that times were hard.

Those like Hugh Wise and Harry Basore weren't the only ones glad to have a place at the little school during the Depression. Even teachers were grateful.

One such teacher was Annabelle McMaster (Fig. 28). "I needed a job," she said. "The bank folded and did not reopen...there were so few jobs. Dr. Good called me and said they were taking fifty more students...they could add three teachers--a home economics teacher, a manual training teacher, and an agriculture teacher. And would I be in-

terested? I said, 'Oh, my, I sure would.' We were about to starve to death, you know. Dr. Good added, 'Which would you rather have? The food or clothing?' I said, 'Your regular teacher gets her choice.' She was a friend of mine, and I

Fig. 28 Annabelle McMaster, teacher who started fruitcake tradition

knew she should have her choice. So...she chose clothing and I, of course, would rather have foods; that's my line of work."

With a second home economics teacher, The School could deal with the burden of more students. But the addition of Annabelle McMaster was more than an extra teacher. She brought new ideas, one of which would be institutionalized as a very important part of the future of The School. It was during these hard times of the Depression that a new teacher was responsible for the tradition of student-made fruitcakes. Annabelle McMaster fondly explains how it all came to be. "Dr. Good's office was just above the Home Economics Department in the old administration (Green) building. Dr. Good would smell an odor coming up and would come down and say, 'Now what are you girls cooking? What are you fixin' today?' He came once in early December and he said, 'There sure is a nice odor coming up from this department. What are you making today?' I said, 'Well, it's December; we're making fruitcakes.' He left and in a few minutes came back and he said, 'If you will make me six of those fruitcakes, I will mail them out to people who are interested in The School. And if we get some money back, I will buy your department its first electric stove.'...We got $1,125 from those six fruitcakes. So, he bought our department its first electric stove!"

Obviously, Annabelle McMaster became well-acquainted with R. M. Good and Mrs. Good. It left a lifelong impression on her. "They were a wonderful couple. They both gave their lives to The School...they took those children (students) in, just as if they were adopting them.

And, those that showed promise, they saw that they continued their education."

Annabelle McMaster did remember one flaw in Dr. Good--his driving. She laughs, "He was a wonderful man but a terrible driver. One day he came down and said, 'Mr. Cave and I have to go to Kansas City, and we want you to go, too.' We drove up there, and he would dart in to get a Coke, and off we would go. So, we got up there, attended a meeting, and drove right back home just as fast as we could. I said, 'Doc Good, if you have to go again, don't ask me to go, because I can't ride with you!'"

Mrs. McMaster not only admired Dr. Good, but she respected the hard work of those who helped Dr. Good at The School. Several of the fruitcakes eventually improved the lot of everybody, because funds were generated for items desperately needed. Annabelle McMaster worked hard along with those she still remembers as just getting started in life. "I lived in the hospital because there was no room in the teacher's quarters for me. Miss Downs (Fig. 29) was the nurse. Most of the teachers were not married. The French teacher was Miss Feaster, not married. The history teacher

Fig. 29
Constance
Downs, Nurse

was Miss Sanders, not married. Shorty Farrell was the coach. Mr. Cave was next to the president, and not married. The girl that taught clothing was from Berea, Kentucky, and it was her first teaching experience. She was younger. It was very hard for her to have dates, because the gates were locked at ten o'clock. And, she only stayed two years. It was difficult for her."

No doubt, Annabelle McMaster was right in her characterization of the sacrificial living conditions of the teachers. But, this was true for every member of The School's family. None complained, going about the everyday business of improving the lives of the students.

It became very difficult to operate The School as the Great Depression tightened its grip. The Trustees had no choice but to impose more and more austere financial controls to ensure survival. The Board's deliberations clearly reflect this. In fact, at a special Executive Committee meeting, the signs were ominous. "R. M. Good presented the urgent needs occasioned at this time, especially by the closing of the Bank of Branson...tying up some funds for which checks had already been written...." Deliberations of the Board continue to reveal just how difficult matters had become. "The President presented a plan by which the faculty had very cheerfully accepted a suggested additional cut of ten percent for those salaries under forty dollars, fifteen percent for those salaries under seventy dollars, and twenty percent for all salaries seventy dollars or above."

This recommendation was accepted and the Trustees were deeply grateful for the sacrifices being made. They also urged that special appeals be sent out to friends to meet obligations. R. M. Good must've been fearful that The School of the Ozarks wasn't going to get by, because he suggested to the Trustees "that the teachers be paid their salaries in installments as their salary was needed along through the year." The Trustees felt this was borrowing from the teachers and that such should not be done, and that the salaries should be paid promptly when due.

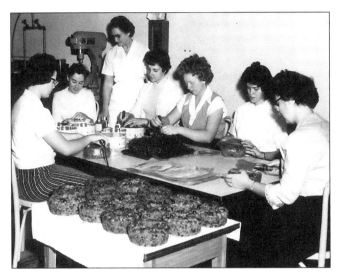

Fig. 30
May McFarland
(standing)
supervises students
making famous
fruitcakes.

It is noteworthy that the Trustees saw a limit to what could be done. Whereas The School attracted donors willing to fund special needs, such as a manual training building or another boys dormitory, getting operating dollars was not only difficult but crucial. So, the Board resolved that the president of The School "was authorized to borrow for The School in cases of emergency to be determined by him, without a specific authority...." Such a motion as that reflects not only the desperate conditions of the times, but also the great trust they had in R. M. Good. He was a man of responsibility, and no one at any level doubted it.

The Trustees explored every avenue for additional funds. The little fruitcake project (Fig. 30) started to grow and it helped with increasing gift income. A program to entertain tourists during the summer was even presented to the Board by President Good. What little money The School received for its small endowment was carefully watched. Even in the midst of the greatest depression the world had ever known, the Trustees voted to put twenty-five percent of the meager holdings in equities, sensing that survival would win the day and the future would be better for The School as the nation pulled out of the terrible slump.

All connected with the Ozarks school could see the position they were in. Even the students understood. Hugh Wise captured this understanding by saying, "There was no surplus of food, and Dr. Good was always talking about the need for money and how the one dollar and two dollar contributions were keeping the institution going...We knew when we worked in the canning factory and turned the checks over...it [The School] was in dire straits. But we never thought there would be any question whether it would go on. It had a purpose."

Chapter V
"I Will"

As the nation struggled with the Depression, storm clouds darkened over Europe with the rise in Germany of the Third Reich. Concern for the nation was soon added to concern for the survival of The School of the Ozarks. Like families everywhere, those in the Ozarks were already in difficulty. Some probably thought things couldn't get more difficult. They were wrong.

Margaret (Willbanks) Applegate (Fig. 31) will never forget this period of time. "I was born in Quapaw, Oklahoma." She had three brothers--Paul, Rolland, and the youngest, Kaney. "When Kaney was eight months old, and I was two years old, our father died...a form of tuberculosis. One day my mother decided to go work in the children's home...so she could be with us. While we were there, they discovered we all had tuberculosis. But, three of us--our systems threw it off; we just had scar tissue. But Rolland [middle brother] had it active."

Mrs. Applegate continues, "Well, my earliest memory...I must have been about five when mother had to bring Kaney to Kansas City because he had a bad kidney which

Fig. 31 Margaret (Willbanks) Applegate

plagued him the rest of his life...We lived in a pretty poor part of town in Kansas City. In fact, you would go down the stairs beside the sidewalk and go in a small apartment. We lived under the sidewalk...the little bitty place had a small living room and a bedroom...I don't think the bathroom had a shower or tub. The three boys and myself slept crosswise in the one bed. My mother slept in the other. And, Kaney, with his kidney ailment was always wetting on me, because he couldn't control it.

"My mother worked real hard; she worked all night on her feet, standing in a bakery. She did that all night long and took care of four children. She got some sort of illness and had to go to St. Mary's Hospital. So they put us in the Gillis home in Kansas City. She [Mother] got well...then... got real sick again. She had bad ear infections, and they didn't have antibiotics in those days. She just didn't have resistance enough to throw it off. Her doctor said she just worked herself to death. So she died."

A guardian was appointed for the Willbanks children. According to Mrs. Applegate, they wound up in the Presbyterian Orphanage in Farmington, Missouri. "But," she explains, "Paul [the oldest] didn't like the idea. So, he took his bicycle and ran off to Joplin before they could stop him. The reason our relatives couldn't take us in is my aunt had eight children of her own and no husband. My uncle Tom had twelve. Paul told me a lot of times all they had to eat at night was bread dipped in bacon grease; that was their dinner. Anyway, they were all so poor they couldn't take him or us in."

In such circumstances, Rolland, Margaret, and Kaney Willbanks came to stay in the orphanage for a number of years. "I stayed for eight years; Rolland left to come here before me. That left just Kaney and me."

The Willbanks story continues as Margaret recalls, "Kaney and I always seemed closer than the older brothers did." Since her older brother had been taken in at The School of the Ozarks, it was only natural that Margaret, then Kaney, would follow. Margaret's time at The School was typical of others who came during Depression years. "I worked at the canning factory." All wasn't work, though, she laughs. "We sat down on the floor and skinned those tomatoes, and then we had tomato fights--threw tomatoes at each other. Then, for a while I waited tables in Thompson Dining Hall." When her younger brother enrolled, she remarks, "Kaney would get so hungry--a growing boy. So after everyone would leave the dining hall he would say, 'Ret, can't you find some more syrup or biscuits on the other tables?' (His name for me was Ret, for the last syllable in my name.)"

Mrs. Applegate, like her contemporaries, knew that the little school's president was doing all he could do to keep The School operating and put food on the table. It must have been taking its toll, but R. M. Good never wavered. He had provided monumental leadership to The School for over a decade. Perhaps the Trustees were worried. At the Fall 1936 Board Meeting in September in the midst of the Depression...a motion "to work with the Executive Committee in the selection of a man to assist in the administrative work of The School to be trained to ultimately take over the presidency of The School" was passed. Of course, the Trustees had no way of knowing what the immediate future held. If they thought R. M. Good's service to The School was nearing an end, the next few years would dispel that, for Dr. Good would soon have to carry an even greater burden than running The School--dealing with the ripple effect of the greatest war the world had ever known. Scores of students from the tiny Ozarks work school were about to answer their country's call. Some would never return, some would spend time in POW camps, others would return highly decorated; all served with honor. A few of their stories have been told, and by taking a glimpse of them, Americans of today can see the price paid for their freedom.

Fig. 32
Kaney
Willbanks

One such story is that of Kaney Willbanks (Fig. 32), younger brother of Margaret (Willbanks) Applegate. As she clearly revealed, Kaney's life was difficult before he came to The School of the Ozarks. He is but one example of the many who died for our country. She remembers well, "Kaney was a kind of 'happy-go-lucky' person. He came to school here the summer before his junior year. He liked it here, and everybody liked him, 'cause he was so easygoing and he didn't let things upset him or bother him...He was sort of an average student, kind of like I was, working hard for grades. Things were sure hard sometimes. He only had one pair of good trousers. So, the night before he graduated, I had to wash those out and iron them dry, so he could have them to put on the next day."

Like so many others, a few months out of high school he enlisted in the Army. By the middle of 1941, Kaney Willbanks was a long way from the Ozarks. He was out in the Pacific. Before Kaney left the States he wrote to his sister Margaret: "As I am writing this letter, I am thinking of the day when the train pulls into Union Station and I get off...Ret, about this war problem, I want to tell you to not believe all this stuff that comes over the radio and in the papers. I am right over here in the actual war zone, and I still believe that I will never see a bit of action. So take it from your little bud and don't be scared."

No doubt Kaney Willbanks was trying to reassure a worried sister, the relative who was his closest companion from childhood. She recalls, "The last time I saw him, we took him out on the highway and let him out so he could hitchhike a ride...We waited to be sure he got a ride. That was the last time I saw him, standing on the highway."

Margaret, ever the faithful sister, constantly wrote to her brother. Just a few months after Kaney tried to reassure his sister that everything would be okay, the Japanese on December 7, 1941, bombed Pearl Harbor. The immediate effect of this on The School is evident in The School's newsletter, *Our Visitor* (December, 1941).

> As this little paper goes to press, the United States has been attacked by Japan. The war comes very close to our door, because we have boys in the Philippines, in Hawaii, Guam, Midway, and all over the Pacific. Probably seventy-five of our boys are in the Pacific. Concern for them and concern for our country makes all of us here at The School feel that we should work all the harder....

That is just what they did. And, setting the example was President R. M. Good, himself having seen war and knowing that a high price would have to be paid by many; no doubt some of his boys would lose their lives. Kaney Willbanks is an example of many who did not return. By the time of Pearl Harbor, Kaney was in the Pacific. And, unfortunately, he was on the island of Corregidor, which was surrendered to the Japanese in May of 1942. Margaret (Willbanks) Applegate kept trying to find out more about the whereabouts of her brother Kaney. A letter to her dated May 22, 1942, from the War Department, Washington, D.C., relates the seriousness of the problem:

> I regret that it is impossible for me to give you more information than is contained in this letter. In the last days before the surrender of Bataan, there were causalities which were not reported to the War Department. Conceivably, the same is true of the surrender of Corregidor... The department cannot give you positive information... The War Department will consider persons serving in the Philippine Islands as 'missing in action'...until definite information to the contrary is received.

Months passed before Margaret knew if Kaney were alive or not. But by March of 1943 she wrote to the Provost Marshall, "I just received word...that my brother, Private Elkanah H. Willbanks, 17.023.849 is now a prisoner of war of the Japanese government in the Philippine Islands...." Margaret wanted to know how to write to Kaney, which she did.

She received special encouragement to write to her brother from an unlikely source, the daughter of General George Patton. General Patton's daughter, Beatrice Patton Waters, knew firsthand how important this was. "My husband was first reported 'missing.' For three weeks I heard nothing more. Then a telegram came telling me that my husband was a prisoner of war in Germany...Cheerful letters from home mean everything to a prisoner." Mrs. Applegate knew this and made every effort. Finally, she heard back from Kaney--by way of censored "letters" from

Philippine Military Prison Camp No. 10-D. "He reports excellent health, not under treatment...and hello to all." These were no doubt reassuring words to his dear sister Margaret, who had to endure month after month of worry. She sent Kaney a package and many letters but received few replies.

The last communication Margaret received from Kaney was in February, 1945. In it he says, "I am all right and still living, up to May 5, 1944. Received a letter from... Dr. Good...please tell them I am well and will see them again some day." Tragically, this was not to be. Just a few months later, tearfully, Margaret remembers, "They delivered it [a telegram] to me...We lived in a house that was made into apartments; we lived on the third floor. They rang the bell, I think, and the landlady downstairs took the telegram and brought it to us." Shortly, Margaret received a card from General Marshall, the Chief of Staff, extending his sympathy: "Your brother fought valiantly in a supreme hour of his country's need. His memory will live in the grateful heart of our nation!"

Margaret received other words of encouragement, one she especially remembers. "I wish I could find it. A lady sent me a letter, and she wrote a poem. It was about her son who had died in New Guinea. Today, it sends chills over me. She had read about Kaney being killed. It was so touching--such a young boy and everything in his life lay ahead of him...."

The news of the death of Kaney Willbanks must have weighed heavily on R. M. Good. The School's *Our Visitor* (June, 1945), reports, "Elkanah Willbanks was captured on Bataan, and so far as we know he has been heard from

only once. We are especially concerned for his safety...."
That very month word had come that Kaney Willbanks
had been killed. As a memorial, R. M. Good printed in the
August (1945) newsletter a copy of a letter to Margaret
(Willbanks) Applegate from General J. A. Ulio. Its con-
tents tell the tragic circumstances of how Kaney had died:

> The International Red Cross has transmitted to this gov-
> ernment an official list obtained from the Japanese gov-
> ernment, after long delay, of American prisoners of war
> who were lost while being transported northward from
> the Philippine Islands on a Japanese ship which was sunk
> on October 24, 1944. It is with deep regret that I inform
> you that your brother, Private Elkanah H. Willbanks,
> was among those lost when that sinking occurred and, in
> the absence of probability of survival, must be considered
> to have lost his life. He will be carried on the records of
> the War Department as killed in action October 24, 1944.
> The information available to the War Department is that
> the vessel sailed from Manila, Philippine Islands, on Oc-
> tober 11 with 1,775 prisoners of war aboard. On Octo-
> ber 24th the vessel was sunk by submarine action in the
> South China Sea, over 200 miles from the Chinese coast.
> Five of the prisoners escaped in a small boat and reached
> the coast. Four others have been reported as picked up
> by the Japanese, by whom all others are reported as lost
> (1,766)...You have my heartfelt sympathy.

R. M. Good struggled to keep spirits up at The School.
So many of his boys were scattered all over the world, over
200 of them. And bad news continued: Kenneth Collier
(Fig. 33) was killed in Normandy, Dickie Spears (Fig. 34)
died when his bomber crashed, Earl Woodard was missing, Roy Hopper and Raymond Leigh (Fig. 35) were being
held as prisoners of war (POW) in Germany, others were
wounded, and many were being decorated for uncommon
bravery. Such a tiny school was contributing greatly to

Fig. 33	Fig. 34	Fig. 35
Kenneth Collier	Dickie Spears	Raymond Leigh

the cause of freedom.

All during the war years, R. M. Good never let up. But he must have known the schedule he was keeping was taking its toll. For a second time in five years the Trustees thought help must be found. As early as the Fall 1941 Trustee Meeting, just before Pearl Harbor, "the President was instructed to interview men and submit a recommendation for an assistant not later than the spring meeting of the Board." Amazingly, under such dire conditions, the Trustees were "presented a discussion on the Junior College situation." Clearly, the future of the country and The School itself may have been in doubt, but lack of vision for the future of The School was not!

Every month during the war years must have brought R. M. Good great sadness and great joy. Two of "his boys" survived the most incredible of circumstances, one as a prisoner of war. Their stories are riveting.

Roy Hopper was able to attend The School because of his mother's determination. "I'm very anxious for Roy to enter The School," Mrs. Hopper wrote to R. M. Good. "I have been so helpless...They were all so small when their father died. The older ones have had to work to help support the younger ones...." "I have placed your son on the waiting list," was the reply. "I hope your son will not give up hope."

Roy Hopper's dream to attend The School came true, his only chance for an education. His journey to an education, to serving his country, and to an incredible escape from a POW camp is forever in his memory. "I grew up in Harrison, Arkansas, about a mile and a half north of town, Oak Grove...It was a one-room schoolhouse. Thirty students divided into eight grades. Just one teacher carried in the wood, swept out the school building, and taught eight different grades! My father died when I was about a month before my sixth birthday. My oldest brother was eleven. We lived in an old hillside farm. We gathered wild food and berries. I don't know how we did it."

Because of his mother's persistent letter writing to R. M. Good, Roy Hopper ended up on The School's doorstep. "We only had about two pairs of what you call clothes you could wear to class...only had about one pair you could work in. I came the first day of July in 1940."

Roy's work experience was pretty standard stuff. "I worked helping build the girls dorm, and later that fall, I worked on the dairy. I was good at that. But it wasn't as much fun as I thought it would be because our dairy superintendent had to get us up at four o'clock." Roy Hopper was not only a hard worker on the job but in the classroom as well. "I managed to make the Honor Roll twice," he said. "But I got kidded too much because mostly girls made the Honor Roll. The guys said, 'Hopper, you were just doing that to be up there with the girls!'"

Not only does Roy remember his work both inside and outside of class, but he distinctly remembers R. M. Good.

"I tell you," Roy recalls, "he could eat you out and still inspire you. And, he had those little signs hanging in the study hall. We had to go to study hall every night. Dr. Good had little signs to remind us about life. Such as, 'When the boy goes bad, the good man dies' or 'Put boots on; the summertime's not made for sitting down,' or 'Empty the pot, the quicker it boils.' They were on little plaques."

Roy Hopper remains grateful to R. M. Good for more than reminders. "He had Mr. J. C. Penny, himself, send us shoes. We would sign up for a pair of shoes, but we had to work so many extra hours to pay for the shoes...."

Things weren't so serious with Roy Hopper that he didn't find time for fun, especially at one of his work assignments. "We had to go down and help quarry out limestone. Our boss was Mr. Bates. He had this old, I guess you would call it, bulldozer to push rocks around...it had a big old metal steering wheel that had round holes in it, I guess to keep it from getting so hot. So, we caught this long grass snake and when Bates wasn't looking, we folded the snake into the steering wheel; it just crawled right in. Now, Mr. Bates always chewed on his tongue and was so busy working it took him forever to notice. Finally, when he did notice, he just slapped it and cut the snake in half...." No doubt Bates almost swallowed his tongue!

Unfortunately, the good times didn't last long for Roy Hopper and a lot of other boys. Roy had enjoyed working during the summer. The first two summers he worked on campus. The third summer he worked in Kansas. "I went out and worked in the wheat fields because I could make ten bucks a day," he chuckles. Roy returned to Kansas the summer before what would have been his senior year.

When he returned, it was obvious to him that his time of deferral from the draft was running out. "I had to notify the draft board. They said, 'We'll be calling you!'" And so it was in August of 1943 that Roy Hopper entered the Army. What would have been his senior year in the Ozarks was to become what he later described as "the time spent in hell."

What Roy Hopper (Fig. 36) experienced is an incredible story. "My oldest brother was in the Army. My other brother was in the Navy and stationed in the Canal Zone. I was the third one to go. My oldest brother was drafted; the next one volunteered. I was drafted." No doubt such a sacrifice by one family wore heavy on Roy's mother. "My mom was a worrywart. Her health was bad, so everything was stressful on her. I always say that she was the one woman that lost a life in World War II because her health went to pot when my oldest brother was wounded real badly and I was a POW...She only lived four years after the war."

Fig. 36

Roy Hopper

At the tender age of eighteen, Roy Hopper joined thousands of young Americans who came to the defense of their country. He went to boot camp in Texas with a friend, Dale Hambright. A few months later, Roy got a rude awakening. "I got up one morning, I think in March, and my right leg was partially paralyzed. I was embarrassed. I had to guide my right foot into my boot." Roy would not be deterred. "The drill sergeant would march us down the road a mile or mile and a half. I always made sure I got in the inner ranks, so the sergeant wouldn't see my leg flopping.

The only time it hurt was when I was walking. I had never heard of multiple sclerosis--MS."

By concealing his condition, Roy found himself a few weeks later on a ship bound for Europe. "They packed us in there real tight. We departed the U.S. on April 10, 1944, and arrived in Europe on April 19th. We got off the ship in Scotland, got on a train, and wound up in a cow pasture north of Bristol Bay. By the time I got to Europe, my leg was working." Roy vividly remembers the conditions in England. "We had tents out there in the cow pasture. No plumbing, no nothing. We had a bag of straw for our mattress; we had an old kerosene lantern and an army cot."

Roy's time in the cow pasture could not have portended what was to follow. "We did nothing but wait," he said, "until the first part of June came and D-Day, and they announced it. They brought us all together and gave us a report on the invasion. They told us the Allies made a beach landing--that we had pushed in slowly, maybe a hundred yards." Roy had missed the initial Normandy invasion by a few days. But he knew his time was coming. "We knew and started preparing."

On June 13, Roy Hopper found himself going ashore at Utah Beach. He still recalls clearly the devastation. "You could see the war, knocked out tanks...." Quickly, Roy Hopper's unit, the 357th, joined the big push inland, and heavy combat ensued. "I don't believe we were more than a couple of miles; we were at the front lines. You could hear the big guns going off before we got off the ship. But I only got scared when I got to the front lines. It was kill or be killed."

Even in such a fierce battle, Roy felt blessed. "You may

not know this, but the Lord was with our landing forces in Normandy." Roy believes it could have been worse, if they had landed where Hitler expected. But it still required heavy combat and heavy loss of life. Roy knew his unit was at a disadvantage in the fighting. "The Germans were good soldiers. They had been dug in there for years. They knew every crick and crevice, every gully. We would push them back, and the next thing we knew they were back. Normandy was made up of little hedgerows and brush. They would put rubber bands in their helmets to hold greenery, twigs. We couldn't camouflage. Our tactics were medieval. We were in wide spaces. It was a bloody fight."

Roy didn't think his green troops were any match for the dug-in Germans. "We were green as a gourd, ran into the 5th German Paratrooper Regiment, and they were reinforced with SS troopers. They were doped up--a leg would be blown off, and they would keep coming. Otherwise, they would have died from shock. There were two companies...."

Roy Hopper and his buddy Dale Hambright were in the same company. "L Company was our company--took the brunt of the attack." Tragically, Dale Hambright died in the fighting, along with 166 other Americans. Roy didn't know about Dale's death until later. Providentially, years later, Dale's sister was to become Mrs. Roy Hopper.

Roy's recollection of what happened in the battle is riveting. "Twenty-five of us held out. We held out the longest. We lost contact with the others; they had been killed or captured. We held out until almost dark. We wouldn't surrender, but we ran out of ammunition. And, the Germans brought in their tanks." Roy's holdouts were surrounded with no ammunition. "They captured us."

Roy must have wondered about his friend Dale. "I didn't know he had gotten killed until I was captured and some of the guys told me...." But Roy had little time to think about it. "First, they marched you with your hands in the air; you thought your arms were going to drop off. They took us back probably a mile and put us in a little circle." What happened next is even worse. "They asked for commanding officers. Three lieutenants stepped forward. Then they asked for Jews. Three Jews stepped forward. They didn't know any better," Roy regrets. "We never saw them again."

During the early part of his captivity, Roy thought of escape. "I could have escaped when we were walking. But they said for every one of you that escapes, we're going to kill ten of your comrades." They even explained how it would be done. "They would bunch us real tight together and throw pebbles in the air; whoever the pebble hit would be shot. So you don't do that." Roy's ordeal continued, "Anyway, they walked us. No food. They walked us for three days. On the fourth day (we didn't get to sleep at night), they kept us huddled in a pasture...they put us in a big old warehouse building with a concrete floor... gave us our first meal--for four guys, one can of horse meat, no bread."

Things continued to go downhill for Hopper and his fellow POWs. "Finally, we got to Paris; they put us in boxcars." Conditions indeed worsened. "It was hot. They shut the doors and packed us in there with no bathroom facilities. People had dysentery; no water. We lay there day and night. We were without water three days in a boxcar.

I bet the temperature was over one hundred degrees. You almost go into seizures; you almost go hysterical...They had water and they had air. I can give the enemy credit for not feeding us. But they had as much water and air as anybody in the country...They violated every Geneva Convention rule for how we were treated."

Roy further explains, "They didn't mark the boxcars; they should have had 'POW' on the boxcar. So, our fighter planes would come down and strafe the boxcars, and we lost lives...Finally, they moved us out. We weren't priority freight. Eventually, we got to a big stalag in Germany... every nationality. They had Russians; they had French... And we were there for two or three weeks. Then, all of us kids with no rank were trucked out to labor camps."

Life in the labor camps was dreadful. "They divided us into three groups. My job was with a group of about twenty-five. We worked on the railroad, repairing tracks, tilling up bomb craters, and putting the tracks back together. My boss was mean. We didn't know what he was saying...We would just stand there. He would grab us by the hair of the head and shove our head down...."

One event Roy says he could never live long enough to forget, "It was deep in the heart of winter. Our labor camp was right below the railroad bank...about eleven o'clock at night...we heard machine gun fire and hand grenades. We wondered, 'What in the world?' We were hoping Americans were coming. After a while it quieted down and they [Germans] came down and got us, ten of us prisoners...These people were oriental-looking...They had killed them. It was cold, and a lot of them were just dressed in thin stuff; those people were probably freezing. They had caused some sort of uproar, and the Germans had just killed them and switched the trains back and forth."

It must have been a gruesome sight, as Roy said body parts were everywhere--arms, legs, heads. He painfully recalls, "We had to clean it up with picks and shovels and burlap bags."

It was in the cold hard winter of 1945 that Roy Hopper endured another kind of inhumane condition. Probably in an act of desperation and a cry for freedom, Roy Hopper and a couple of other soldiers bounded over a fence and escaped. "We ran up the hill and then into the woods. They didn't know we were gone until we were 'too' gone," Roy says. "The forest was thick--like a whole bunch of Christmas trees, about eight feet high and thick. We had only a loaf of bread. We started going north. We were afraid and always stayed under cover. It was cold and sleeting. Every day we were getting weaker. One day we came to a barn... came across a big pile of straw and chicken litter, crawled under it, and stayed all night."

No doubt the three escapees were nearing exhaustion. "The next morning, before daylight, we got out but we couldn't walk. We were cold and stiff--had to roll on the ground to get our circulation going before we could walk. We were getting to the point where we were going to give out walking through this brush...then there was this railroad track. We were going to walk this because it wouldn't be as hard."

The three hoped the tracks would wind up on the Allied side of the fighting. They rounded a curve, Hopper explains. "It was rainy."

They came upon an outpost and feared they were Germans. "They had their helmets off; they were goofing off. I had old fuzzy whiskers...looked terrible, scared. We saw them reach for their rifles." When the POWs got closer they must have breathed a deep sigh of relief because they noticed, "They had American helmets. We yelled, 'Are you guys American?'" The reply was direct, "'Yes sir, who the hell are you?' We were scared, and we were safe." Hopper laments, "We had gotten away from the Krauts [Germans]. I asked, 'Where is your main line?' They said, 'Right up there after the turn.' I said, 'We're going to go home.' One of the guards replied, 'No, if you go any further you're going to get shot. You stay right here.'"

Eventually, the three arrived safely escorted to the main line. "That's when we got to heaven," Roy says. "You have to imagine being in hell and waking up in heaven."

At Allied headquarters Roy and his two comrades were told, "Now pick out the nicest house you can see. Go in there and make yourself comfortable." "So," Roy says, "we went up to this nice house. I still feel guilty. We were filthy; they had their white sheets on the bed...we opened the cabinet...all of this canned fruit. We started eating. We stayed there that night."

The next morning a load of German POWs arrived in town. The three Americans were told they could ride with the Krauts. "We rode about twenty-five miles with them."

Later Roy says he and his comrades found their way to an apple orchard. "Here on a box about four feet high was a captain; he was the air traffic controller! He looked at us; we looked awful. We said, 'We're POWs; we would like to hitch a ride back to London.' He said, 'You guys deserve to go anywhere you want. There's an evacuation hospital up there. There are nurses there. Go up there and get your coat because it's going to be another hour before I get another plane.'"

So they did. Winding up in England in a hospital, they were nursed back to health. Roy Hopper experienced a surreal return to the United States and to Arkansas. "We were put on a troop train marked with red crosses. People were crying at railroad crossings looking at the happy soldiers, many with missing arms and legs."

How Roy Hopper survived is known only to God. But his dear mother never gave up hope. In a letter to R. M. Good at The School, Mrs. Hopper wrote, while Roy was a POW, "As for us, we have found hope in prayer...I felt like it was my duty to write and inform you about Roy when we first received the news...." Ever faithful R. M. Good wrote to Roy and received notes from Roy. One such note reads, "I am praying the time will come when I can see you again...." Dr. Good, by way of the *Our Visitor* magazine, had reported on Roy's captivity, and as soon as he heard that Roy had escaped the POW camps, Dr. Good wrote directly to Roy's mother some very touching remarks. "I feel that I'm not the only one by far who is still praying for him, and all of those who have suffered and are still suffering that we might still have America."

Roy Hopper, known as POW #50160, was discharged from the Army as a Private First Class with two bronze stars. Almost fifty years later he was recognized with the Jubilee Medal of Liberty from the state of New Mexico. And, The School of the Ozarks (now college) awarded him his high school diploma.

Many other products of such a small Ozarks school lost their lives or had their lives changed forever. Many knew each other or had been classmates like Kaney Willbanks and Earl Woodard, coming to The School from the same orphanage. Kaney tragically lost his life in the Pacific, but  Earl (Fig. 37) was miraculously spared in Europe by the French underground after his bomber had crashed. Like Roy Hopper, he was one of the lucky ones. He lived to tell his inspiring story in *The B-17 of LaGoulafriere:*

Fig. 37
Earl Woodard

"I woke with a start. Mac Dickinson was shaking me. 'Woody,' he said, 'Come alive! The 457th is leading the 94th wing today. You're the lead navigator.'

"After little more than an hour's sleep, it was not easy to 'come alive' as Mac directed. A good breakfast helped... Briefing for the mission began about 0300. Our pilot, Ed Bender said, 'Woody, we've got it made! It's something different, a "milk run" [a routine mission, not expected to be dangerous]. We won't know how to deal with it!' I agreed. After missions like...Hamburg and Berlin we could cope with this one, our seventeenth.

"The briefing proceeded...partly overcast in England, eighty-five percent in France. We saw photographs and got a physical description of the target, including the location of anti-aircraft installations and were told what kinds of bombs were being loaded.

"When the briefing for the mission was complete we proceeded by Jeep to the flight line and our airplane 'for the day'...Our B-17G, as usual, was carrying a maximum load, 2500 gallons of gasoline and twelve 500-pound bombs...a test for the flight engineer's skill!

"The plane shuddered as it began taxiing down the take-off runway, gathering every bit of power Ed Bender could muster from the four engines. We cleared the woods and began our ascent. This was the thirty-ninth mission of the 457th Bombardment group, and we were leading two hundred Flying Fortresses...our target, a German air installation at Nancy, France.

"Once we had assembled above the overcast, it was my job as lead navigator to give the pilots a heading for our destination. As we set out over the English Channel, I was not as tense as I had been on previous missions. We were on our 'milk run.'"

It became clear pretty quickly that things would not be according to plans. Earl Woodard continues the story, "We were practically flying blind. Circumstances were seldom ideal and this day's eighty-five percent overcast made it impossible to use the terrain to verify our positions...we maintained silence. As we approached Nancy-Essey Airdrome we encountered heavy flak. The target was completely overcast and dropping the bombs was out of the question. We turned back...we turned west and were, as usual, faced with one hundred mile an hour headwinds....

"Suddenly, we heard on the intercom, 'Number four engine on fire.' And shortly thereafter, 'Number three engine on fire.'... From my position in the nose of the plane, I could see fire in both engines...Soon we heard 'smoke in the bomb-bay.' Then, 'Abandon ship!'" It was obvious to all that the big bomber was on fire and was going to blow up or crash or both. "At the signal to abandon ship any delay could be fatal. Hearing it, I had lifted off my heavy flak jacket and helmet, and unhooked the oxygen line...I was at the escape hatch in no time....

"We stepped out of the burning plane into the quiet of the 25,000 foot altitude." Earl still admires the captain of the doomed plane. "Ed Bender was true to a captain's tradition...He was the last to leave the plane." Eventually, eleven parachutes floated down to French terrain below. Earl recalls, "The parachute opened with a jolt on the harness...I had pulled the cord at four or five thousand feet. The rate of descent had slowed dramatically. Fields and orchards passed beneath. I landed rather abruptly in an apple tree unhurt, except for a wrenched knee."

Finding one of his buddies nearby, they had to make a decision. "Feeling sure the Germans were not far away, we decided to move off in opposite directions." Earl was right. Soon thereafter he remembers, "Two or three Frenchmen appeared and directed me to a hollow tree in which to hide. I was barely hidden when a German patrol swept through the woods. Had they looked back, they surely would have spotted me."

It must have been a good omen, because Earl was not abandoned. "The patrol passed and a lone Frenchman came to my hiding place in the tree." Earl was taken to the Frenchman's home, and they explained that the Germans would be searching the village carefully that night. In order to spare Woodard, the Frenchman took him in a horse-drawn carriage to a farm and passed him on to a new host. Woodard knew the risks to these people. "Needless to say, he risked his life and that of his family by sheltering me."

Incredibly, the next evening brought a big surprise.

"There at the front door stood Jack Hotaling, fully recovered from his fiery exit and frigid fall." His buddy Jack told Earl what had happened to him after landing and hiding in a barn. "Within minutes two Germans on motorcycles zoomed up the drive and...began searching for the American whose parachute descent they had been watching. According to Jack he dropped on to the first German to enter the barn and broke his neck. The farm's owner made sure the second met the same fate!"

Unbelievably, two more of the fliers were reunited. According to Earl, "Eleven parachutes were seen floating to the ground. SS troops from the garrison at nearby Tremblay Chateau were combing the area in search of downed fliers." Earl Woodard knew that he was one of the lucky ones. "The Germans had captured six of our crew, but the courageous Frenchmen had snatched five of us from under their noses. The six men who landed closest to the wreckage seemed to be the ones who were captured. They were taken to the garrison at Chateau Tremblay and thence to prison camps in Germany and Austria."

The lucky five fliers remained hidden from the Germans, but they had to be careful. "Boredom was difficult to deal with. An occasional walk in the forest would have been a relief, but Germans from the nearby garrison hunted in the area and often came within a few yards of our hiding place. Our isolation was relieved by almost daily visits from members of the 'underground'...After almost two weeks after the five of us had been gathered on...the farm, we were visited by four men from the 'Resistance' organization...It was obvious that the 'Resistants' had close contact with British intelligence."

A plan to get the fliers out was devised, according to Earl. "Five weeks after we parachuted into the French countryside, the morning of departure dawned." Hidden in a flatbed truck, the fliers were smuggled past German after German patrol. "The day's journey would take us on a circuitous route to the railway station at Ste. Gauburge." Later the group arrived at a young couple's cottage. They were fed and grateful. "We were deeply moved by the young couple's generosity and honored to have been their first guests."

The next step on an incredible journey to freedom was more of the same. "Into another vehicle...this one with a canvas cover. We were soon bouncing down the road."

At a village railway station they met three 'Resistance' leaders. "We were to take the train...to Paris. Knowing our escape route would take us across the Pyrenees into Spain, we had assumed we'd be traveling through more lightly populated areas...." The fliers donned disguises and made it to a modest hotel in Paris. "Five of us shared one of the few rooms the owner had been allowed to rent. A distant view of the Eiffel Tower was our only reminder that we were, indeed, in Paris."

The next morning the fliers were to board a street car with coins given to them to find "the departure point south" by train. They did. They also were careful to follow instructions. "We were to exit the train when the military police entered and re-board when they had passed through the car." It worked. The group arrived at a safehouse in Toulouse (called 'gateway to the Pyrenees'). As Earl explains, "This was the point from which final preparations would be made for our journey to Spain. Allied intelligence was supplying funds to pay the mercenaries for the safe delivery of evading fliers. They were risking their lives but for a fee significantly larger than the profit from their usual occupation, smuggling."

After being joined by a British flyer, Earl tells what happened: "A group of six (of us) headed into the mountains with two guides. It was cloudy and very cold as we walked single file, in the pitch darkness, each holding on to the man in front of him...Snow began to fall as we climbed and our scant clothing was not sufficient protection...no overcoats...no boots...we gave little thought to the cold. We were determined to get through the mountains to freedom...The sun rose as we crossed that last mountain barrier."

What happened next makes the story even more nerve racking. Earl explains, "The local gendarmes were awaiting our arrival and led us without ceremony, to jail! Collapsing exhausted, we were oblivious to the stark surroundings."

After being led from jail and passed from town to town and finally to the town of Lerida--location of a U.S. Consul's office, someone from the Consul arranged for the fliers to board a bus to Madrid, and a few days later they found themselves at Gibraltar. Mercifully, as Earl Woodard remembers, the end of the ordeal was near. "We had been at Gibralter less than twenty-four hours when we boarded a British military transport to London."

What the fliers saw when they got to London, they will never forget. "We arrived in London at the height of the German 'buzz bomb' activity. The damage was horrendous. At least a half million people slept on the subway platforms at night...." After being interrogated by Allied forces, Earl Woodard had returned full-circle. He soon learned the price. "When I returned to the base it was pretty glum to learn how many friends had been shot down and died or were missing in action."

As if Earl Woodard had experienced every twist and turn of war, his journey home added a new one. On the final leg home he waited in the train's dining car. "I waited with an attractive brunette in an unfamiliar uniform. She explained she was a Cadet Corps Nurse...returning to Washington University School of Nursing...and we had dinner together...We were married three months later."

Earl Woodard's safe return no doubt encouraged a weary R. M. Good and all The School of the Ozarks family. The year before the end of WWII had strained everyone. In the little school's July 1944 newsletter, R. M. Good reported great relief about Earl Woodard in an article entitled, "Lt. Earl Woodard Missing." A little P.S. appeared at the end of the article and reads in part, "It is with great rejoicing that we are able to amend this article, just as the paper goes to press. Lt. Woodard's mother has informed us that Earl is now safely back in England. The details of his experience are something that cannot be told until after the war...."

It is evident that a tiny Ozarks school paid part of the high price for freedom. Many stories could be told of bravery and sacrifice. The ultimate sacrifice made by Kaney Willbanks and many others is now a part of history. And the incredible stories of survival of Private First Class Roy Hopper and Lieutenant Earl Woodard serve as a constant reminder of hope and freedom paid for by their classmates, friends, and countless others who answered the country's call. The willingness of all in uniform who served, those who survived and those who did not, is perhaps best captured in a poem that President R. M. Good included in his little newsletter distributed just six months after Pearl Harbor. It was sent in to him from one of "his boys" from an American base, location censored. Here is the quotation the soldier enclosed:

"I Will"

America *must* win this war.
Therefore, I *will* work; I *will*
save; I *will* sacrifice; I *will*
endure; I *will* fight cheerfully
and do my utmost, *as if the issue
of the whole struggle depended on
me alone.*

A very small school in the Ozarks, under the leadership of one of God's greatest servants, R. M. Good, had done its duty. It was time to face the future.

Chapter VI
"The Wizard of the Ozarks"

The decade following World War II was a time of change at "the School that lives on faith." Thanks to the untiring efforts of R. M. Good, the little school had taken root from its auspicious beginnings, having now survived two major fires, a change of location, a major economic depression, financial crises, and the greatest war the world had ever seen. Through it all Dr. Good never wavered, and his total commitment inspired everyone.

Over a ten-year period (1946-1956), the minutes of the Board clearly indicate the challenges before The School. The constant demand for funds to operate The School didn't change. But funds were needed for better facilities, because a "dream" of some board members seemed paramount--that of adding a junior college program. Trustees still knew that Dr. Good needed help. After a quarter century of leadership, time was taking its toll. The little school had also been dependent on a small board of trustees with some very prominent business leaders among them. Not only had Dr. Good given years of strong leadership, but so had some key trustees, such as L. W. Hyer and J. M. McDonald, Sr., to name only two.

So, it must have been with great apprehension that The School forged ahead. The most pressing need seems

Fig. 38 Robert M. Good (left) and M. Graham Clark

to have been finding someone to take the place of R. M. Good (Fig. 38) eventually. This need had come before the Board earlier but now took on more of a sense of urgency. Dr. Good never complained and was more than open to bringing in someone to help him and, in due time, take over the reins and meet the future.

Some trustees had previously had someone in mind, even contacting him a few years earlier. Then the war came along. They decided to try again and contacted M. Graham Clark (Fig. 38), a young insurance executive in Atlanta, Georgia. He was a committed churchman, and a person of great speaking ability, fund-raising acumen, and definite leadership potential.

Some fifty years later Dr. M. Graham Clark fondly recalls his first dealings with The School of the Ozarks, prior to coming to the Ozarks.

"I was active in interdenominational work in Atlanta." Dr. Clark first heard about The School of the Ozarks, in a somewhat unusual manner, at a National Presbyterian Mission Conference in Atlanta. "They brought in...very prominent clergymen from this country. And the first open meeting was in the brand new facility of Atlanta's First Baptist Church, called the most ideal church plant in the United States. I was asked to preside at the first meeting," Dr. Clark recalls. "I guess being the youngest one around, I did! E. Stanley Jones, a famous Methodist missionary to India was a speaker. When that meeting was over, four men walked down front...Dr. Ed Grant said to me in the company of the others, 'You do know about The School of the Ozarks,' and I said, 'No gentlemen, I don't.' His response was, 'You ought to...' and he started telling me about it, and I said, 'What has that got to do with me?' 'Well,' he said, 'Some years ago I promised the Trustees, with the President Robert M. Good, that I would be on the lookout for a successor to Dr. Good. Tonight I felt moved; God's spirit moved in my heart.'" Dr. Clark vividly recalls being told by this very prominent man that he believed, "That's the man we want."

Dr. Clark was no doubt taken aback by such a revelation. But he remembers responding, "Well, I tell you, I decided early in life that I would try to find what God wanted me to do, and I think I have found it. In fact, my wife and I signed a pledge before we were married that we would seek God's will for our lives, and finding it, we would follow it where it takes us, cost what it may." Dr. Clark says the four pastors asked to visit with him the next day. They did and Dr. Clark never forgot. "I heard the story...a mountain school educating young people who were found worthy but without sufficient means to pay for an education...to give them the benefits of a Christian education." Dr. Clark told the group he would think about it. After speaking with his wife, Dr. Clark also remembers more. "I started getting letters from Dr. Good and from the Chairman of the Board. One very prominent trustee, Dr. William Crow, came to see me in Atlanta. That gentleman had a big bony finger and was putting it in my face and said, 'Young man, I am convinced it is God's will for you to go to the Ozarks.' I said, 'I wish it was that easy for me!' I didn't want to leave. I loved the city of Atlanta. But The School never failed to send me fruitcakes, hams, jellies, and preserves...just overwhelmed me. I never knew of a place that did things like that. I don't know anything that won my heart any faster than just kind treatment and candid letters. But World War II came along.... 'You need to get an educator or preacher or someone who will fit in.' I didn't hear from them quite as often beginning in the '40s."

The search for Dr. Good's successor intensified after the war. Dr. Clark says, "The day I got home...there was a Western Union messenger there about the same time I got to the porch. He had a telegram...from the Board and it said, 'Let's settle this matter. We need you. Please consider coming out and looking at us and meeting our board.' I did both. I had been out once earlier. I took my wife...it was the first of May, all the flowers were blooming and the weather was perfect. It was one of those beautiful spring days...Well, we headed back to Atlanta by train...."

Obviously, young Clark had a difficult decision to make. It must have been a struggle, for he described a near "Pauline" experience. "I was over at the main auditorium of Atlanta's First Presbyterian Church, just about the time the sun was setting...I had been down on my knees, the light pouring through the windows...and, of all things, the first words that hit my eye were 'not my will, but Thine be done.' It couldn't have hit me harder...I felt pulled, tugged, and I called and told them I was coming. My minister told me I would regret this." Perhaps Graham Clark's minister didn't know Clark well after all. M. Graham Clark had no regrets; he had a mission. The little school in the Ozarks had found the right man for the future, and The School would never be the same.

Coming to the Ozarks school exacted a price from Clark. "I had to sell my controlling interest in a good-sized business...insurance. I prayed that the cup might pass from me, but it didn't. We burned bridges behind us. My salary [at The School] was $200 a month. I paid a lot more than that in federal income tax...But I've not regretted it. I felt that it was God's will...there were times when the road seemed hard."

And so it was that M. Graham Clark was called to the Ozarks. Within a year of the close of the war, The School had met its goal. M. Graham Clark became vice president of The School of the Ozarks, knowing that one day he would have to carry the load.

Dr. Clark definitely didn't forget the move out from Atlanta. "I loaded the vans. We had more furniture than we could put in the house. I left an eighteen-room house, with a lot of comforts and a good staff of people working for us.

We had had a chauffeur...I was disappointed in the house... When we got here they had gotten behind and hadn't finished the cottage they were building for us to live in. It burned on Christmas Eve. It was not located where I liked it, but I didn't burn it down...We decided to offer to build a house, my wife and I did." Dr. and Mrs. Clark and their young daughters were determined to make The School their home, and they did, although it was a challenge.

"Doc Good couldn't have been more gracious...But he couldn't have given me a worse send-off! The first night here in the dining hall he said, 'Well my successor has come on board.' That's the last thing these kids wanted to hear...a man from Atlanta...'We don't want anything to do with this city slicker.'" But the Clarks were determined. "We won the hearts of the students, and they won ours, my wife and I. She was a great help. She taught the biggest Sunday School class we had here. She was the superintendent, as well."

Dr. Clark persevered the initial year, recalling, "I sat out on that bluff that first year, the winter...sitting there looking at the lake and up the river, and that mist froze in my hair...I was praying for courage...." Clark showed no indication of anything but confidence as he and Dr. Good worked closely together to meet the Board's expectations, as well as keep The School on the straight and narrow. But the Board sensed the time was right to consider seriously adding a college program. Dr. Clark quickly picked up the challenge and became a driving force in this direction.

The School was not only fortunate to have attracted a future leader such as M. Graham Clark, but others as well. One who joined The School shortly after the Clarks

Fig. 39 Beulah (Gutridge) Winfrey

arrived was Beulah (Gutridge) Winfrey (Fig. 39), a young business instructor who became one of The School's longest and most loyal servants and benefactors. Her recollections of this period reveal a lot, not only of herself, but The School of the Ozarks and its operation. "The Placement Dean at Central Missouri State University called me and said there was an opening in just the right place for me. I interviewed with Dr. Good and Dr. Clark...The ride from Springfield was quite an experience on a very slow bus all the way through Forsyth, the long way around...after the long layover in Springfield. Then, an all-day and night experience. Shortly thereafter, I got my appointment letter from Dr. Good."

Even a casual reading of Dr. Good's letter suggests the hiring process was taken seriously and in a no-nonsense manner. Beulah remembers, "Their expectations were quite high. The emphasis was that I would be doing more than just teaching a class...."

> As we have explained to you, we need more than a commercial teacher. We need someone who would take an interest in outside activities...This is distinctively a Christian school, justified, only in the desire to give boys and girls a well-rounded intellectual, social, vocational, and spiritual training.

His letter went on to say that Beulah would be paid $150 a month and be furnished a separate room with steam heat, a shared bathroom, laundry, and board in the dining room. To point out how serious her would-be employer was, Beulah laughed, saying, "Only if you worked out would you be asked to stay."

Beulah Winfrey wasn't married when she arrived but was married within a year. It just increased her usefulness to The School. "They asked us to manage the boys dormitory. We were called Ma and Pa...I was teaching full-time, and my husband was working construction full-time." Beulah Winfrey's workload was typical of those times, and she never forgot. "Six classes, study hall, and any secretarial work they needed done for the office--nights, weekends. My class did the church bulletin on the typewriter and mimeograph; my class did the special letter gram sent in the fall to recruit funds; and all these were done on manual typewriters and had to be proofread." Such a workload, along with running a dormitory, made Beulah one of many "workhorses" The School depended on. But Dr. Good set the standard and Beulah admired him for it. "He had a heart as big as all outdoors. We shared things, and he was never too busy to take time to listen to a student or an outsider who came in. It didn't matter if it was a workman or somebody well dressed."

The little school needed all the leadership it could get. More was going to be required; the task of adding a college program signaled that. The Trustees must've believed in keeping the plate full. In the spring prior to Dr. Clark's arrival, the Board expressed its big goals and more. They "unanimously and enthusiastically passed a resolution that the college, when established at The School of the Ozarks, be named the Lewis W. Hyer Junior College...." This was based on "enthusiastic testimony of Mr. Hyer's many years of unselfish service and devotion to The School and of his study and plans for the establishment of a vocational junior college."

After the Trustees passed their resolution of intent, Dr. Good wrote confidential letters to special friends to solicit their views as to how they felt about this and how Mr. Hyer would view it. One of Dr. Good's letters, written to Mr. John Swift of Kansas City, exemplifies Dr. Good's long-range plan for The School:

> There is a matter I have had on my mind for a long time, and that is the suggestion that we name the junior college the Wilk Hyer Junior College, and that in the catalog pertaining to this junior college we have a picture of Mr. Hyer and a little history of his life; how he came from a large family, how his father died, and how the family was very poor. He had to quit school in early life to work for a living for himself and his family, but he never ceased to study or prepare himself until today, in my opinion, he is better educated than many college students. I believe this would be a real incentive to boys and girls in the future to struggle and strive to accomplish...at best Mr. Hyer will not be with us a great many more years....

Evidently the idea didn't take root immediately. Mr. Hyer likely made it known he didn't want his name used, as he was a very private man. No doubt, Dr. Clark had been informed prior to his coming about such plans. He recalled, "I kept being told that we weren't ready. Well, I really think that if we would have waited until we were totally ready, financially speaking and every other way, we never would have a college and I told the Board that. Maybe I stuck my neck out a little bit...I had been told way back that I was to someday make this into a college. Well, that someday, seemed to me, was on us."

It was probably not a coincidence that such a strong leader was around only a few years as vice president before taking over. Dr. Clark verifies this. "I had a good time breaking in, and when I felt like I had learned the ropes,

Dr. Good said, 'Well, I am going to retire.' He became President Emeritus (1952) and stayed right up until he died."

It is obvious that Dr. Clark bonded with Dr. Good. "He was always a great help to me and a great friend; I appreciated him so much. I will always know that somehow, God had it in His plan, and in His will and purpose, for us to come to the Ozarks. I don't think we would have been happy doing anything else."

Thirty-one years after coming to the Ozarks, Dr. Good took on a new role, that of president emeritus. This undoubtedly had been well planned as Trustee Wilk Hyer proposed a by-law change whereby The School would be run by a president emeritus and a president, with final authority on all matters reserved by the Board. It was a natural transition of leadership and worked well, for most believed that the two kept whatever differences they ever had out of public view. It served the little school well, allowing for more fund-raising and carrying out the plans for a college.

The same year (1952) that Dr. Clark assumed the presidency, the Board passed an historic directive. "It was moved to...make a diligent study of junior college plans and methods of operation, to present this at the next meeting of the Board." At the same meeting, a resolution of appreciation to Mr. Hyer was approved, but no mention was made of attaching his name to the junior college.

The plan was accomplished with a lot of hard work. "We did a study," Beulah Winfrey recalls. "We worked late night hours; sometimes committee meetings would end at 1:30. He [Dr. Clark] pushed us on it." Within a year, a study report was presented to the Board. This report was made with the consultation of the Committee on Accreditation of Junior Colleges. It was thorough and direct, and it was pointed out that the addition of a science building would make the plant adequate, library supplies would be needed, and that all teachers must have at least an M.A. degree with appropriate credentials. It went on to cite some danger points. "Four junior colleges had closed in the state last year...the difficulty in securing teachers is not to be underestimated." The report included a warning from the committee. "It would be better not to start than to start and fail."

The Board called for continued study and another report, no doubt to the consternation of Dr. Clark, who likely never considered failure an option. But the Trustees were a cautious lot, and they wanted to be assured before they jumped into such a big undertaking.

Although Dr. Clark took on increasing levels of responsibility, Dr. and Mrs. Good's presence did not diminish. Beulah Winfrey worked with Dr. and Mrs. Good for many years, and she emphasized Mrs. Good's role. "We called her 'Sunshine.' She could tell you a student's name, their parents' name, others who had gone to school here and who were related to them, and things they did while they were here. She was not only a wonderful math teacher... they [she and Dr. Good] hosted people in their home. You may have heard the term, 'they carried it on their back.' They went out of the way." Beulah Winfrey equally admired Dr. Good. "He would always share something with you--maybe it was made by The School, or maybe it was something that was made in his home. He was a very sharing person. I mean, if you went to his house, he probably would give you something before you left, whatever it was. It might be a gourd; it might be a pen; it might be a Coke."

Dr. Good's work ethic was inspiring to all, especially Dr. Clark. Dr. Clark fondly adds, "He was a loyal friend, and I respected the man as family; he worked as hard as anyone could know, and, I think [that was] one reason I didn't think anything about working every night. If I got to my office at seven in the morning and left at eleven at night, I thought I was fortunate. He worked the same way, even after he retired; he went on and worked long hours... He loved students...Had what we called a hard luck fund, and I respected that. If students had a hard time, they could go to him and if they needed a little money, he'd give it out and wouldn't make you pay it back."

Dr. Clark added, "This is a story worth putting in... Dr. Good had been taking money out of his pocket, and I'd been taking it out of mine. This boy said he'd had a hard time and he didn't have anything; he was desperate. A student later said, 'I saw the man take it out of his own pocket and hand it to me.'" Dr. Clark was just following the example of Dr. Good.

Those who attended the little Ozarks school shortly after World War II never forgot Dr. Good, Dr. Clark, and what The School of the Ozarks did for them. Countless

numbers of students saw The School as a beacon of hope in their lives. One such person was Stan Dixon (Fig. 40), later a craftsman who gave forty years of service to the institution. His story is typical of the times.

Fig. 40 Stan Dixon

105

"I grew up in a little town called Mincy, near Kirbyville. I went to grade school there. There were thirteen students in the school and the old building is still standing...We had kerosene lights...a wood stove right in the middle of the building." Stanley's family background was not unusual. He said his mother and dad "were little farmers" and that he had "seven brothers and two sisters." Raising a family of ten children was difficult. Stan says, "It was pretty tough. We raised a garden, and we did all our farm work with horses. When I was five years old, my dad traded twelve pigs for forty acres of land. He cut logs off that...and we cut shakes out of the oak and put a roof on. We lived on that farm; we were living there when I came to school here. My dad worked for Henry Skaggs. Dad earned fifty cents a day for twelve, fourteen, sixteen hours of work."

Before Stan enrolled in The School, he had watched his family deal with tough times, including the war. World War II added a terrible burden to Stan and his family, Pearl Harbor especially. Stan could never forget, "I was home; we had an old battery radio where we heard it. I had a brother at Pearl Harbor--Glen, my older brother. When Pearl Harbor was bombed a lot of them were moved to the Aleutian Islands off Alaska. Glen (Fig. 41) was moved there, and we didn't hear from him for a year and a half. The Red Cross couldn't find him." Incredibly, Stan's brother survived, though his family thought he was dead. Stan remembers how they found out Glen was alive. He said his parents "worried to death. They thought he

Fig. 41 Glen Dixon

106

was dead. We got a letter from him that was sent maybe six months prior." The Dixons didn't have a mail box, but he remembers getting it. "We had a general store there at Mincy, a little old store."

By the time Stanley was ready to go to high school, his choices were limited. "There wasn't any high school other than Branson and The School of the Ozarks," he recalls. It wasn't that he was unfamiliar with The School. "I had two aunts that had come here back in the 1930s. But my mother couldn't go...she couldn't go simply because she had to stay home and take care of the little kids." It must have been a relief and a blessing to Stan's family when he was able to enroll at The School of the Ozarks; he vividly recalls how he got to Point Lookout. "I hitched a ride with the mail truck and made it over here. And of course, you know, I had all of my belongings in a brown paper bag...I had two pair of jeans, maybe some underclothes, a tooth-brush, and a razor I thought I might need. It was like going to the far end of the world. I was scared. I worked; it didn't cost a penny, of course." Not unlike most of the students of the time, young Stanley depended on The School for about everything. "At that time, they had a used clothing room. That's where I got a lot of my clothing, and most other people did, too."

Stan Dixon knew some of the other students when he got here. They must've helped. But, as he repeated, "I was scared. I knew Don and Ed Baker. I worked with Don in Foster Dormitory." For young Stan Dixon, it was his big chance. The School was structured for success. "Very, very strict," he remembers. "Oh, room checks, the whole works, students accepted it. They were taught at home the same thing--obey your elders. I got exactly what I needed to get at home if I got in trouble." There was, of course, the ever watchful eye of Dr. Good. For example, Stan says, "Dr. Good, he would have a dream that you'd gotten in trouble, and he'd have you called in the next day...." Not unlike his classmates, Stanley occasionally went over the line. "They were always catching some of us, maybe caught smoking or something." Punishment varied but was always swift and sure, usually extra work. "Plenty of it," according to Stan. "I was late coming in from a weekend, a little late. I got a dock called a three-fifteen [three demerits and fifteen work hours]. That was the only one I got."

For Stan Dixon and his many friends, work seemed never to end and was very much a part of their lives. "One year I worked on the farm all summer. I was the only one that knew how to work the horses; The School had two big Belgian horses, big horses, workhorses. So, I got the job of planting and harvesting and cultivating the Irish potatoes, about six acres. I plowed hard, and harvested them with those horses." That's not the only work assignment Stan had; he helped to construct one of The School's main buildings during his time, and he worked some at the dairy. The summer seemed long, and so did the school year. "Eight to ten hours a day all summer, all summer. Then, during school it must have been twenty to twenty-four hours a week, plus a lot of times on Saturdays all day."

Many students, including Stan Dixon, got to know donors who made their educations possible, "scholarshipped," according to Dr. Good and Dr. Clark. Stan remembers who underwrote his time. "The Jordan sisters were my sponsors...They had dinner there with Dr. Clark and Dr. Good at the bull pen, an area of the dining hall, a chained off area in the old cafeteria. That's where the donors and the president and people like that would eat lunch. It was exciting to eat in the bull pen with important people. It was always a very exciting time for a poor country boy, you know...They were really good ladies. They would bring us down a five dollar bill, a necktie, or something like that for Christmas."

While getting an education, students like Stan got to be a part of some very special projects. Several big projects were on the Board's agenda during Dr. Clark's and Dr. Good's early years together. "I worked on the McDonald Hospital and I worked beside Ralph Bates, the old fellow that taught me how to face those stones. I faced a lot of those stones on the McDonald Hospital when I was fourteen to fifteen years old," Stan states proudly. The McDonald Hospital is but one example of the many contributions made by Trustee J. M. McDonald, Sr., who built the hospital as a memorial to his wife Josephine, a registered nurse.

J. M. McDonald, Sr., or "Mr. Jim," as he came to be known on campus, was attracted to The School originally by his good friend and associate at the J. C. Penney Company, Mr. Lewis W. Hyer. Like Mr. Hyer, Mr. McDonald was a prominent businessman devoted to the cause represented by The School of the Ozarks. They were called by Richard G. Price and Beth Bohling, in *The J. M. McDonald Story,* "guardian angels" of The School. They wrote much about J. M. McDonald, Sr.'s life and contributions. A glimpse of his story provides a clear idea as to why he

Fig. 42

J. M. McDonald, Sr., (right) welcomes J. C. Penney to campus.

joined Mr. Hyer on the Board of Trustees.

J. M. McDonald, Sr., (Fig. 42) joined J. C. Penney in launching Penney's first store in 1905. McDonald and Penney had known each other since childhood, attending Sunday School together. Mr. McDonald was very instrumental in building up the J.C. Penney Company. He was depended on to do much of the buying for the company, often done by a buying committee--a group of businessmen who went to New York for that purpose. He often worked with Wilk Hyer who subsequently interested him in becoming a trustee of the struggling little Ozarks school. Mr. McDonald knew what hard work was all about. After retiring from the J.C. Penney Company, Mr. McDonald continued working as a consultant, helping build up the Brown-McDonald Company and establishing a farm in New York with outstanding cattle herds. The McDonald Farm, like his other business endeavors, became a big success. Mr. McDonald had a long tenure as a trustee of The School of the Ozarks and was attracted by the work ethic which provided opportunities for youngsters that he and Wilk Hyer well understood from their native Ozarks.

J. M. McDonald, Sr., was so committed to The School that he established a private foundation to include The

School in its philanthropy after his death. The McDonald name was ultimately to be found on six buildings at The School and is reflected in many other ways. For example, Mr. Jim even loaned The School money to buy land. Not only did Mr. McDonald give of his money but gave also of his time. His attendance at meetings was regular, and he served as a trustee officer prior to his death. Mr. Jim enjoyed preparing publications to support The School. One of them, *The Story of a School,* reveals a dedicated Christian man seeking to honor the founder's intentions for The School he was helping build. He was very specific in describing the kind of education involved: "A well-rounded Christian training...the development of minds? Yes. Tremendously important...To do with their hands? Yes. There is no substitute...for the ability to do a job and do it well... Physical fitness? Of course. But the heart of its program is, has ever been, Christian education...of course, there is no separating this Christian purpose from all other aims of The School."

Fig. 43
Josephine Armstrong McDonald Hospital

The Josephine Armstrong McDonald Hospital (Fig. 43) was built, like most other buildings, with student labor. The dedication speaker for the occasion, Dr. Ralph C. Lankler, praised Mr. McDonald, Sr., saying, "Mr. McDonald's interests went beyond materialism." He said Mr. McDonald was interested "in building better people, in developing their minds and bodies and spirits."

The hospital was to become heavily used, The School having an annual tonsillectomy day (Bloody Saturday, as it was fondly called). On one occasion, twenty-three tonsillectomies were done in one day! Shortly after the hospital opened, a young fellow by the name of Frank Moreno (Fig. 44) had his tonsils removed. His story reveals how the hospital played a part in his skipping chapel.

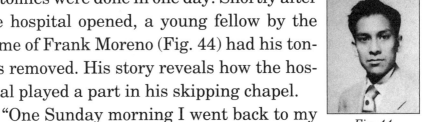

Fig. 44
Frank Moreno

"One Sunday morning I went back to my room after breakfast. My roommate looked at me and said, 'What's wrong? You look bothered!' I said that I did not feel like going to church but did not know how to get out of it, and they may check attendance. 'Hey,' he said jokingly, 'they are taking tonsils out at the hospital.' We had just opened the Josephine Armstrong McDonald Hospital (which I helped build). I picked up my coat and went and got in line for tonsil removal. One of the nurse's aides, a student and a friend of mine, said, 'What are you doing here, Moreno?' I explained that I had come to get my tonsils removed. 'You are not on the list,' she said. 'Why are you here now?' 'I do not want to go to church,' I confided in her. She looked at me and added my name to the list.

"I was back in class on Monday morning with a very

sore throat and could barely talk. Ms. Hocum was a teacher in one of my classes. She asked me a question which I knew required a lengthy answer, which I did not want to try. I do not recall the noise I made in response, but I saw her make a note and pass the question on to someone else. I wrote a note saying that I had had my tonsils out on the day before and that my throat was very sore. I showed Ms. Hocum the note after class. 'Open your mouth,' she said. I did. She opened her book and scratched out an 'F' which she had jotted next to my name for not answering her question!"

As The School of the Ozarks neared its Fiftieth Anniversary, it was obvious that J. M. McDonald, Sr., had joined others in making a difference. It was a start of a long relationship among McDonald family members and the institution which Mr. McDonald called "The School that runs on faith."

Dr. Clark and Dr. Good continued to have their hands full, trying to get a science building built, along with the hospital. For many years it had also been their hope that a beautiful chapel could be built in the center of the campus to represent the focus of the heart of The School.

It is abundantly clear that Dr. Good (and Dr. Clark) took seriously the religious commitment of a school to which they had dedicated their lives. They did their best to keep the most important things in perspective. A wonderful example can be seen in a letter to Board Chairman Wilk Hyer, written in the year Dr. Clark assumed the presidency (1952). Dr. Good writes:

> Over the weekend, we had one of the finest series of services we have ever had since I have been at The School. A

young Baptist minister named Jack Wilson, of whom the youngsters are very fond, came and preached twice Saturday and then delivered the meditation for communion Sunday. Yesterday morning forty-one youngsters were baptized, including some of the older boys who we believe will be especially helped. This was really a very inspiring occasion.

Dr. Clark thought that since the Presbyterians had started The School, they would build a chapel. Although Trustee Frank Thompson had left some money in his will for a chapel, it apparently wasn't nearly enough to build what Dr. Clark had in mind. Mr. Hyer had helped get it started, according to Dr. Clark. "God put it in his heart to give the bell tower, when we were trying to build the chapel and trying to find the money for it." Actually, the Trustees started the chapel project so that faithful workers could have work, but shortly decreed, "Tower and chapel will have to be built separately, when the foundation is completed, on account of lack of funds for the chapel."

Dr. Clark thought he had a logical answer to the dilemma. "The Women of the Church had what they called a birthday offering that amounted to thousands of dollars every year, nationwide. I went to Dr. Jane McGaukey, whom I had known before I came here, asked her to come out, and she accepted the invitation. She was sold and made this statement before she left: 'This is just a little bit of heaven!' So she went back and sold her board of the General Association of Women's Work on the idea of taking us [the chapel project] on." Dr. Clark recalls his desire to see the church built with quality. "I said that we wanted this chapel, and I wanted God's house to be the nicest."

Although with the best of materials and intentions,

Dr. Clark was bitterly disappointed. "The Presbyterian Church turned down the Board of Women's Work; it was blocked by the General Assembly Council on Stewardship/ Budgeting; they said, 'No, we won't do it.'" Evidently such a rejection bothered more than Dr. Clark, who had been pleading for support. "Well," he said, "Dr. McGaukey resigned her job as a result. She said they just weren't willing to go along and do things that seemed right and reasonable; she took early retirement. I wrote her and said that even though it had been turned down, God certainly had another plan."

Dr. Clark was certainly right. As he remembers, his faith was rewarded pretty quickly. "It wasn't but two weeks after the turning down by the General Assembly that I had a call...from a Judge Jacob Lashly, a very prominent St. Louis attorney. Lashly asked that I come to meet an early flight on Ozarks [Airlines]; that he had something important to talk about."

Dr. Clark recalls meeting the plane and some of the discussion that took place on the way back to campus. "While coming down from Springfield, he asked a hundred questions at least...But I could see that, lawyerlike, he was asking almost the same questions, like you cross examine a witness trying to trip them up...but it didn't make any difference as long as you're telling the truth, no damage."

Apparently, Judge Lashly had met his match in M. Graham Clark. "He evidently liked what he heard, got to my office, sat down, and said, 'Clark, I have a very dear friend who was a U.S. Senator from Missouri; he's retired in Florida and has a very large gift he wants to make. Would you have a particular project?'" Dr. Clark wasted little time in bringing up the chapel project, saying, "This is providential; God sent you here...'How much have you got in mind, if I may ask?' And he told me."

Surely, Clark's sharp mind was at work in anticipation. He recalls, "Well, I just reached in the desk there and pulled out the estimate which showed the exact amount of what he wanted to give! The Judge said, 'You got another estimate in that drawer?' and I said, 'Well, help yourself.' He looked; there was nothing else." No doubt the Judge was dumbfounded. "May I use your phone?" he asked. "Sure," Dr. Clark replied. Dr. Clark continues with his recollection of events. "He called Florida, where Williams was living in his retirement. Lashly said, 'I have come across something here that amazes me...This man says that God sent us, and I believe him.'"

Dr. Clark went on to say that Judge Lashly told Senator Williams, "What we had in mind seems to be the exact amount they need for this project, and they are willing to put your name on it." Dr. Clark thought he had just finished the chapel project. He must have been ecstatic, but his elation was short-lived. As he recalled, "We ran into one who acted like he was going to knock us out of that gift."

Dr. Clark reports that not long thereafter he was on the East Coast and received a disconcerting phone call. "I had a call from the office that said that Judge Lashly was on the phone...and he wanted me in St. Louis that afternoon. I said, 'Well, that's almost impossible...tell him that I'll do the best I can, but it doesn't look like it will be possible. I'll come as soon as I can.'"

No doubt worried about the call, Dr. Clark would not

wait any longer than required to follow up. "I had a friend take me out to the airport. I had my secretary cancel my speaking engagements...got out there and asked if I could get a seat on this new flight to St. Louis." Dr. Clark says the airline ticket agent laughed at him and said, "We are already booked solid, and I have got twelve on the waiting list." Dr. Clark was not willing to take no for an answer, remembering, "I said, 'Would you put me on that waiting list and put DAP by it?' The agent laughed again and said, 'You know airline call-ups, don't you?' I said, 'Yes.' That [DAP] used to mean 'do all possible.' I said, 'It's very important to me.'" The agent told Dr. Clark to "have a seat; I'll call you if we find something."

Miraculously, Dr. Clark says, "I was the only one they called. About five minutes before the flight, he called my name, and I jumped up and went to the counter. He said, 'I've got a seat for you. You seemed real anxious.' I said, 'You'll never know what this means.' I got on that Super G Constellation, and about halfway to St. Louis the pilot came on and said, 'I have interesting news. We are setting a record for the time between Washington and St. Louis... today we've got a jet stream from east to west [unusual], and we are going to make an all-time new record.' I just said, 'Thank you, Lord, thank you.'"

Dr. Clark remembers what happened next, "I got off that airplane, got in a cab and said, 'Take me downtown,' named the building and said, 'Just get me there as quickly as you can.' The driver said, 'If I get a ticket, you going to pay for it?' I hesitated, but said, 'Yes, I'll pay for it!'...And I never had such a taxi ride! I got downtown in record time, went inside, and called from a pay phone in Lashly's building. 'Oh,' he said. 'Clark, you're in the East, and we needed you here so badly this afternoon!' I said, 'I'm in your building.' He said, 'Can't be!'...He said, 'Let me just meet you at the elevator.' So he met me at the elevator at the back door of his office."

No doubt Judge Lashly was bewildered at how Dr. Clark managed to do this. Dr. Clark continues his tale. "He said, 'Tell me what happened.' So I started to tell him... and about the time I got started they called and said, 'The delegation is here from Florida.' And it was Howard Williams, the son of Senator Williams; he was an importer/exporter. He had been in South Africa for quite a while and had just found out a few days before about his dad's big gift, and he was protesting it. He said it was taking too much out of the corpus of the estate at one time. He had with him his banker; he had his lawyer, some other staff...He [Howard Williams] said he was worried about taking too much out at one time." Dr. Clark must have been caught off guard by all of this. But he believed deeply it was his duty to build the chapel and that, in fact, God had ordained it.

Dr. Clark explains, "I think God puts thoughts in our mind and hearts when we need them the worst, so I was certainly in an attitude of prayer. And I said, 'Gentlemen, I know what the prime rate is now...a little under four percent. We can borrow money at prime from Mercantile Bank; we have a line of credit, but, I said, 'It would be nice if we could have the money now....'" Clark had sensed that his big donor as well as his dreams were slipping away. Dr. Clark forthrightly suggested that instead of a lump sum gift being made outright, it could be paid over a peri-

Fig. 45 Chapel, under construction

od of years. Dr. Clark remembered how the dilemma was solved and how he saw his solution. "I said, 'The benefit seems to me would be greater to have this spread out... and he'd save more on his income tax.' That's when Lashly said, 'Well, I didn't know you studied law.' 'Well, I didn't,' I said. Lashly said, 'I've got a young lawyer, who is a tax man. Let me get him in here. Got to run it by him'...And afterwards he [the tax lawyer] said, 'It would work...I recommend he do it.' Well, Howard Williams said, 'That's all I want to hear and recommend that we just go ahead.'"

Dr. Clark must have been relieved. He had the money in the pipeline to finish the on-again, off-again construction of the chapel (Fig. 45). Starting a bit early with the best of intentions to provide jobs for faithful workers, running out of funds, and having the bell tower separated from the chapel building had been discouraging enough. Also, the rejection by the Presbyterian Church was a disheartening blow. Yet Dr. Clark had faith that a way would be found, and a way was found, however incredible it seems. God had, indeed, provided a way for a chapel to be built that would constantly remind the Ozarks school of its roots and the desires of its founders.

In addition, all who were watching Dr. Clark must have been impressed. For within a short period of time since his arrival in Point Lookout, Dr. Clark had engendered the support of Dr. Good and the Trustees and had moved smoothly into the presidency. The beautiful McDonald Hospital was built, and now all eyes were shifting toward the starting of a college program. On the eve of The School's Golden Anniversary, it was clear that the pace had quickened and that The School of the Ozarks was being carried into the future. This momentum was due in no small part to M. Graham Clark, a man whose remarkable achievements later led to his recognition nationally as the "Wizard of the Ozarks."

Chapter VII
"No Greater Gift Can Man Bestow...."

The Golden Anniversary of The School of the Ozarks was not just a celebration of the first fifty years. It was the beginning of fifty years of yet another miracle--that of a college! In the January 1956 issue of the *Ozark Visitor,* college officials sent a clear message:

> From a single building on a contributed plot of ground to a campus of 1,400 acres and fifty buildings...That is the proud fifty-year record...Those fifty years are filled with stories of near-miracles...Seeing The School as it now stands, no one can doubt that a Higher Power has been looking after this greatly-needed school...Surely, goodness and mercy shall continue all the days of The School's life.

Dr. Clark remembers starting modestly with the college program. "We graduated our first two-year (college) class in 1958. The first college level class had a handful of people. We took what's the upstairs of the McDonald Hospital and put a big eight-inch block partition through the center...And, the boys entered it on one end, and the girls entered on the other. They had an equal number of rooms, and we didn't fill it up...it was a while before it took off. Bob Hicks was our first dean, college level. For many years, I didn't have a single dean...It was kind of crazy; I tried to do it all by myself...."

Adding this college program alongside the still burgeoning high school was no simple matter. As reported in the September (1956) issue of the *Ozark Visitor*, the complexity of the endeavor showed through. "This year, the start of our school year could have been even more difficult since it marks the opening of our junior college. Thanks to President Clark and Dean Hicks, who worked out all the details, through many months, the college classes started off smoothly as the others."

Dr. Clark must have been relieved to see the dream coming true. He was the driving force behind the establishment of a college program. But he had the help (and confidence) of many others who believed in The School and what was being undertaken.

Mrs. Beulah Winfrey recalls, "We felt like there was a place for us. Our graduates [two-year] could go on to the University of Missouri, the University of Arkansas, Southwest Missouri State University, Drury, and complete their work. Some of them went other places. In planning our general education program, we tried to make it so it would transfer...."

Unfortunately, the Golden Anniversary school year (1956-1957) brought some very sad news along with the good news of beginning the college program. The sad news was the passing from the scene of two trustees who had contributed much more than money to The School. The death of J. M. McDonald, Sr., in the fall, when the very first college students enrolled, must have been a jolt to all concerned. But the death of Trustee Lewis Wilkins Hyer (Fig. 46), less than six months later, no doubt added to the anxiety of the times. Each man was known to have con-

Fig. 46 Lewis Wilkins Hyer (center), Trustee

tributed generously, not only of his means, but also of his time. It had been through the influence of Mr. Hyer that Mr. McDonald, Sr., had become a trustee. "Mr. Jim," as J. M. McDonald, Sr., came to be known, was loved by all. Mr. Hyer, though a different personality, made impressions that some former students vividly recall.

One such student was Judy (Mackey) Morisset (Fig. 47) who attended The School during Mr. Hyer's last years. She recalls one very special occasion prior to Mr. Hyer's death. "It was the fall of 1954 or spring of 1955 before we graduated that Mr. Hyer asked Dr. Good to bring some

of the kids up to his house so he could encourage them and see us one more time. Mr. Hyer knew he had very little time on this earth. Dr. Good loaded up a car full of kids from his office, Dr. Clark's office, and the

Fig. 47 Judy (Mackey) Morisset

treasurer's office to visit Mr. Hyer. When we arrived, he gave us a pep talk and gave us all one dollar bills; he kept rolls of them hanging on his bed post. This was one of the highlights of my days at S of O." Judy also remembers another distinguished friend of Wilk Hyer and J. M. McDonald. "Another happy day for me was when some of us girls prepared a meal for J. C. Penney at our Home Economics Dining Room...."

The record of the Trustees is laced with the contributions of J. M. McDonald, Sr., and Wilk Hyer. It was far more than the McDonald Hospital or the Hyer Bell Tower (named for Mr. Hyer after his death) or any number of other buildings or projects. Each spent countless hours at The School and both were role models for all to follow. Perhaps their lives are best summed up in a short poem written by Wilk Hyer entitled *Let's Help 'Em*. Its words are simple, yet profound:

> No greater gift can man bestow,
> Than giving of his life to help others grow.

For a long time, this little poem appeared, along with the seal of The School of the Ozarks, in the *Ozark Visitor*.

Both men, J. M. McDonald, Sr., and Lewis Wilkins Hyer, made generous long-term provisions for The School-- Mr. McDonald by creating the Armstrong McDonald Foundation and Mr. Hyer by creating the L. W. Hyer Trust. The continuing interest of the McDonald family was evident as J. M. McDonald, Jr., was already serving on the Board, with other family members to follow. However, the carrying out of Mr. Hyer's Trust provisions was, unfortunately, delayed. As Dr. M. Graham Clark said, "We could have starved to death because of the delay involved in carrying out Mr. Hyer's Trust."

Dr. Clark's view, though harsh sounding, was not without merit. In fact, at a special called meeting of the Trustees in June (1957) following Mr. Hyer's death, it was obvious that trouble was in the air. The minutes of the meeting make this clear: "Judge Hennings and Dr. Good reported on their negotiations...respecting claims against the Hyer estate." At this meeting the Trustees authorized the continued negotiations "to settle on behalf of The School." At the same meeting, the Trustees also authorized the borrowing of $50,000. Funds must have been scarce.

It was during this period of time that The School opened its college program. A quick settlement did not occur. At a full meeting (fall 1957) of the Trustees, yet another resolution was made with respect to the Hyer estate: "...to negotiate further with those claiming to be heirs of Lewis Wilkins Hyer, deceased." Yet another loan was authorized by the Trustees to "borrow any necessary amount of money in connection with the forgoing settlement, using securities of The School's endowment fund as collateral...." Evidently The School had run out of unsecured money, as collateral was being required.

The process was to drag on for several years with the Trustees at one point recording, "A compromise settlement has been effected." Since money was in short supply, they passed yet another motion in which Dr. Good and Dr. Clark "were granted authority to borrow $200,000 to take care of the payment on the settlement with Hyer relatives, and an additional loan of $50,000 for necessary operating expenses of The School."

Clearly, the little school didn't have enough money to

effect a settlement and operate The School at the same time. All of this financial anxiety was going on while a college program was being implemented and the chapel was being completed. The ultimate settlement was not only a relief from increasing financial pressures, but also, no doubt, the relief of a heavy burden on Dr. Good and Dr. Clark.

As Beulah Winfrey remembers, the days of working at both a high school and a junior college were challenging, to say the least. Nevertheless, she was left with fond memories about the day-to-day happenings at The School during this period. "One time we had to leave campus for the funeral of Wayne's [Mr. Winfrey's] grandfather. When we got back, a boy met us at the gate and said, 'We've been good just as long as we could, so we flooded the dorm while you were gone!' They [students] always had the excuse that they couldn't go to church, because they didn't have a clean shirt, or they didn't have a tie. So, Wayne's shirts and ties always made it to church, while he spent his time rousting the students...They got pretty good at figuring out how to get out of class, too."

Everyone took Mrs. Winfrey's classes seriously. And she was more than up to the challenge of catching students, regardless of how creative they were. "We had people who were known for [giving] scholarships; the money they gave went to cover the cost of a particular student. Dr. Good always liked for scholarship people, when they were on campus, to see the students they were sponsoring. So, a note would come to the classroom door that so-and-so's sponsor is here. Well, it got to be a racket to figure out how to get out of class.

"I remember the first year I taught, we had a faculty meeting and discussed how students were overdoing it a little bit, and we had to be more cautious. So one day right after that faculty meeting, within a day or two, up comes a student that says Dr. Clark wants so-and-so excused to go see the [scholarship] donor. On the basis of what we had just heard in the faculty meeting, I refused to let the student out. In about four minutes, Dr. Clark was at my door, so I knew I had goofed. After that, I tried to make sure if it was legitimate.

"Another time I had been on to my students about strikeovers in typing class. I got this note that was typed very poorly, so I criticized it. So the principal said, 'I did not have a secretary; I typed it myself!'" Mrs. Winfrey must have been relieved to begin teaching college students who were not quite as mischievous and a little more focused!

Both high school and college students had a big part in constructing the chapel. Concurrent with the implementation of the college program (1956-58) was the finishing of the beautiful chapel. Ironically, the chapel was dedicated in the very same month that The School of the Ozarks produced its first junior college graduates in May of 1958.

The dedication service for the Williams Chapel and Hyer Bell Tower must have been a splendid event. There were many guests that day, including Senator George H. Williams and Judge Jacob M. Lashly. Unfortunately, J. M. McDonald, Sr., and Lewis Wilkins Hyer did not live to witness this meaningful occasion. But they certainly knew it was going to become a reality.

Dr. Clark led in the dedication liturgy, and Dr. Good

introduced Judge Lashly. In his address, Judge Lashly wasted little time in crediting Senator Williams (a long-time friend) with supplying the strategic gift that made possible the completion of the project. Perhaps the most meaningful statements made by Judge Lashly were, "The School of the Ozarks itself is a living example of that which always occurs when faith and works are joined in a single, unselfish purpose. Upon the principle that he is best helped who helps himself, this unique, educational experiment was founded...." These were certainly insightful observations from one who had limited exposure to The School, but one who had been well-informed by M. Graham Clark.

One of Dr. Clark's dreams had now come true. It had taken years of perseverance and hard work. Some probably thought such a magnificent gothic structure was too much for such a small school. Anyone who thought this surely didn't know what Dr. Clark had in mind or just how much a visionary he would turn out to be. He once said, "I know it seemed much too lavish, but I knew our student body would grow, and I wanted to be ready for that time." Though the dedication program of the Williams Chapel was careful to credit Senator Williams and many, many others for their contributions, perhaps enough wasn't said about Dr. Clark (Fig. 48) and his

Fig. 48

Dr. M. Graham Clark,
in front of Williams Chapel

determination to build a chapel that would inspire generations and stand as a testimony to the faith of The School's
founders. The chapel, though still called Williams Memorial Chapel is, in effect, the M. Graham Clark Memorial.

The chapel, duly dedicated, was followed in the month
of May (1958) by the graduation of the first college class.
Twenty-three graduates received their junior college diplomas, an important achievement shared by faculty and
students alike; forty-eight graduated from the high school
program.

From the start, the college program attracted some
very talented and dedicated faculty and staff. For example, Dr. Alice Nightingale (Fig. 49) joined the faculty with
the enrollment of the first class. She held a Ph.D. from
the University of Chicago and eventually gave decades of
service to The School. Attracting a faculty member of such
standing definitely sent a signal of the serious academic
intentions of those in charge. Dr. Robert F. Hicks was the
first dean of the junior college. Shortly after the junior college program was started, The School attracted yet other
capable workers. Good examples were Dr. Stanley Fry
and Dr. William D. Todd. Dr. Fry recalls much of the life
of The School as its college program began to take root.

"Dr. Stanley Skinner...was in need of a band director.

He phoned me and said, 'I need you, so
would you come down?' I said, 'Well, I'm
very happy where I am...I'm really not interested in moving.' He said, 'Well, come
on down and look us over.' So, we came
down and my wife [Jean] and I really fell

Fig. 49 Dr. Alice Nightingale

129

in love with the place, because we saw so much potential here...."

Apparently, Stanley Fry believed coming here to have been providential, for he remembers an important event in the life of his family just before Dr. Skinner's call. "We had an evangelist at our little church who invited people to make a real commitment (about their life's work). My wife and two little boys walked up to the front. And then, we got this phone call. So, we feel it's definitely a calling for us to be here."

Married to his lovely wife Jean and with two little boys, Stanley Fry (Fig. 50) might have seemed to have had an easy time in life. No one could've known how quickly he had "grown up" as he recalled his military service. "I got deferred from the draft to finish high school...I knew I was going to be drafted, so I volunteered for two years. After basic training, I went to Japan and spent most of the two years over there in the country we had been at war with. I grew up in a hurry. I vowed that if I got back to my country, I would never say anything bad about it. I walked down the gangplank in Washington when we got back and got down and kissed the ground."

Fig. 50 Stanley Fry and family

With such a background, Stanley describes coming to join Dr. Good and Dr. Clark and the team of "builders" of the college program. "So...we decided that we would come.

Our first home...was in the faculty apartment in the dormitory. And, since we had two children, we got two apartments." Though Dr. Fry spent most of his career as a top level administrator, he had come to The School as a faculty member. "I came in music, part in instrumental music and band." He taught for a year before Dr. Skinner died, thereby creating a position as department head. Stanley served in that capacity, but before long, The School had other needs for him.

As the junior college program settled in, Dr. Fry was called in by Dr. Clark and told, "'If you're going to have a college, you've got to have a dean of students.' So, rather than bring somebody in from the outside, they invited me to be dean of students...they saw that I had some administrative ability."

Dr. Fry recalls challenging but interesting times, being in charge of discipline for high school students and college students at the same time.

"We had growing pains at the time. Because when you have students of high school age, say fourteen and up, and college age--say twenty or twenty-one--you can't have the same set of rules for everybody. At the time, I think, when we came here, there were about 200 students in high school and about seventy-five in the junior college. So, high school outnumbered. We worked at it the best we could, and I think, did a good job, because the people still come back today and give me a big hug and thank me for giving them a second chance."

For over a decade, Stanley Fry served the call admirably as dean of students. He remembers that although those were heady times, they were also hard times. "We went through some difficult times...The money coming in from the Hyer estate was still in court. There was a lot of controversy...I don't think there was ever a time we didn't have food on the table...It wasn't as bad as it was during the Depression years when...I've heard Dr. Good say that they would open the morning mail to see how much money they had to spend for food that day."

Dr. Fry added that many workers at The School were frugal, citing Dr. William Todd (academic dean in his early years at the institution). "He was very frugal. He would go to Jefferson City and get surplus stuff...and go anywhere he could to save The School money...I always admired that. He was a hard worker. He didn't want to waste The School's money."

Stanley Fry, like others around, revered Dr. Good. "We were in Rotary...Dr. Good, Dr. Todd, and Dr. Clark...We all rode to Rotary together. I remember that between here and Hollister, before you get to the bridge, nearly every time we'd have to stop for Doc Good. He'd have a little bouquet of flowers that he would take in to this little old lady that lived there...that was his nature. He liked to help people and give them encouragement. He was always taking or sending flowers to somebody, usually flowers that were grown here [on campus]."

As dean of students, Stanley Fry worked hard to uphold The School's expectations of its students. He remembers Dr. Clark directing that a "green line" be established, a line beyond which boys and girls could not cross while together. "He ordered that it be done...Actually, there was no physical green line." The idea behind it was pretty simple: "It's off limits," Stanley recalls.

As the 1960s dawned in America, Dr. Fry believes that the Ozarks was still a very traditional place. "You know, in the '60s on college campuses over the country, students were burning buildings down and having all kinds of uproar. There was a visitor who came on campus, a tourist, and he stopped one of our students. He said [to the student], 'Say, do you have any problem here on this campus with students burning down buildings?' He [the student] looked at him and said, 'Mister, when you help build these buildings, you are not interested in burning them down.'"

Up until and through the implementation of the junior college program, The School of the Ozarks was approved or accredited through the University of Missouri. This was very important, as it attested to the quality and/or transferability of the credits awarded. However, such a recognition was gradually replaced by a regional accrediting agency--the North Central Association of Colleges and Schools (NCA). Dr. Clark, Dr. Good, and the Trustees, joined by faculty and staff, were most concerned and eager to meet the new standards. Beulah Winfrey certainly remembers the expectations of the completed new accrediting process. "That's why we had all those late-night meetings!"

Dr. Clark showed no interest in being satisfied with only a two-year college. In fact, even before being fully accredited by NCA (1961), a report to the Board of Trustees a full year earlier revealed that "The proposed plan for a four-year college program was discussed. No official action was taken." Apparently, the need for better library facilities was a concern of the accrediting agency from the start. How Dr. Clark managed to finesse this is legendary, and Stanley Fry remembers when a visiting accreditation team came to The School, staying in the guest house. "Dr. Clark knew they were coming along the sidewalk [next to where the library would be built]." During the night, Dr. Clark got all the work crews out and started the project while the committee slept. "They were digging with the backhoes along the sidewalk. Dr. Clark made sure they saw it. I think it was a good move on his part, in that it showed--here, we've started on it...We're going to do it. It showed, I think, faith that we could get it done." And they did.

It must have been with a great deal of pride and a sense of accomplishment that Dr. Clark read a letter to the Trustees from the North Central Association during the Spring 1961 Board Meeting "regarding the full accred-itation...." This led to a resolution of appreciation from the Trustees "to all who had a part in the hard work and the labor necessary in bringing about the full recognition of The School's college program by the regional accredit-ing body--the North Central Association of Colleges and Schools."

There would be no resting on The School's achievement. Dr. Clark kept pushing, both the Trustees and those inside The School. The Trustees were concerned with plans for the McDonald Administration building, putting up a field house, and the provision of an addition to the Thompson Dining Hall, just for starters. But one project that came up for trustee discussion scarcely a year after The School's junior college program was accredited was "the matter of the airport which the city of Branson has proposed and which will involve certain properties owned by The School and other properties adjoining The School. It was stated that it is hoped this matter will be worked out very soon since a good airstrip adjoining the campus will be quite an asset to The School." The area was still isolated, but the city of Branson apparently thought The School should address this need. As the record will show, The School of the Ozarks certainly followed through with this idea, but the city never assumed any financial responsibility commensurate with its expectations.

The fledgling school had more immediate needs and ambitions than building an airport for Branson. There were so many competing demands on The School during this period that it must have taken two miracle workers like R. M. Good and M. Graham Clark to manage them. Dr. Clark knew that he was having to manage change and maintain direction at the same time. So, it is no surprise that he asked the Trustees to authorize a "comprehensive re-study of The School of the Ozarks philosophy, structure, functions, and procedures...." The Board passed such a directive, authorizing the use of consultants as necessary and appointing Trustee David H. Nicholson as Chairman. Dr. Clark told the Board, "During the past fifty years and more, this school, currently entrusted to our care, has been transformed from a small, struggling self-help school to a college. Changes in philosophy, direction, organizational structure, functions, and procedures have been made as necessity pointed the way. To better insure, preserve, and increase for the future the values of that which has been begun, it has become my earnest conviction that a comprehensive re-study should be made."

The record shows that Dr. Clark's wishes were granted.

In fact, more than one study--five studies, to be exact--or report was done, and more than one consultant was used. The content of these reports or papers speaks to the wisdom of Dr. Clark's thinking. Dr. Clark must have sensed the many transitions going on around him, including the passing of some of The School's most important friends.

At the April 1964 Board Meeting, the Trustees sadly acknowledged the passing of Senator George H. Williams, Dr. John Crockett (early president of The School), Dr. James F. Forsythe (founder of The School), Reverend Roy Johnson (a Baptist preacher and favorite speaker of students), and Mrs. H. B. Hooper (a generous donor). Yet during the same period, The School gained new leaders and benefactors such as Mrs. W. Alton Jones and Mr. Henry R. Herold.

In the April meeting, Trustee David Nicholson gave a rather exhaustive re-study report (the first of many such reports to come) to the Board. It made numerous recommendations, not the least of which was "Recommendation No. 8" that "the administration prepare a feasible budget for a four-year college program, including a recommended starting date for a four-year college to begin." The Board adopted this recommendation, thereby assuring that Dr. Clark's four-year plans would not be delayed.

In the fall of the same year (1964), the Board received another report. This one was prepared internally and was called "A Projection for The College of The School of the Ozarks, 1964-70." At the fall meeting, "the four-year college plan was discussed in detail and thoroughly considered." The Board voted its unanimous approval. Ironically, at this meeting, the Board seemed concerned about cash flow or fiscal matters. "By common consent it was agreed upon that no new major capital expenditures, for which money is not in hand, are to be undertaken prior to the next semi-annual meeting of the Board." But, at the same meeting, it was reported that "a full explanation of the airport project was made by Dr. Clark." In his report, Dr. Clark pointed to tentative FAA approval, the sale of the airport property in Branson, the strip of land to be donated by The School, the use of school equipment, matching federal funds, and finally that "the City Council of Branson had agreed to build the airport...." The Board authorized Dr. Clark and Dr. Good and the Chairman of the Finance Committee to close the deal when they felt ready.

The School was clearly taking on more and more and the Trustees were uneasy. After all, transition to a four-year college was no small task. But continuing with construction projects while possibly taking on an airport project added, no doubt, a heavy dose of uncertainty. Evidently, some were worried about holding on to the character of the unusual college, all the other distractions notwithstanding. A report or paper given to the Board at the fall meeting was followed by a December 10, 1964, letter to trustees summarizing concern in the report about the religious life and admissions requirements of The School, and concern that The School might not hold on to its Christian orientation during this time of transition and growth. As stated succinctly in this paper, "We have a most earnest and deep-seated concern that these factors will not characterize our institution." Among factors cited was how many so-called Christian colleges had lost their way, had drifted away and become secularized. Also cited was that in many colleges, as the prestige of the colleges in the academic world had increased, emphasis on the Christian faith had decreased. It was pointed out that a continued Christian commitment of a college couldn't just be assumed.

Trustees wanted no part in any such mission drift for their school. The Board adopted the principles set forth in the paper, and trustees were challenged to elect only trustees who professed the Christian faith and administrators to employ those with similar convictions. Given the turbulence of the '60s, it is not hard to understand why this was such a concern during such an exciting time of growth and transition. The country itself was in a state of turmoil, with all that was traditional being severely tested. History shows that the Trustees were wise to be concerned.

With philosophical and financial issues at the forefront, no one was prepared for what was about to happen on December 26, 1964. Disaster struck The School by way of a terrible fire which destroyed the A. P. Green Classroom Building (Fig. 51). It was one of The School's major aca-

Fig. 51
A. P. Green
Classroom
Building

demic facilities, and it happened on the eve of transition to four-year status.

As dean of students, Stanley Fry lived through it all. "We heard the fire alarm, and I immediately came over and watched it burn. It was a big fire. It was just too much for the fire department." Dean Fry knew it was a heavy blow to The School. "It was a much-needed building." Dr. Fry places credit for getting past such a disaster with Dr. Clark. "I think one of the most impressive things that I can remember Dr. Clark doing was, the very next morning, he had all the administrators down in a meeting, planning where we were going to have class and what we were going to do when the students got back from Christmas vacation." Dr. Clark was determined to forge ahead, for the scheduled beginning of the four-year program was scarcely six months away.

At a special called meeting in January (1965), the Trustees reviewed what had happened. Someone had filmed the Green Building burning, so the Board watched this and then heard from the indomitable Dr. Clark. "The President told about heroic efforts on the part of the members of our own fire department...." After much discussion, the Board voted to procure and install one large siren on campus.

Dr. Clark knew the big academic building had to be replaced, and quickly. He expected $200,000 of insurance, and Trustee Nettie Marie Jones pledged to match all gifts of $1,000. The message was clear: The School would not stumble. And it didn't. It charged ahead. It was committed to taking in its first juniors in the four-year program for the fall of 1965, come what may.

The School accepted a consultant sent by the North Central Association. This consultant was Dr. George Arbaugh of Augustana College, and his was the fourth paper or report of one sort or another. His "Report on College of The School of the Ozarks" was highly positive on the progress being made toward becoming a senior college. This report was read by the Trustees at their Spring 1965 Board Meeting. It was announced at this meeting that Mrs. Jones was giving additional funds to The School. Also, three new trustees were added: Ben Parnell, president of a local bank; Harry Basore, vice president of a Kansas City company; and Elmo B. Hunter, a federal judge. Subsequently, all served The School for generations.

With the way cleared to build a new facility to replace the burned out Green Building and encouraged by Dr. Arbaugh's words, The School jumped into the four-year transition. The first juniors enrolled in the fall of 1965. At the fall Board of Trustees meeting, faculty and staff alike were thanked for their hard work, especially with the accrediting agency. Trustees also had a long discussion about the high school program.

Concurrent with the transition from the junior college program to a senior college program was another transition, that of the surrounding area. For a number of years roads and public schools were improving, and the need for a boarding high school was decreasing. Consistent with these facts, along with the cost of maintaining a secondary program, a decision was made to begin phasing out the high school program. This seemed to be a logical step with few objections.

It was during such a time of rapid change that Dr.

Clark received yet another consultant's report, this one done by Dr. N. H. Evers, Dean of The School of Education at the University of Denver. This report was written in the context of The School of the Ozarks already having been given provisional senior accreditation by the North Central Association and preparing for full accreditation. Planning for the future was the theme of Dr. Evers' report. He was complimentary of the progress being made and especially, "a willingness to do whatever will be necessary to mount a quality upper-division curriculum."

After making a number of observations, Dr. Evers stated clearly in his report that there existed a great threat to this unique institution. He cited and explained his concern in the report:

> ...finally and perhaps most important of all, the ability of the institution to remain true to its fundamental mission, that of educating students who would otherwise be denied an opportunity for higher education. The temptation to make The School of the Ozarks into just another liberal arts college fighting to enroll only students of superior academic ability with a much-diminished concern for the need factor in admissions is already present and will, if let develop, negate much of what is the unique quality of The School of the Ozarks.

This consultant had his hand on the pulse of the institution and knew that the temptation, though well-intended, to make The School of the Ozarks just like any other was lurking in the shadows and probably always would be. Dr. Clark certainly was vigilant of such temptation. He knew that as the college gained senior status and additional programs, more faculty and staff would be brought in to join the effort. The kind of people recruited to staff the senior college program would either help maintain and reaffirm the mission or else undermine it. It was the '60s and many institutions lost their way in this tumultuous decade.

With the senior college transition underway, all eyes were on the future, and Dr. Clark was determined to keep The School on a steady course. During the first year with junior students, the Trustees gratefully authorized the naming of the new academic facility, the Nettie Marie Jones Learning Center, recognizing the significant financial support of one of The School's newer trustees.

By the spring of 1967, all who had doubted that it couldn't be done had to give credit to Dr. Clark for leading The School to four-year status. At its spring meeting, "The list of graduates for bachelor's degrees was presented. Upon motion by Harry Basore, seconded by Mr. Anderson, the graduates were approved for certification by the President." So as the last high school graduates received their diplomas from The School, the first students received their four-year diplomas. A new day was dawning, and there were many challenges ahead. But even during such a time of rapid change, the Ozarks school was still making a profound difference in the lives of deserving students.

Dr. Stanley Fry (who after years of serving as dean of students, served as chief development officer) believes that many of those helped, at both the high school and the college level, had their lives changed for the better, some-

times in ways not known until years later. Dr. Fry recalls that students received both reprimands and words of encouragement. One student (Fig. 52) wrote to Dr. Fry many years later, he recalls: "At the time I was

Fig. 52 Gary Hughey

142

getting ready to retire, I received a letter from a former student, and he told me about my making rounds in the dormitory and coming into his room. He was studying. He said, 'I guess you were surprised to see me studying. You gave me some words of encouragement and turned around and walked out. I want you to know my life turned around at that point'...That boy became Lieutenant General Gary Hughey of the United States Marine Corps. It just really grabbed me, because it pointed out to me, you never know [the influence] when you say a kind word or Christ-like thing or encouragement. And look how this man turned out!"

The letter received by Dr. Stanley Fry from General Hughey clearly shows how, as a boy, The School (and concerned friends like Stanley Fry) changed his life:

This letter is prompted by the article in the *Ozark Visitor* announcing your impending retirement...The conclusion of my freshman year was the turning point in my life. I returned to the dormitory with my grade slips, all Cs and Ds feeling a little ashamed. The shame turned to guilt, which worsened as the night wore on...I thought no one really cared. I realized, on that brisk November evening, sitting in my room in Foster Hall, that what success I achieved in life was solely up to me. Shortly thereafter, during one of your evening tours, you stepped into my room. As I was not on restriction at the time, I think you were shocked to find me at my desk, actually studying. You offered a few words of encouragement and left. A small act of leadership on your part, but what an impact. Suddenly, somebody did care and it made a big difference in my life. I attacked my studies and made the Honor Roll every quarter until graduation...I'm confident you don't recall this incident...We used to have a slogan that we printed on most of our publications at The School: *No greater gift can man bestow, than giving of his life to help others grow.* It must have meant as much to you as it did to me, for your career has epitomized that slogan.

Clearly, something very unusual was going on in America's heartland. What had been, through most of its history, a struggling high school was now a four-year college. Already passing through its halls were future

Tommy Bell

leaders; Brig. General Tommy Bell and Lt. General Gary Hughey were among the first. Another youngster at the time named Terry Dake (Fig. 53) would later become known as General Terrence Dake, Assistant Commandant of the United States Marine Corps. Jerry Ragsdale (Fig. 54) was another, later to become Maj. General Ragsdale. Yet others like Doyle Childers (Fig. 55), and Maynard Wallace (Fig. 56) would serve in the Missouri legislature. Alumni were to become leaders in all sectors of public life.

Within a short decade, a dramatic transformation had obviously taken place. But as the first senior college graduates emerged, so did the big financial challenge of operating a senior college, especially for those willing to work but unable to pay for their higher education.

Fig. 53
Terry Dake

Fig. 54
Jerry Ragsdale

Fig. 55
Doyle Childers

Fig. 56
Maynard Wallace

Chapter VIII
Hard Times *at Hard Work U.*

The decade immediately following the graduation of the first senior college class was a time of growth and challenge. As the country struggled to deal with the Vietnam War and Watergate controversies, The School struggled to deal with the growth of its physical plant, faculty, and ever-present fund-raising needs. Very little slowed down after the first seniors marched down the aisle and out into a troubled world. Within a year of the historic graduation exercises, a report by Dr. Clark to the Trustees revealed just how much was going on. A student-run restaurant was being completed, The School's museum expansion was underway, and the old canning factory was being turned into a printing building. Grading for an airport was proceeding, the work being done by The School and not the city of Branson as some had envisioned.

On top of all this, the Trustee Building and Grounds Committee "hoped" for the immediate start of four more major buildings: a science building, a men's dorm, a college union building, and a field house. These projects, along with many smaller ones, must have seemed impossible and surely signaled that Dr. Clark needed help managing so much. It became evident that such ambitions, along with the growth and demands of a four-year college, would exact a price, and it became abundantly clear that The School would have to slow down a little bit, recruit critical staff, and raise even more money. Even Dr. Clark's chasing all over the country, day and night, to secure funds, wasn't enough.

The financial needs of The School took on critical proportions. In a memo to trustees, dated May 27, 1968, the Chairman of the Executive Committee presented some sobering facts: "Current liabilities amount to $222,566.95, but current assets amount to $33,197.64, plus $20,000 in accounts receivable. Total disbursement for the 1966-67 school year revealed a shortfall of $956,463.82...Similar figures for the first eleven months of 1967-1968 revealed a shortfall of $781,267.40."

The Chairman characterized the situation citing, "the immediate problem of satisfying the May payroll...repayment of special and restricted funds...repayment of a bank loan...." He went on to conclude, "It's considered that the root of the overall problem lies in the requirement to operate a higher level school in the face of steadily increasing cost levels...." The bottom line was that $1,250,000 had to be withdrawn from a long-standing contingency fund. The Chairman explained, "I can see no other alternative...." The financial crisis of the late '60s passed only to reappear a few years later--even as The School began to attract fame, as well as more supporters.

Perhaps nothing pointed to the future fame of the institution more than a visit by the First Lady of the United States (Fig. 57). Most colleges could only dream of such a thing, but Dr. Clark made it a reality. He recalled, "I simply wrote a letter and addressed it to her [Mrs. Rich-

146

Fig. 58
Dr. John Mizell

Fig. 57
Mrs. Richard
M. Nixon, First Lady of the United
States, with student Jerry Brannan at
the Graphic Arts Department

ard M. Nixon] at The White House. She had been visiting a few colleges...she came. We had good weather [March, 1970]. We got all kinds of national publicity." Dr. Clark made sure that The School was ready. "Several hundred students lined the entire way down the hill."

Students waved big American flags. And Dr. Clark joined Mrs. Nixon in planting a tree in the center of campus. But the program in the chapel must have been the focal point of the visit. It certainly stands out in Dr. Clark's mind. "When the Chapel Choir did a rendition of *The Battle Hymn of the Republic* that Dr. John Mizell (Fig. 58) had arranged, Mrs. Nixon sat there on that platform; tears ran down her face. She was just so moved by the rendition."

Students played an important role in accommodating the First Lady. They served as escorts and attended to her every need. One student escort was Jerry Brannan (Fig.

57). He had arrived at The School from the tiny town of Chadwick, Missouri.

Jerry describes his hometown as "the copperhead capitol of the world; that was our only claim to fame. It was about one hundred people. We had a general store with a pot-bellied stove. My high school had about sixty-four students. I was valedictorian." Jerry Brannan was typical of so many students coming to The School from small Ozarks towns. "We didn't know we were poor, because everybody else around us was similar." His dad encouraged Jerry to go to The School. "He said, 'Why don't you think about The School of the Ozarks? It's close. If you can get accepted, it's pretty tough competition to get in, but it's a work-your-way-through school'...It was the best choice I could have made."

Jerry Brannan could not have known what was in store for him. His first job assignment was digging the footings for a new building. "Then, I went from there to the power plant. I stoked coal, and I worked midnight to 4 a.m. During breaks, I worked in the dairy when they needed people; I shoveled manure. Then, my senior year, I became a dorm counselor. And, I worked for Dr. Keeter; he had just come. I was his assistant, kind of a 'gofer' to do various things. If Dr. Keeter was short on a job or needed somebody, they would send me."

What really stands out in Jerry's mind is being sent to help Dr. Clark. "He was very much a people person, a super salesman...But we always said if he had one hand on your shoulder patting you on the back, you better watch your wallet!" Given Jerry Brannan's work experience, it shouldn't be a surprise that he was selected, no doubt with

Dr. Clark's influence, as one of the student escorts for the First Lady of the United States. But he thinks he knows another reason why he was selected. "I think probably I got the nod because I lost the Student Body President race by one vote--the vote was 350 to 349. So 700 out of 800 students voted."

In the buildup to the visit, Jerry Brannan remembers a stranger coming to campus who asked a lot of questions. "He looked out of place, because he was so nicely dressed... a very Ivy League look--oxford shirt, red tie, and suit. He said, 'I'm a prospective teacher and they've offered me this position. I'm thinking about it. But, it sounds too squeaky clean to be true.' He said, 'We've got riots and colleges being burned; I just don't know. I've got the ad-ministration's viewpoint, so I'd like to get yours.' So we talked about The School, did we agree with the war, was there any anti-government syndrome. I was still working on and off with construction. I said, 'No sir, if you think about it, if we burned down a building, we could be back the next day re-building it. So, that doesn't make good sense.' So he kind of laughed." As it turned out, the "visi-tor" was a Secret Service agent doing background checks before the First Lady's visit.

When the big day arrived, Jerry found himself in the back seat of a big limousine beside the First Lady of the United States. He recalls, "She was so disarming. We re-ally didn't feel uneasy. I was worried about us stammering or saying something wrong. She had been visiting other self-help institutions. Ours was the only college, I think. She talked a little about that."

On the way from Springfield to The School, people were

lining the road to get a glimpse of Mrs. Nixon. "There were farmers in their bibbed overalls and wives standing at their property lines, hat over heart as she went by. I thought that was pretty touching...still brings tears to my eyes." The day was carefully planned. "When we came in, they had the hill going down into the campus lined with flags, must've been two hundred flags. We stopped at the Friendship House [student-run restaurant] and she [Mrs. Nixon] made a speech."

Included in the event was a demonstration by the student-run fire department. Jerry still thinks the First Lady felt at home at The School. "I think she thought all the students were unpretentious, had a goal, and were working toward it. That impressed her that students were pulling themselves up, because that was the mission of her whole trip--self-help."

Mrs. Nixon dined with the students during her visit and was gracious upon her departure late in the day. "She thanked us for accompanying her and for background information. She said she would send us some pictures. We had wanted an autograph but were afraid to ask," Jerry remembers.

There were plenty of pictures in the newspapers, and the small Ozarks college basked in the national limelight. Students like Jerry Brannan had a memory for a lifetime. "I got letters from all over the country--from people that either knew of The School or had gone to The School. One lady sent a clipping from *The Kansas City Star.* She had been in Chadwick, her husband had proposed to her in Chadwick, or they had spent their honeymoon night there when it was just a turnaround spot in the railroad. It was just a nice commentary on humanity." Jerry's family was proud to see their son by the side of the First Lady. "My folks were honored. I mean they were die-hard Republicans. They always said they voted for the best man; he just always happened to be a Republican."

Although Jerry Brannan and Lola (Jones) Fritts were student escorts, yet another student was a tour guide for the entourage once it reached campus. Gary Wortman was Student Body President his senior year. Like Jerry Brannan, he had worked at various campus jobs and was very knowledgeable of The School. He recalls, "I started out in the furniture factory. We made sandboxes, doll furniture, and stuff like that for Western Auto and Montgomery Ward. I went from there to the dining hall for a year. I then went to the dairy for a year. My last year I was Student Body President; the first year it was a full work assignment."

Gary's recollections of First Lady Pat Nixon's visit are similar to Jerry Brannan's, although Gary's role was different. "I was basically the tour guide from location to location." Like Jerry, Gary was impressed by the work of the Secret Service before Mrs. Nixon's arrival. "They were looking at everything. I don't think they missed anything. It was a lot of excitement...basically, they spent probably a week here, just looking at the campus, and we had a schedule of the entire day's activities; every step was choreographed. Everyone who was to be within a certain distance of her wore a special lapel pin. You could see the Secret Service agents the moment you got near where she was going to be. I sat next to her at dinner. Of course, everybody that sat at the tables on either side had one of those little pins. She didn't eat very much; she was very polite."

Gary dutifully served as tour guide. "I basically gave her a thumbnail sketch of each location throughout the entire campus...She decided she didn't need to take a nap or take a break; she just went on. She was very gracious."

Gary Wortman's remembrances are sprinkled with his observations about the heavy security. "I was extremely impressed with the Secret Service. The White House guys were just publicity hounds. But the Secret Service guys were very professional--very smooth about what they did and very concerned about what might happen. They basically didn't want to have an incident, because they didn't want to have to react to it. The student body was impressed because they had never seen anything like that." Jerry Brannan, Lola (Jones) Fritts (Fig. 59) and Gary Wortman were no doubt fortunate to have had such an experience.

Although the visit of First Lady Pat Nixon cast a glow over The School and generated more press and contributions, it didn't make Dr. Clark's continuing struggles go away. In fact, at the Spring 1970 Board Meeting (April), only a few weeks after the historic visit, yet another budget had to be passed containing a deficit. The School needed more operational funds and looked for them in every

direction. The Trustees were concerned about a recently-passed Tax Reform Act and what effect it might have on colleges and their endowment funds. The School

Fig. 59
Lola (Jones) Fritts, Gary Wortman

was only using interest and dividends from its small endowment, but some thought a different approach was in order, thereby taking advantage of capital growth as most schools did. With such thoughts in mind, an investment committee was established to come up with a prudent policy. But this would take time, and the uncertainties of the times must have given Dr. Clark great concern. He was carrying a heavier load than might be assumed (or accepted) by many of his colleagues. As well as attracting the rich and the famous, he needed to attract someone to help him manage a growing, complex enterprise.

Such a person was found in Dr. Howell Keeter (Fig. 60), an administrator from nearby Arkansas and one with a background in management, construction, and especially dealing with people. His coming to The School was critical, for he quickly gained Dr. Clark's confidence and tackled every task given to him, considerable in

Fig. 60
Dr. Howell W.
Keeter

number. The economy of the country was not good and neither were the financial operations of the growing college. It must have been sobering for Dr. Keeter to hear the report given by Dr. Clark to the Trustees during Keeter's first year (1970). "While our financial structure is solid, we are having difficulty with our operating capital. This is not a new development...an operating budget showing a deficit of $660,000...for 1969-70...a cash operating deficit of $397,417.65." The Board authorized borrowing up "to $750,000." It also granted a request from the Alumni Association for the "setting of a date for a symbolic groundbreaking for the Lyta Davis Good College Union." Undoubtedly, young Dr. Keeter found out what was going to be required: a lot of hard work, substantial funds, and, no doubt, a lot of prayer. The School didn't have on hand enough funds for the construction of the College Center or a number of other projects being discussed. But Dr. Clark was determined to move ahead, believing that a way would be found.

Dr. Keeter recalls his early years at The School and the magnitude of the challenges. "I'd known about The School forever. I grew up just down the railroad tracks, over in Arkansas. In high school, I think I came up here a time or two to play basketball in the old Green Building; also, I came up here in summer--I played American Legion baseball, and we played down at the Mang Field in Branson... of course, when I came here Dr. Clark was President of The School and Dr. Good was Chairman of the Board."

After his arrival, Dr. Keeter had plenty to do. "The first day I was here, we broke ground for the field house. It was a big project for us--about 100,000 square feet; and I was very involved in working with Mr. Elmer Braswell who had been here about six months when I came...We had a lot of problems to address with the physical plant all over campus."

Dr. Keeter became more and more valuable to The School as Dr. Clark gave him more and more responsibility. "I had been Work Coordinator; I was moved to Associate Dean of Administration. They were wanting me to take a little bigger role in construction, and the building end of the thing as Associate Dean of Administration, and several other areas. And, there was a lot of strain." Although The School had turned to bonds for financing construction, money remained tight both for operations and capital projects.

Before long, Dr. Keeter found himself trying to manage the finishing of one construction project and starting others at the same time. Dr. Clark wanted things done quickly because he thought the need was so great. "We had other big projects going. We stopped construction on the science building at one time, probably for about six months, because of cash flow."

Dr. Clark believed conventional fund-raising couldn't do the job on the College Center, even though the alumni had come up with $250,000 for the project. He told the Board that without some unexpected windfall, it would take at least ten years or more to provide sufficient funds to complete the building. His solution was the use of bonds which the Board approved. The Board also approved changing the proposed naming of the College Center to honor both Dr. R. M. and Mrs. Lyta Davis Good.

Not only were the Trustees occupied with the physical growth pains of The School; they were equally concerned about holding steadfast to its founding purposes, with an uncertain future looming ahead. The Board wisely, under the direction of Trustee Judge Elmo Hunter, appointed an institutional study committee to look at the growth of The School, the maintenance of its purposes, and the general operation of the institution. This charge was taken seriously, and the committee reaffirmed (by report) just what, in fact, The School was to reflect.

The committee's report is most noteworthy in that it gets to the heart of the matter by addressing the issue of hiring practices:

In choosing faculty and staff members, preliminary consideration is to be given to their Christian convictions and experience, with the expectation that these will mark their teaching and their contacts with students. It is expected that life on the college campus will lead each student into an increase of his Christian experience.

Their report also zeroes in on the type of student to be served: "Need, primarily financial, coupled with a willingness to work." The committee clearly expressed that students should have a "capacity to undertake college level work," "good character," and exhibit "personal responsibility" in the area of morals and citizenship.

At the Fall 1973 Board Meeting, the Chairman of the Planning Committee, Judge Elmo Hunter, requested and received by the entire board a reaffirmation of the committee's actions. In addition, by unanimous vote and upon the recommendation of Judge Hunter, a fifth goal of patriotism was added to academic, cultural, spiritual, and vocational (work) goals. Adding patriotism during the Vietnam era as an additional goal of The School was consistent with the values and character of an institution whose alumni had served the country in every major conflict throughout The School's history. The Trustees were strengthening the uniqueness of The School which the consultant Dr. N. H. Evers had indicated, a few years earlier, must demand continued vigilance.

It was at this critical meeting that the Board received a proposal from a staff member ostensibly "for strengthening the spiritual growth objectives" of The School of the Ozarks. This document could not possibly have been well-received, as it contained many ideas that amounted to the loosening of the current chapel expectations. The Board appointed yet another committee to study what they, no doubt, viewed as unacceptable.

The Trustees seemed in no mood for such things, especially after Dr. Clark had "presented a frank analysis of the financial situation"...stating that, "It may become necessary to curtail severely both administrative and academic operations." Trustees had received a report indicating that the deficit approved by the Board for the year was for $127,000" but that the "net result was a cash deficit of $302,000" with the complaint that, "We continue to be plagued by the fact that costs continue to rise faster than does income." In other words, The School was still struggling, continually running operational deficits.

While Dr. Clark, Dr. Keeter, Dr. Todd and others labored internally, The School continued to shine externally. During the same year (1973) of so many problems, a major newspaper did a story that would forever brand The School in the eyes of the nation. *The Wall Street Journal* published a story entitled *"Hard Work U.*--at School of the Ozarks, the Students Flunk Out If They Shirk Chores." The article pulled no punches: "Like many private colleges and universities, The School is in a deficit right now...." But that was completely overshadowed by the positive American value image created by the paper and communicated to millions. *The Journal* article proclaimed that The School of the Ozarks was "one of the most unusual little liberal arts colleges in the country. Commitment to the good-old-fashioned work ethic, in fact, runs so deep here that honest toil is an integral part of the curriculum." A prominent executive was quoted by *The Journal* saying, The School "represents an idea whose time has come."

Clearly, *The Wall Street Journal* had hit a nerve and many responded to the article. That such a school existed in America during such a tumultuous time was refreshing to many and made a strong case nationally for its support. Quoting Dr. Clark, *The Journal* wrote, "We obviously can't continue to operate this way indefinitely, but I'm convinced God will provide." The message from *The Wall Street Journal* was clear: Here's a truly American institution that is carrying out an important purpose and deserves support. Many who read the article became ardent supporters of The School. One person who read the article was later to become one of the greatest benefactors in the institution's history.

Somehow, despite worsening financial problems brought on by growth and a terrible economy, The School managed to plow ahead, but it was becoming more of a load than Dr. Clark could carry. So it might not have been a surprise when Dr. Clark stated to the Board in the spring of 1974 that in his opinion, "the Board of Trustees should be giving thought to naming his successor." Although Dr. Clark was sixty-five years of age, in good health, and willing to continue, he advised that the Board might want to appoint a chancellor as an operating officer for The School. This would obviously free up Dr. Clark for more fund-raising.

This is exactly the course of action followed by the Trustees at the Fall 1974 Board Meeting--a committee was appointed to search for a chancellor so that Dr. Clark could continue as president and work even harder to raise yet more needed money. After settling that matter, the Board, among other actions, returned to an unresolved issue and unanimously approved a proposal for strengthening the religious commitment of The School. Their document entitled "Religion on Campus" reaffirmed the long-standing Christian commitments of The School and states:

> A Christian College is not such by the mere declaration of such character in a charter or catalogue...The absolute prerequisite of a Christian college is a Christian commitment, manifested in the life and practice of all persons charged with the management of the affairs of the college and teaching of the students...Faculty and staff who accept positions of responsibility with such a college must expect to be both committed and active Christians in their private lives. They must also expect, and be expected, to participate in campus religious activities in such a way that they may share with students their own Christian convictions...A highly developed respect by the student for his own person, and that of others, as children of God in Jesus Christ may be the greatest accomplishment of a Christian college.

Anyone could tell that the Trustees intended for the institution to continue honoring its most cherished goal. It did.

The spring of 1975 was significant in more than one respect. First of all, a projected deficit for the next school year exceeded $1.2 million. And second, the Board unanimously elected Dr. Howell Keeter as chancellor, the chief administrative officer, whereas Dr. Clark was to remain as president and chief executive officer. What the Board envisioned was pretty simple: Dr. Clark would be directing his effort at raising more money, and Dr. Keeter would be directing his effort toward spending less of it. Dr. Keeter was willing to take on this responsibility, but served notice he didn't want to be positioned for a move up to the presidency. He believed the endless travel and fund-raising did not appeal to his interest or considerable talents.

Things got focused pretty fast with the new arrangement. Chancellor Keeter was soon told to prepare a budget for the next fiscal year indicating a deficit of "not more than $400,000." The Board, with the leadership of Dr. Clark and Dr. Keeter, sought to stabilize the financial operation of The School.

Dr. Keeter has a very clear remembrance of such challenging times. "The year I came in as chancellor, we had a budget on the table that had a deficit of $1,216,000, and that's on a budget of about $6 million or so...that was a major, major deal." What Dr. Keeter knew, few others knew internally, as Keeter verifies. "I don't know that anyone internally other than Colonel Hackett [Business Manager] knew...In fact, when I was brought in as chancellor, until I had a chance to look the situation over, I really didn't know the extent of the problem."

Dr. Clark and Chancellor Keeter had an immediate problem that was likely to get even worse. There seemed to be no alternative but to do again what was so distasteful scarcely ten years earlier, a bitter pill for Chancellor Keeter to swallow early in his new position. "We borrowed a million dollars out of the endowment...I was having to borrow money when I came into the chancellor's job; I was having to borrow money to make the payroll. This accumulated into a million dollars down at the bank. That is in addition to this budget that was on the table that had a deficit of $1,216,000."

Undeterred, Dr. Clark and Dr. Keeter found a way to survive. "We had hard times," Dr. Keeter explains. "We went without raises. People cooperated with me--the staff, the faculty, everybody. We got through some lean times. Dr. Clark and I had agreed that he was going to hit the road and try to raise additional funds to meet the shortfall. I was going to get down to the business here to try and operate on less money. I found myself doing a lot of different jobs on campus, and so did a lot of other people. It wasn't just me."

As a result of the belt-tightening, The School stabilized over the next few years. Dr. Clark's fund-raising efforts paid off as well. Dr. Keeter recalls, "I set out as a goal while Chancellor to operate The School and pay back what had been taken from the endowment. We weren't adding to it. I knew we weren't going to add to it, but [we needed] to try to keep it where it was. Dr. Clark came up with a fellow by the name of Foster McGaw in Chicago. He [Dr. Clark] and I went up there. Foster wrote us a 'little' check for a million dollars...I took that and paid back the endowment for the million we had taken out." Things must have brightened quickly for the two men. They were operating in one of the most difficult financial environments in the nation's history. Interest rates were increasing faster than The School's deficit! Dr. Keeter remains grateful. "We had it [The School] above water, barely. We were just barely making it." But The School moved forward.

Not only did Dr. Clark and Dr. Keeter have to face The School's precarious financial situation, they had to do it without Dr. R. M. Good. Just after Dr. Keeter was named chancellor, Dr. Good passed away. The summer issue (1975) of the *Alumni News* carried the story: "We are saddened to announce the death of Dr. R. M. Good, President Emeritus...." A special edition of the *Ozark Visitor* re-

Fig. 61 Dr. R. M. Good

ported that "over 1,200 friends, relatives, and guests filed into the chapel for the service." In Dr. Clark's statement, he seemed to speak for everyone, "I have lost a friend, so have you."

No other person in the history of The School of the Ozarks had played such a vital role not only in building its campus but in building its character. His office, usually filled with pictures of alumni, attested to the "family" over which he had presided. Dr. Good (Fig. 61) had seen The School grow from a tiny high school in 1921 to a fledgling college of the '70s while still maintaining its character. A man of strong faith, he depended on the Lord to get them through times of war and struggle. He had fought

162

the good fight; he had finished his course. But most of all, he had kept the faith.

Fig. 62
Dr. Marvin
Oetting

Fig. 63
Mr. Jerrold
Watson

In the midst of perhaps one of the most trying decades of its existence, The School managed to attract more and more capable faculty and staff. And they didn't stand still. Dr. Marvin Oetting (Fig. 62) started the agricultural degree program, whereas Jerry Watson (Fig. 63) began graphic arts. Dr. Marilyn Graves came in and joined Dr. Keeter in getting the intercollegiate athletics program off the ground. Amazingly, much was accomplished in the academic program during very difficult times. Academic Dean Wayne Huddleston worked hard at recruiting faculty who supported the mission, a necessary and difficult job. Concurrent with the progress that went on in the academic program was the equally important improvement of the work program. When Dr. Keeter assumed the position of chancellor, young Dr. Mayburn Davidson moved up.

Dr. Davidson had arrived during hard times and remembers them well. "At our first administrative council meeting, Dr. Clark mentioned that times were tight, that money was tight. I remember him mentioning that things were so tight that...if any of us got a good opportunity to take another job, we ought to give it serious consideration. I thought, 'Gosh, what have I gotten into?' I was sitting there thinking how I had borrowed money from my wife's mother to rent a U-Haul to move the family up here. As

Fig. 64 Dr. Mayburn Davidson

the new man on the totem pole, I wondered which one would go first, if somebody had to go...I figured it would be me. I said something about it to Dr. Keeter afterward. He said, 'Ah, I wouldn't worry too much about that. I've heard that before.' And, nothing came of it." Apparently Dr. Davidson hadn't been told about any financial crisis. "I didn't have any idea!" he asserts. But he remembers Dr. Clark well, "He was a mover and a shaker. He was very much in charge. You could tell that!"

Dr. Davidson (Fig. 64) was allowed to run the work program, and Dr. Clark, as well as Dr. Keeter, had confidence in him. Dr. Davidson became known for working long hours and taking a personal interest in students. He recalls many stories about students he worked with, bad times and good. "Yes, we've had several who would go home, either on grades or disciplinary suspension, or work suspension, who would come back and do real well--go ahead and graduate. Nearly every year at graduation there will be one or two that we've seen have difficulties, who came on back and did well."

Davidson recalls one student asked to leave who came

back and did well, both at The School and afterward. His name is Wiley Hendrix (Fig. 65), for whom one of the athletic support awards is named. "He just didn't go to work [at the Friendship House] like he should. He wasn't a stinker or a misbehaver; he just didn't

Fig. 65 Wiley Hendrix

like going to work." So, Wiley was sent home. "Oh, Wiley did well when he came back. He's one of those success stories. He tried hard, he kept his nose clean, he went to work, he did what he should." Wiley Hendrix, who became a popular sports editor in the region, always remained grateful for his second chance. He apparently missed being at The School. "I called Dr. Davidson and Dr. Cameron (Admissions Dean) so many times that they told me that if I didn't call back again, they'd let me in!" Having followed instructions, Wiley came back and blossomed as a student.

All was not just work in Dr. Davidson's capacity as dean of work. He lived on campus and, like others, occasionally had to do weekend duty in the administration building--answer calls, greet guests, help students, etc. One such weekend duty he will never forget. "A fellow called wanting to bring his mother-in-law's body over here, for her will called for it to be donated to The School. This was about the screwiest one I ever ran into...I was on duty one Saturday morning...the phone rang...he didn't sound serious...I thought someone was pulling my leg...But the longer I talked to him, the more I could tell he was serious. He said, in her will, she had it set up this way...and he wanted to get details as to where he should bring her.

"I didn't know what to tell him. I finally became convinced that he was not someone joking me. I said, 'I can't understand why we would have ever made such an arrangement; we don't have a medical school here--don't have any facilities to accept the body.' So, I took his phone number and told him I would call him back.

"I ran into Dr. Keeter. He laughingly said, 'Just tell

them to throw her on the back of a flatbed truck and bring her on over here. We'll do something with her.' I said, 'Howell, he's not kidding; the guy is serious.' 'Nah,' replied Dr. Keeter. But I said, 'Yes, he is.' So we did some digging around. He said, 'It sounds like something the development officer would cook up!' We spent some time, and I haven't told anybody this: We went over to the development office and did some poking around in some of those records to see if we could find anything; didn't find anything.

"The guy called me back late in the afternoon...by then I just didn't know what to do. He was just as apologetic as he could be. He had said something about it to his wife, whose mother was the one. His wife said, 'No. No. No, honey!' Said it wasn't The School of the Ozarks; it was the University of Missouri where the body should go. He just kept apologizing. I said, 'I'm just too relieved to be offended.' I said, 'Well, that makes sense. They have a medical school and so forth.' He said, 'Well, she [his mother-in-law] was quite a donor to your school.' We got a kick out of that."

As The School moved closer to the end of the decade, its finances were up and down. Dr. Keeter and Dr. Clark did yeoman's duty, and it showed. Unfortunately, by the spring of 1978, the Chairman of the Board "called the Board's attention to the fact that for the first time in three years The School is faced with a budget deficit for 1978-79 in an estimated amount of $634,000." Dr. Keeter again tried to tighten expenditures, with some degree of success. By the turn of the decade, he reported that a deficit projected that year (1980-1981) at $500,000 would be reduced and that the financial picture had brightened. Considering that high interest rates and inflation were wreaking havoc on the economy, this was no small accomplishment.

All of these struggles were clearly taking their toll on an aging Dr. Clark. He had health concerns as well as concerns for the future of The School. At an executive committee meeting prior to the Fall 1980 Board Meeting, it was clear that a transition of leadership was being set in motion:

> The Chairman reported to the members of the Executive Committee on discussions held during the past few months, among Dr. M. Graham Clark, Dr. Howell Keeter, and the Chairman, concerning successor management at The School of the Ozarks. It was their decision that steps should be taken to phase in a new president of The School of the Ozarks, and the name of Dr. James T. Spainhower has been presented to the Nominating Committee as a candidate for this position.

Also, the Chairman reported that the Nominating Committee envisioned Dr. Spainhower serving as a visiting professor for the upcoming spring semester, with the plan that he would assume the presidency in June.

The Chairman allowed the plan to go forward, but only after being told by Dr. Keeter (again) that he did not want the presidency. Dr. Keeter knew only too well what was expected, and he felt as if his skills were elsewhere. "I was pretty well familiar with the duties of the president at this particular institution...It's very much a fund-raising function. I had traveled with Dr. Clark and knew what that was. Before they offered the position to Dr. Spainhower, they offered the position to me again."

Within a few months the plan began to unfold. At the Spring 1981 Board Meeting, with President-elect Spainhower, in attendance, Chancellor Keeter reminded the Board that the budget included a projected deficit of $680,000. This must have been sobering for President-elect Spainhower to hear, for it clearly signaled that he would face challenges far beyond standing in the classroom.

Though the inflation-riddled American economy was making things difficult for colleges and universities across the country, all concerned with the transition of leadership were confident that the challenges faced by The School would be met just as they always had. However, this was not to be the case.

Dr. Spainhower assumed the presidency in the midst of much pomp and circumstance. A grand inaugural was held to signal the changing of the guard for a very capable new leader. Since Dr. Spainhower had previously served for many years as treasurer for the state of Missouri, many thought him ideally suited for The School and its challenges. Expectations were high and optimism prevailed. At his very first board meeting, a resolution was introduced, "commending his performance during the first five months of his administration." A ten-page management letter from The School's auditors may not have seemed so troublesome. But, beneath the glow and euphoria were real problems to be dealt with, and no one knew for sure how Dr. Clark would adjust to a new president from the outside with new ideas and the task of dealing with so many challenges. The answer was not long in coming. At the very next board meeting, Dr. Spainhower tendered his resignation.

With the community, students, and alumni upset, The School found itself back to where it was a few months earlier--looking for a new president. Again, Dr. Keeter stepped forward to carry the load while a new presidential search committee was formed, after again serving notice that he did not wish to be considered for the presidency.

Over the next few months, the Search Committee worked diligently to identi-fy the right person. Several were carefully interviewed, and Dr. Stephen Jennings (Fig. 66) was chosen. This young administrator had a background with educa-tional institutions, as well as having the usual aca-

Fig. 66
Dr. Stephen G. Jennings and family

demic credentials. He got off to a strong start, and the Board joined him with the development of a new long-range plan. Within a few months, this likable young man was gaining the confidence of trustees, staff, faculty, and students.

By spring semester (1984) of his first year, progress was being made. Dr. Jennings (along with Dr. Keeter) was giving serious thought to how best to solve this school's long-standing operational problems. Noteworthy are the comments of Board Chairman Dr. Clark at the springtime meeting (1984). "Dr. Clark expressed his and Dr. Keeter's complete confidence in Dr. Jennings and the job that he is doing as president. Mrs. McDonald stated that she had the feeling that Dr. R. M. Good was the more or less founder, Dr. M. Graham Clark the builder, and that Dr. Stephen Jennings would be the polisher." Clearly, the new president was off to a good start.

The School was still struggling with its budget, yet much progress was going on in the financial arena. Endowed chairs were being established, and a new business building was in the pipeline.

Both Dr. Jennings and Dr. Keeter took the planning process very seriously. Dr. Keeter had long figured out how to address many of The School's financial problems. It involved changing the year-round academic calendar which included summer classes. Dr. Keeter explains why this critical issue had not been faced. "We were really operating on the basis of saying, 'This [budget] is the bare bones that we can operate on,' and then trying to go out and raise the money to cover it. Well, of course, this is a difficult procedure if you are ever going to make improvements. You can't do that forever...So, I worked out a plan whereby we eliminated the summer term. It was so expensive. I put together all these stats concerning how much could be saved if we eliminated the summer term. That was the plan, along with how much we were going to save on utilities during the summer...We were going to close most of the dormitories. Of course, if we eliminated the summer term, we're going to eliminate quite a bit of payroll."

But Dr. Keeter had never tried to implement such a plan, no matter how hard times had gotten. "I sat down and talked to Dr. Clark...Dr. Clark and I were very close. I'd have to say he tried to support about one hundred percent of anything I ever wanted to do. The summer school idea wasn't one of them. It was just too much change for him to accept. He thought we would be de-emphasizing the work program, although he could see where the savings would be." Knowing Dr. Clark's position had always kept Dr. Keeter from trying to get it done. "I wasn't about to bring that to the Board if Dr. Clark didn't concur. Dr. Clark would tell them straight up that he didn't want to do that. I didn't have even close to the votes. If Dr. Clark didn't support it, it wasn't going to fly. It was just that simple. So, I kinda put it on the back burner." Dr. Keeter knew that The School couldn't just tread water forever. "Operationally, The School was struggling."

With the arrival of Dr. Jennings, a committee charged with planning for the future seemed like a possible way of creating momentum, and hopefully Dr. Clark's support, for changes that must have appeared more and more obvious as they were more and more needed. Dr. Keeter explains, "During Dr. Jennings' time, things were beginning to turn around a bit...I went to Jennings and said, 'Now, here. I have a plan...But it has to do with eliminating the summer term.' His answer to that, of course, was that he wasn't too sure of the situation either. He said, 'Well, I'm going to start the Strategic Planning Committee, and we'll have them take a look at it.'"

No doubt, Dr. Jennings knew something had to be done. Trustee Jack Herschend had raised concerns about how trustees could be comfortable with the current financial condition, revenue being down and expenses up. Gifts from bequests no doubt made it up that year, but such budgeting was unpredictable at best. To Dr. Jennings' great credit and leadership, the Board received, at its Spring 1985 Meeting, the recommendations of the Planning Committee. Recommendations touched on many areas of The School's operations and included a proposed calendar change. Since the plan had worked its way through the committee system, it no doubt had become public knowledge. As Dr. Keeter recalls, "Some things about it weren't well-received, especially the dropping of the summer term and attendant savings. The Strategic Planning Committee, chaired by longtime faculty member Dr. Kenton Olson, presented a very well developed report with many recommendations.

Unfortunately, unbeknownst to Dr. Jennings and Dr. Keeter, a petition had been delivered to Dr. Clark. It contained over 150 names of students who objected to a calendar change. Students were likely encouraged to do this; such a change undoubtedly would have affected faculty compensation. Dr. Clark brought the petition up at the Trustee meeting. The result was predictable. A few trustees asked for "further study and research." Although Dr. Jennings and Dr. Keeter "answered questions about the proposed change," it wasn't enough. This must have been very discouraging to both men, as they knew The School must change structurally to flourish. Dr. Jennings worked tirelessly to manage The School and its complex operations. Within a year of seeing the plan sidetracked, the Finance Committee reported to the Board that "there was a deficit of receipts last year; expenditures exceeded receipts by roughly $90,000." In other words, not addressing the structural changes backed by Dr. Jennings and Dr. Keeter had the obvious result--a continued struggle with the budget.

Another matter addressed by Dr. Jennings and Dr. Keeter managed to stay "below the radar." They filed with the Secretary of State a registration for a name change--from The School of the Ozarks to College of the Ozarks. Like the proposed calendar change, its time had not yet come. Had this action leaked out to the public, no doubt other petitions would have been forthcoming. But both ideas were right and their time would eventually come.

To the consternation of many and the surprise of some, Dr. Jennings resigned at the Spring 1987 Board Meeting, having accepted another college presidency in Iowa. In his comments to the Board, Dr. Jennings stated that a number of factors influenced his decisions, that he had not applied for the position in Iowa, and that "he felt he could be more effective there."

For the third time during the decade, the Board found itself creating yet another search committee for new leadership. In the meantime, at Dr. Keeter's urging, Dr. William Todd (Fig. 67) was named interim president, and his long affiliation with The School must have been reassuring. His presence alone assured fiscal restraint. "Bill always spent The School's money just like it was his," Dr. Keeter says.

Ironically, the decade of the '80s had come to resemble the earliest decade of The School's history, a time when the rapid turnover of leadership became problematic. It

carried with it an uneasiness about the future and lingering doubts about whether long-term leadership was attainable. Dr. M. Graham Clark, a charismatic leader who had created the college program and done so much to sustain it, had thus far not been able to adjust comfortably to emeritus status.

Fig. 67 Dr. William D. Todd

Chapter IX
Change

No doubt all associated with The School took a collective "deep breath" when the Search Committee made its recommendation to the full board in the spring of 1988. When Trustee Jack Justus moved "for the acceptance of the Presidential Search Committee's report, which included placing Dr. Jerry Davis in nomination for president of The School of the Ozarks," some probably thought, "Here we go again!" Although Dr. Todd had done an admirable job as interim president, The School had not been able to address its underlying problems. It was heavily dependent on bequest income to stay even, and many were concerned about the future if changes weren't made. So, why would anyone want such a leadership challenge when many thought failure was a distinct possibility?

"This is the ultimate opportunity for what I see is my purpose in life," were my words in Michelle Katzenell's article carried in a Springfield, Missouri, newspaper, scarcely thirty days after I took office with no inauguration, but plenty of determination. Few really knew much about my past, other than I had come from the presidency of Alice Lloyd College, a small work college in the hills of Kentucky. But if the personal statement given to the Trustees had been public knowledge, perhaps the depth of my commitment and identity with a school such as this would have been known.

> I was raised in the home of my grandparents in rural north Georgia. The doors of education were opened to me by The Berry Schools, a self-help boarding school for low-income mountain youth. It was at Berry that my ultimate educational philosophy began taking shape. From the work program, I learned the values of self-reliance and other qualities so necessary for success in life. The Christian faith has provided me with the spiritual framework for success, and this was ingrained in me by family, church, and the schools I attended. Self-help and Christian values, when coupled with high academic expectations, form the heart of my educational philosophy. To me, this is the *American Way,* and I am a product of my own philosophy....

My background provided me with the advantage of identifying with those for whom The School of the Ozarks was founded. Also, I was acquainted with Dr. Clark, and we shared many common bonds. At the opening convocation for fall semester (1988), Board Chairman Harry Basore looked at me and said that I was charged with the responsibility of maintaining and enhancing the purposes of this school. In concluding his "Charge to Dr. Jerry Davis," he said, "As you can see, the 'buck' stops at your desk." He could not have known how well I understood that, nor could he have known how seriously I would take my responsibilities.

Before the end of one year in office, all doubt would be removed as to whether change would occur to address the needs of the institution. Although these changes touched most aspects of the institution, the underlying financial problems were addressed first. The ensuing years found The School caught up in controversy and conflict as decision after decision was made to enable The School to better do what it was founded to do and face the future. These decisions were mission-driven and had to be made.

My idea for restructuring The School went far beyond the calendar change (dropping the mandatory summer session) and included creating an option to work off room and board in the summer by staying on campus and working off campus. Also, it seemed as if some belt-tightening was in order in several non-academic areas that had gotten too big. All involved difficult personnel decisions, but I knew from experience that only a narrow window of opportunity existed to effect real change or the effort would end up like the previous admirable strategic plan, more plan than action.

Of those entrusted with the operation of The School, it was obvious that no one came close to understanding it as well as did Dr. Howell Keeter. He understood how badly we needed to modify The School's financial operation; he also knew how difficult it was going to be, as he and Dr. Jennings had found out. I regarded Dr. Keeter's advice as sound and savvy. He said, "If I were going to try to do this, I would get together a well-thought-out plan, a package that encompasses what you see as the future of this school. Incorporate all of this [needed change] in there, and drop it on the Board at the next meeting without a bunch of committees and people trying to protect their turf...there's probably still enough influence out there by the people who are opposed to it, namely Dr. Clark." He made clear who had to do it. "You understand it like nobody else. This change has got to take place."

Dr. Keeter obviously thought that we should plan an

October surprise and that there was a yearning on the part of the Trustees to see the leadership settle in. "We were getting tired. Every time we would have a search committee, we would say, 'We're getting tired of this swinging door where presidents are running in and out. This institution was built on people like Dr. Good with a long tenure, Dr. Clark with a long tenure, and we need to support someone and start developing another long tenure.'"

Fig. 68 The Davis family

During early fall, while my family and I (Fig. 68) were adjusting to life in the Ozarks, every night Dr. Keeter and I would go over and over my plans and ideas. By the time of my first board meeting, a plan to restructure--and recommit--the entire school had been formulated. No one knew anything about it, except Trustee Joe Basore, whom Dr. Keeter and I thought would support us by making a motion. We were afraid the Trustees would be caught with their mouths wide open, since the plan was so sweeping, and they would be afraid to do anything at all other than appoint a committee to study it. After all, they didn't know the new president very well, and they would be caught off guard. Also, my friend Dr. Clark would be sitting there (as emeritus trustee). With much apprehension we faced the meeting.

After all the committee reports had been made, it was time for the President's Report, near the end of the agenda. In a business-like way, I gave them my analysis of our condition saying, "The only reason The School is not in serious financial trouble has been this unusual bequest income." I thought spending needed to be curtailed in a few areas, and I didn't like the way budgeting had been done because it entailed a greater and greater dependency on bequest income. Right away I asked for a motion, "to authorize the President to bring expenditures more in line with revenue." It passed.

Next, discussion followed on how this could best be accomplished. I told them our yardstick should be to ask, "How does it serve the mission?" No one disagreed. Then came the critical part, a plan upon which so much would depend: the need to change the calendar (a holdover from high school days); the commitment to help truly needy young people by charging no tuition; and the provision of options for paying room and board during the summer by simply adapting to the changing Branson tourist scene which provided many summer jobs (especially Silver Dollar City). One trustee stated for the record his compliments about the proposal and the thorough way it had been presented. Without pausing, Trustee Joe Basore made a historic motion, to make *all* the changes recommended. During the discussion that ensued, I restated my convictions: that this must be done, that I was absolutely committed to what The School of the Ozarks was about, and that little room was left for retreat. The motion passed.

As if revealing the reservations of many, a motion was then made asking for more information at the next meeting or before. We planned on moving quickly to make the changes, knowing full well that the institution would either flourish or else my tenure might very well be less than some of my predecessors. Dr. Keeter reported after the meeting that a skeptical trustee said to him, "We did the right thing, didn't we?" The answer would come more quickly than even I dreamed.

Before the Spring 1989 Board Meeting many changes had been announced: the controversial calendar change; options for payment of room and board; personnel cutbacks at the airport, radio station and computer center; and food service changes. Many of these were as unpleasant as they were unexpected. But all were needed. At board time, a major article in the *Springfield News-Leader* started out by saying The School "can take a breath now--the cutbacks are complete." It went on to note the trimming of the budget by about $2.5 million in bequest money and quoted my reasoning. "The bequest money will be put in the bank. It's our future. If you are spending your bequest money, in essence you are spending your future." All eyes were now on the future, but with great anxiety. I had done my best to make good decisions. In my own quiet time, I had been praying that everything would work out, that good things would happen, and soon.

At the time, my secretary Ruth Raley (Fig. 69) often said that the Lord was looking out for this school, that everything would be okay. So, in early summer, we both had our prayers answered in an unusual way when Dr. Joe

T. McKibben came through the office door, into my life, and subsequently into the history of *Hard Work U.;* to us it was a prayer answered.

Ruth recalls, "I well remember the day

Fig. 69 Ruth (Cheek) Raley, as a student

Dr. McKibben came into our office...he asked if the President was here. I told him 'No'...He sat there a minute. I said, 'I can get in contact with him. I'll be glad to, and ask him to come back and visit with you.' He began asking questions...about students...were boys and girls dormitories separate, and a few things like that." I was at a meeting at the Holiday Inn, when Ruth called. While on my way back to campus, Ruth tried to converse with Dr. McKibben. "He seemed almost uncomfortable to be in the office. Very modestly dressed. He seemed to be interested in all about our students, not only about their housing, but their working."

Upon my return, I invited Dr. McKibben (Fig. 70) into my office and closed the door. Little did I know I would be talking to one of The School's future great benefactors. "Tell me more about this school *The Wall Street Journal* called *Hard Work U.*" I did, and we discussed the future needs of The School, but especially my view of what The School was all about. Finally,

Fig. 70
Joe T. McKibben, M.D.

I got up the courage to inquire about a gift he was considering. He said he was looking at ten different schools for the disposition of his estate. "With respect to what we might do if you chose us, could you give me some idea of what we might be talking about--just a guess?" I asked him. With a sheepish grin he said, "Son, we'd be talking about millions." My heart seemed to stop. So I said, "Do you mind if I reach out and pinch you to see if you are real?" He laughed, and I did, too. Before he left he told me more about himself. He was a retired medical doctor

180

from Missouri and had invested well in California real estate. I asked if I could have a little time to formulate what we could do with his trust. I told him that we needed to start a campaign, and that I would bring my ideas to him. He agreed and gave me his phone number and address in California and left.

Ruth remembers what I asked her to do before Dr. McKibben had gotten very far. "'Check on this number. See if there is such a person.' I did, and found that it was a working number, to our relief!" She also vividly recalls her feelings, "We wondered who he was...I think he mentioned *The Wall Street Journal*, but why was he here?"

Given the timing of the event in the life of The School, Ruth Raley saw more to it. "To me there were two things about this; that's just my own personal feeling. It was a confirmation that you [Dr. Davis] should be here, and a confirmation that the finances and this uneasiness [due to changes] would all begin to settle down. I've said through my years with The School, God's hand of Providence was in Dr. McKibben coming into our front door." The future would prove her definitely correct about Dr. Joe T. McKibben, but when we first met I was not so sure.

Off to California I went. It was to be the first of many visits over a period of about ten years. My first visit astounded me and gave me pause. He lived in a tiny, somewhat cluttered apartment. One of my field reports noted:

Unbelievable...Suggested a place to eat--Motel 6 restaurant. Ate diet plate with him...Dislikes lawyers...has first degree heart block. Beeper...We traded stories of hard times. Told him we never ate at a restaurant when I was a boy, no money. He said he got "all you can eat" for 35 cents during the Great Depression...looks good and it's real.

On yet another trip out to see him, he insisted on taking me to Bakersfield to see some property that The School would one day own. He revealed more of himself to me. My notes read:

> Dr. McKibben is very conservative in his views, especially economics. Very disgusted with what is going on in D.C. Very disgusted with people that won't work. His main interest is the work ethic. He doesn't recall fondly his academic days. Didn't think the faculty treated him right... I am sure he has income off stocks, bonds, and cash deposits. He is reluctant to eat in a place that charges very much. In fact, we ate at a K-Mart, and we got a special on two sub sandwiches, if you can believe it. He didn't want the Coke because they were so expensive, so we drank ice water free.

These reports give insight into a most unusual man who subsequently did a most unusual thing. He left his estate to a school he did not attend, that he visited briefly only once, but whose work ethic he strongly admired. My visits were always revealing about this man.

Another report reads:

> This call was just incredible. I found Dr. McKibben in his...apartment; his drapes were closed. He opened the door and greeted me with a smile. He had on his tie and coat, which is an old, old coat with a flap over the pocket and stripes running vertically. I told him he looked good, and I hoped he had been feeling well. He said that he had not.

He went on to tell me more about his heart problems before insisting that I ride with him to see one of his investment managers.

> We got in his small car, a Honda Civic; the back part was folded down with a garbage bag down there and an old burlap bag. Dr. McKibben's driving was enough to give me a heart attack. He would tailgate, and every time he

hit the brakes or a red light came in front of him, my heart skipped a beat. I was relieved to get there alive.

When we entered the big investment building, he introduced me by saying, 'This is Jerry Davis, and he is as conservative as I am' and broke into a big grin. During this meeting, Dr. McKibben reviewed his investments with me sitting by in awe. One of the bankers said, 'Well, Mr. Davis, I understand that if Joe passes on, we will be dealing with you.' I said, 'I guess that is correct, or with The School.'

Over the years my experiences with Dr. McKibben would fill a volume. It was about five years before we ever saw a penny. Ruth Raley certainly remembers, "It was almost like I thought this was going to happen, but I wasn't sure." Probably we both were never sure until the first gift--$100,000--cleared the bank. This was the first of many gifts; he ultimately gave the bulk of his estate. What began at Point Lookout on a hot, summer day in June of 1989 was a miracle in the making and did, indeed, point to better things ahead.

The fall semester of the first "restructured" school year (1989) got off to a better start than anyone imagined possible. An article in the local paper reported "Record Number of Students Enrolled...." and gave my observations. "What is happening here is unheard of in higher education. Our college has rapidly reduced its cost per student, which has a net effect on our budget of more than two million dollars. Endowment will grow, and the institution will get much stronger than it already is." Things seemed to be turning around.

Other areas of The School were contributing to the perception that momentum was moving in the right direction. One very positive area was in public relations. It was obvious to me that the Director of Public Relations, Dr. Camille Howell, was as capable as she was eager to help. Not only did she have an earned doctorate, but she also had media experience and was gifted in her ability to articulate The School's story and tell it nationwide. The first evidence of this was when *U.S. News & World Report* came out with its rankings for *America's Best Colleges* (Fig. 71). We were ranked in the top tier, the

Fig. 71
America's Best Colleges
U.S. News & World Report,
October 1989

first of many such recognitions. This provided a big boost to faculty, staff, students, and the public alike while The School was undergoing a restructuring.

At the next board meeting (October, 1989), it was possible to report to the Board that "all indicators point to a balanced budget this year without using bequest money, which has historically been done." As the year was unfolding, it must have been obvious that we were getting our house in order. But the demand for gift income was great, and some thought this alone was all that was necessary. This, of course, wasn't true, but I needed to show the Board that new supporters could be found. After all, the need to raise funds hadn't gone away. And neither had Ruth Raley's prayers. Another one was answered by an unsolicited letter on December 15, 1989. It was from an old friend who had a family foundation. The letter read, "We are proud to make donations in the amount of one million dollars ($1,000,000) to your building fund. Also, please find enclosed another check in the amount of four hundred twenty-five thousand dollars ($425,000) to be used where you see best fit." Such a surprise was more than a pleasant Christmas gift; it was a godsend. These discretionary funds were divided among the academic (international travel), religious (chapel activities) and work (supervisor training) programs of The School. For me, it was a chance to draw attention to the "head, heart, and hands" philosophy of The School.

When I reported this timely gift to Trustee Joe Basore, he agreed that it would send a powerful message and dispel the idea that no one else could raise money for The School. That idea never came up again.

Whereas all of the financial changes had an immediate, dramatic effect, other internal changes were slower to take effect. In an environment of new accountability, the Trustees wanted assurances that the entire institution measured up--not just for the present but for the future as well. They were especially concerned about the future; that is how the subject of tenure came up. I told the Trustees the policy would be honored until the Board changed the policy. If that policy were going to be changed, it seemed wise to get a little further along. Besides, the faculty was already having to adjust to a new calendar and teaching load, though they no longer had to work year around. Dealing with a new calendar didn't seem to be causing as much anxiety as a new academic divisional organization.

Upon assuming the presidency of The School of the Ozarks, I was encouraged to find a capable and strong academic dean, Dr. Kenton Olson (Fig. 72). He had been ap-

Fig. 72 Dr. Kenton C. Olson, Dean of the College

pointed by Dr. Todd when he was interim president. Dr. Olson was a good choice. He wanted to strengthen and better manage the academic program. To do this, he recommended a shift from twenty-three departments to six divisions, and I concurred. Unfortunately, this was one more change and added to the uncertainty of the times. He recalls, "People were very uneasy about the financial situation. We were spending too much bequest income. It was a slippery slope."

Dr. Olson also recalled having chaired the Strategic Planning Committee a few years earlier when an unsuccessful attempt had been made to effect change. "I'll never forget when, after the Board meeting, it [calendar changes, etc.] got the axe. It took the wind out of everybody's sails. It might have contributed to Dr. Jennings' departure. He had invested an awful lot of time and work." Like Dr. Jennings, Dr. Olson knew The School was being held back because Dr. Clark had not been able to accept change. "He just couldn't turn loose," Dean Olson says.

Dr. Olson soon found out how hard change was to accept by some who resisted the shift to a divisional organization. "In part, people felt threatened; you're displacing seventeen people as chairs. They were very bitter. I had meetings with the departments of all prospective divisions trying to get people on board." Changing the structure wasn't the only thing Dr. Olson did to get better accountability. He asked faculty to post and keep their office hours and even increased them. Of course, the great majority had no problem at all with that. But the Dean had to deal with a few malcontents who resisted change. On the whole we both were grateful to have a preponderance of talented, dedicated faculty members. And we were determined to face any problems we had.

Though this critical school year (1989-1990) had many ups and downs, they were mostly ups. Most sensed the changes were working (and they were). The big surprise gifts enabled us to address some capital needs, and part of the discretionary gift income was used for academic, work, and chapel programs--a way of reaffirming our purpose and that the mission must come first. There was much positive momentum, primarily because of the perception of changing financial conditions. Before the school year had ended, Dr. Keeter and I knew the right thing had been done at the right time. Dr. Keeter explains, "If we hadn't made the changes at that time, we would have continued to dig our hole deeper." And, he said, the Board and Dr. Clark recognized a change of direction. "We were now not only not taking money out of the endowment, we were putting money in. Which, in an institution like this, to maintain the status quo--a status of no debt--you've got to continue putting money in; you've got to at least offset inflation. We've done much better than that."

At the Spring 1990 Board Meeting, the Board approved yet another change. This, too, had been in the back of the minds of a lot of people for years--namely, upgrading the name of The School of the Ozarks. The timing seemed right to bring this up because of an atmosphere of change, and because it would help clarify that indeed *Hard Work U.* was a college. After giving everyone (especially alumni) a chance to recommend a name change, I asked the Board to change only one word; keep it simple. They did with the motion "that the operating name of The School of the Ozarks be changed to College of the Ozarks." It passed unanimously.

This unique occasion provided an opportunity to reassure Dr. Clark of our direction and intentions. He had supported the name change, and he had even learned to live with the calendar change. Our relationship was positive. The minutes of the Board (April, 1990) revealed, "Dr. Davis suggested in view of changing The School's name to College of the Ozarks that the Board go on record in acknowledging that Dr. Clark was president when the college program was founded." The Board graciously did this. It seemed important to let Dr. Clark know that his contributions were not forgotten and that we were all only trying to make things better. He was profoundly grateful and used "Founding President of the College" on his stationery up until the day he died many years later.

As the name change took effect, the efforts of Camille Howell and the Public Relations Office continued to bear fruit. The now "College of the Ozarks" was named to the Templeton Foundation Honor Roll for Free Enterprise Teaching, and the College again made the *U.S. News* listing of *Best Colleges*. Among the top colleges, the College was rated the #1 Best Buy. By Fall 1990 Board Meeting, a story by Karla Price in the *Springfield News-Leader* got everybody's attention. "Californian Gives $10 Million in Trust to College of the Ozarks." Quoting Dr. McKibben, the writer says, "It is my hope that this commitment will enable you to start your campaign to raise substantial sums of money." The perception of financial and academic success was encouraging.

As the College continued to push for accountability in all areas, it was inevitable that the College, while striving mightily to honor its traditions, would bump up against the culture in the country at large. For almost a century the College had refused to accept the descending standards of the culture. Therefore, no one should have been surprised when the College balked at appearance fads that surfaced on practically all college campuses. Basically, long hair and earrings on males was the latest fad on college campuses in the early '90s. But not here. It was contrary to a long tradition of neat, hardworking students.

Our school didn't have very many students of concern, but the College needed to make clear its expectations. It did. An article in the campus paper entitled "Administration to 'Reinterpret' Dress Code" signaled a major controversy. After all concerned had their say, a clear decision was made. Martha Hoy's article in the local Branson paper concludes:

> The recent reinterpretation and enforcement of an appearance code at the College of the Ozarks will remain in place for next year...'The College has stated its position and it will not depart from it,' Dr. Davis said Tuesday... The statement followed meetings of the faculty, staff, and a student committee on the issue...The appearance code came under fire from some students and faculty members last month when about twenty-four male students were kept from registering for the fall semester because their hair was too long or because they wore earrings.

Twenty-four students out of over a thousand seemed pretty insignificant and not worthy of such an uproar. But it did provide the College the opportunity to signal that it would not accept fads or change its principles.

No sooner did the student appearance issue die down than others surfaced. Full-time day students were asked to work the same number of hours as residential students for their "cost of education." This policy was directed by the Trustees at their Spring 1991 Board Meeting. The Board also directed that the *Faculty Handbook* be reviewed and clarified, and froze tenure considerations until such reviews were completed. Both of these decisions were controversial, but again, they were the right things to do, as history attests.

Making the work requirement uniform was not easily done. It represented not only more change, but also a strengthening of the College's unifying concept as a self-help work school. It seemed logical and necessary. There were five commuter students who didn't agree; they filed a lawsuit claiming this change couldn't be made. They were wrong, as a court subsequently decided. It could be done, and it was done, and it was right that it be done, especially in light of the mission of the College.

Some may have had a few things to be unhappy about, but all had plenty for which to be grateful. The endowment was growing, for, as the years were going by, funds were now flowing into the endowment like water from a fire hose--strong and sure. This good fortune was fueling innovative programs such as international travel and the expansion of a camp for underprivileged kids, Camp Lookout. When new Branson entertainer Andy Williams decided to give his opening night receipts to the College, the proceeds were used for expanding the camp.

The constant change and decision-making had exacted a price. Dr. Keeter's reflections show that controversy goes with leadership. "In my thirty-six years here, well, there was usually some controversy going on. Some of it surfaces; some of it doesn't. It goes with the territory. If you're going to be an administrator, you better be ready to accept it; that is just the way it is."

Prior to the April 1992 Board Meeting, the *Springfield News-Leader* ran a major story entitled: "College of Ozarks Simmers Over President's Power." The writer, Christopher Clark, questioned almost every major decision made during the previous four and one-half years. An article (entitled), "Storm Gathers Over College as Discontent Goes to Court" chronicles the complaint of a faculty member whose contract was not renewed and that of a few commuter students not wanting to work the same hours as other students. The fact that the College won both cases was not as prominently reported by the media.

In another of Clark's articles entitled, "Education, Career Began at Similar Institutions," he describes me, saying "Jerry Davis portrays all that is traditional. God, family, work, and a good education." I viewed this as a high compliment; the attempted satire, in effect, backfired.

During such a tumultuous year, the privilege of citizenship was brought home to College of the Ozarks in a most unusual way; it was a big boost and a big thrill when the President of the United States and the First Lady (Fig. 73)

Fig. 73
President and Mrs. Bush, admiring student-made products

made a visit to Branson, Missouri, to attend a rally at Silver Dollar City and departed (literally) from the middle of the campus. It was such an unusual last-minute happening that jotting down some notes seemed to be in order, for it wasn't the scripted occasion surrounding First Lady Pat Nixon's visit. My notes explain:

A Secret Service agent came to campus and we cornered him down in Dr. Keeter's office. He was talking about arrangements being made for the motorcade which they planned to use to bring the President back to campus to catch his helicopter. He discussed their needs, and we indicated we would cooperate in any way possible. I asked him who was in charge of arrangements--that we would like a photo opportunity with the President, if possible. That would be good for the College. He said he had nothing to do with that--that I would have to see someone who was staying in the Palace Inn. She was the only one that could deal with the schedule--that it had already been made out. He said he would like to help, but he couldn't. What followed during the next few days were repeated attempts to reach the right person. After a few days of calling the Chief of Staff and anybody else we thought would help, we were about to give up. I thought I would make one last shot. So, I called Jack Herschend who, with his brother, owns Silver Dollar City, and told him what was going on--that I hadn't been able to get any satisfaction, and that I didn't understand why if the President of the United States was going to motorcade down the middle of campus, that the College couldn't get some press coverage from it. He said his brother Pete had all the contacts, and he would talk to Pete and see if they could help me. Pete called a little later, and I told him what we wanted. He said he would try. He called back again and told us he had made the contacts and told me it might happen... that the final decision would be made that night and that I should expect a call on Friday morning as to whether it could be done. He thought there was a good chance...In fact, a call did come from the Chief of Staff stating he had cleared it and that though this was being called a 'closed departure,' it would now be called a 'greeting departure'... They had cleared it for the President of the College and maybe one student--no more.

That is how it happened. The student, Yvonne Hughey from Kennett, Missouri, and I were ready to greet the President of the United States and First Lady. We didn't really know if it would happen until the motorcade approached, and someone jumped out and came for us. It was surreal. We weren't allowed to carry a basket of student-made products out to the President because of tight security. The White House aide said, "Come quickly," and so we did.

We were standing directly beside the limousine when President Bush got out. I greeted him. "Welcome to our campus. We're glad to have you here...I would like to present you with a special shirt." He said, "Well, let's see it." I said, "This is a new jogging shirt," and he laughed. He continued, "Well, let's hold it up here so the camera can see it." So, I knew then I would get the picture we coveted (the President holding a *Hard Work U.* shirt). President Bush saw the basket (that we wanted to give him) a few feet away. He told the Secret Service Agent to get it. Yvonne and I pulled the items out, and we explained to the President that they were all made by students. He stepped back a few steps and said, "Tell me about your college." I told him about the College and that the nickname *Hard Work U.* had been given to us by *The Wall Street Journal.* "They're [*Journal* representatives] over there in the press corps," he said, pointing to the crowd of media and cameras.

The President invited us to tour his helicopter and then to pose on the steps of Marine I for a picture. After that, they were gone. The media response was predictable, but it would never have happened without the help of Pete and Jack Herschend, longtime friends of the College and the Branson community.

At the Fall 1992 Board Meeting, the Trustees were pleased to see continued progress, especially to note the endowment growth. But they knew there were more challenges looming ahead other than the growth of the College's endowment. The liability attendant to the College airport was an ongoing concern; some felt the facility should be closed to the public.

On a positive note, I reported that the College would implement an ROTC program the next spring, as this would enhance our patriotic goal, a part of the mission statement. The advent of military science was supported by the vast majority on campus. A naval program had been on campus in years past, and I felt that the College and the students would benefit from the ideals of the military, whose presence would promote patriotism. The College of the Ozarks military science program has distinguished itself in many ways and has commissioned (Fig. 74) many

Fig. 74 Cadets from Bobcat Company taking oath

fine men and women as officers since its inception. They serve honorably around the globe.

As the College tightened its arms around its mission, many thought the controversies brought on by needed changes would soon subside. I did, too. We were all wrong. Things were going to get worse before getting better. A lot worse.

Chapter X
Turning Point

Branson, Missouri, is a small Ozarks mountain town that has become a national tourist destination. The College is Branson's neighbor to the south. In the early 1990s, Branson and the surrounding region received national attention caused by the explosion of growth associated with the music shows and recreational activities of the area. It is Middle America at its best and is known as a family vacation destination. Even before the boom of the early '90s, it drew families from far and near who sought to visit Silver Dollar City (a family-oriented theme park), perhaps take in some mostly-country music shows, or enjoy the lakes and streams. The character of Branson was reflected in its shows and entertainment centers--a place where family, faith, and patriotism prevailed.

With the Branson boom came many "new" shows and visitors. Some of the shows made it, and some did not. But there was (and still is) concern in the community about what Branson might become. With the advent of big name entertainers, concern heightened over what kind of entertainment would be offered and the possible advent of gambling. The College did not want to see Branson evolve into just another gambling town, a place where families would no longer be comfortable. In other words, the College wanted to see Branson remain family friendly.

The issue of the future direction Branson might take was involved when the College served notice that it would not accept a "gift" from opening night attendance at a show many thought to be inappropriate. Wayne Newton, though a talented entertainer, had some content in his show that did not fit well with the values and expectations of many local citizens.

In its front page article of May 27, 1993, the *Springfield News-Leader* reported "'No Thanks,' C of O Head Tells Newton." The article continued, "The President of College of the Ozarks Tuesday declined a donation from opening night of the Wayne Newton Theater because the show was not wholesome, family entertainment." It went on to express the College's opinion, "We simply want no part in the image the show is creating. At a recent show, for example, a discussion of the sexual habits of retirees was not only inappropriate, but downright vulgar."

The reaction from the public was swift, controversial, and long-lasting. The day after the College's announcement, the phone never stopped ringing. Multiple lines come into the president's office. All of the lights stayed red, blinking, and eventually more than the switchboard could handle. My secretary (Tamara Schneider), ever so polite, repeated herself over and over, "Thank you,"; "I'll tell him"; "I'm sorry, we have so many calls"; or "I'll pass along the information." The calls came from all walks of life and were supportive of the College's position.

The national media picked up the story, and it was carried all over the United States--in *USA Today,* radio shows, you name it. But the debate it caused in this region was as entertaining as it was insightful. In the newspapers, reaction was all over the map, letters to the editor by the score. Their titles were revealing, "Money Finally Loses to Morals," "Show Offensive and Just Dumb," "Newton Should Get an Apology," "Singer Provides Great Evening," "Visitors Found Only One Show Offensive: Wayne Newton's," "Newton Fan Says There Was Nothing Offensive in Shows," just to show the variety of reactions.

The editorials and opinion pieces were equally plentiful. An editorial in the Branson paper seemed to be pretty much on target, "In the end, it will be public patronage that will make or break the Newton Show. The family market has been the basis for the Branson area's entertainment growth for a long time, and the market will determine which shows survive for years to come."

Meanwhile, the ripple effect continued. Most of the hundreds of letters the College received were from thoughtful people. Most of them were supportive; very few were dull: "We were shocked and very disappointed that a show like this could be in Branson," from a writer in Little Rock. "We had a group of forty-five people at Wayne Newton's fourth performance in his new theatre in Branson. Nowhere have we been so uncomfortable and mortified as with the content of the show," from a tour operator in Nebraska. "I was bitterly attacked by a lady at bridge who was defending Wayne Newton as I took up for you," wrote a lady. "Parents should be thankful to have a college like that to which they can send their children," said a writer from Wisconsin. "We are doubling what we usually give each year to the College, to help replace a little of what you turned down," came from Florida. "Three Cheers for

College of the Ozarks," exclaimed an editorial from Missouri in which the writer asked his readers to send a donation--and they did!

Though the College's mail ran overwhelmingly in support, there were those who didn't agree: "In Las Vegas, he is the only entertainer who can pack a showroom every night--can that many people be wrong?" opined a writer from Texas who boasted of being secretary of the Houston Chapter of WNIFC (Wayne Newton International Fan Club); "Please know that most of us are not the stuffy, narrow-minded, unsophisticated hicks as might be implied by the actions of Mr. Davis," a writer from Illinois expressed; "Get rid of Davis, he's obsolete," directed a writer from Springfield.

The controversy gave rise to an almost comical scene. At the Wayne Newton Theater, tee shirts were being sold advocating my replacement--with Mr. Newton himself. On a large American flag superimposed with a waist-up smiling photograph of Wayne Newton, the message "Wayne Newton for President of College of the Ozarks" was emblazoned across the shirt (Fig. 75). Such a "souvenir" was sold to the College's attorney Virginia Fry, who gave it to me as a keepsake!

And so it went.

Fig. 75
Tee shirt sold at theatre in Branson

While the press was obsessed with a school passing up Newton's $10,000, almost unnoticed was the success the College was having with its capital campaign, "Promises to Keep." A matching grant of $1,000,000 had been met, and the Trustees received word, "A record year has been recorded in annuities...and the gift income picture continues to improve." Improve it did, as the next report to the Trustees verified that gift income was at a record level. Trustee Justus noted "that the endowment has increased six and one-half million dollars (approximate) from last year." A trend had clearly been established, brought on by the many changes of a few years before.

Change continued at the College in the academic areas as well. The Dean had already implemented a new faculty governance system and was implementing an evaluation system. The Board had directed that both be done. Also, a former faculty member had filed suit because the College refused to renew her contract. So it was in an atmosphere of change and controversy that the issue of tenure came before the Board at its Fall 1993 Board Meeting.

The subject of tenure has been one of the most sensitive subjects in academe; it is also believed by many in and outside of academe to be the most abused. Tenure amounts to the granting of lifetime contracts. Although many academics say this isn't so, their arguments are disingenuous, as tenure is regarded as a property right by the courts. It is definitely the "sacred cow" of education, wherever it is awarded, in public or private institutions. The process of how tenure is awarded and how it assures performance is open to serious question.

Organizations such as the AAUP (American Association of University Professors) and the NEA (National Education Association) view tenure as the "Holy Grail." It is not uncommon nowadays for colleges and universities to question, modify, or eliminate the policy. In a decision that I view as one of its most important, the Trustees of the College of the Ozarks unanimously instructed "the administration to terminate the policy of awarding tenure." Thus, a change to a system of multi-year faculty contract possibilities was authorized.

The change in tenure policy received the expected reaction. But most of it came from outside the College. It was one change too many in the eyes of some, and a great controversy erupted which made most people forget the Wayne Newton controversy--at least for a while. Locally, *The Outlook,* the school paper, carried the headlines "College Discontinues Teacher Tenure." Editor Alicia Winkler matter-of-factly wrote, "Everyone would be at ease if they knew they had job security. No worries about making the bills or putting food on the table. But often this type of job is not beneficial to the work site or employees working under a supervisor with that security...Tenure grants a lifetime contract to teachers who have worked at the College for at least six years." That's how a student viewed the concept. Winkler's article went on to quote Dean of the College, Dr. Kenton Olson, "...It is hard to bring accountability into play with tenure." He wasn't necessarily talking about College of the Ozarks faculty, though a few seemed to be bothered by the policy change. How it was viewed outside the "Gates of Opportunity" (inscribed at the entrance to the College) is another matter.

The *Chronicle of Higher Education,* the major "educational" newspaper, wasted no time delving into the matter. A lengthy article included the usual "unidentified" sources but did identify a few: "One longtime trustee, Arthur R. Cahill,... says, 'There isn't any other business that I know of that grants lifetime employment.'" In addition to the abolition of tenure, the article drags up other issues. For example, a faculty member was quoted as saying, "...the president is trying to make the College more religiously conservative."

Others joined in to condemn the actions of the Trustees of College of the Ozarks in abolishing tenure. The faculty senate of Southwest Missouri State University (now Missouri State University) and Drury College (now Drury University) passed resolutions in opposition. Their resolutions just affirmed for many that the Board had made the right decision for all concerned. Other institutions lamented that they wished their boards possessed the courage to do the same thing.

Not to be outdone, the AAUP (American Association of University Professors) took the following position through the comments of Missouri (AAUP) Executive Secretary John Hopper:

> The immediate results of this 'cleansing' remain to be seen. Neighboring faculty governing boards at Southwest Missouri State University and Drury College have protested the actions. The state conference has condemned the situation in the strongest terms, and the national office is investigating the situation with action possible from Censure-recommending Committee A and Sanctions-Recommending T. The immediate results are more obvious. The vitality and openness that marked this little island of learning in the '80s is no more, the campus atmosphere is a strong blend of Orwell and Jonestown....

Although we knew we would be attacked for making changes which included the dismantling of a tenure system, we had no idea this would be compared to Jonestown. Mr. Hopper urged the national AAUP to investigate College of the Ozarks. The lines had been drawn in the sand, but as Mr. Hopper and the AAUP learned, they wouldn't be on campus to investigate anything.

Much of the criticism in the local press came from a former professor. Many faculty members resented the former faculty member's interference. One faculty member, Professor Donald McMahon, had all he could take, and wrote an article in the local paper wherein he said:

> He has the right to state his opinion; however, he has no right or authority to represent the College of the Ozarks faculty...Members of the Board of Directors are people of integrity and continually strive to improve the College... The College's financial position has improved greatly. Since 1989 the College's endowment has increased by $27 million. The College is debt-free and is in the middle of a $7 million building and capital improvement program with the money in hand to complete all projects. The College operates on a balanced budget...retirement benefits have increased substantially...over seventy-five percent of the faculty have received a ten-day expense-paid trip to Europe to visit our sister college...the number of academic scholarships has increased....

Finally, Professor McMahon concludes, "Only a small number of College of the Ozarks faculty is a part of the AAUP...the SMS AAUP Chapter should get a more balanced view of what is really happening on this campus before it casts stones."

Although the storm of criticism subsided temporarily, the lull wouldn't last long. Soon, the College found itself squared off in court against a faculty member who sued the

College because her contract had not been renewed. The College believed right would prevail and that it had made the right decision. Further, I knew that the College had a sharp lawyer in Virginia Fry who had already prevailed against a lawsuit by commuters not wanting to work the same as other students. She knew the College well, as her brother was an alumnus. Under Attorney Fry's pleasing personality was a keen knowledge of school law, a sense for what was right, and a strong will to back it up. The plaintiff would soon find out.

The trial took place in rural Christian County, Missouri, and was covered in depth by the *Springfield News-Leader.* A series of daily articles appeared entitled, "Reason for Non-renewal Still Hidden," "Teacher Didn't Fit, Was Devious, Say School Officials," and finally on the third day, "Former Professor Loses Suit Against C of O." Comments from the final article are indicative of what a jury thought of the suit:

> It took the jury only eighty minutes to reach a verdict. With relative quickness Friday, a Christian County jury ruled against an ex-College of the Ozarks professor who contended the school owed her a reason why her contract wasn't renewed more than two years ago...But all she got in a county courtroom Friday was defeat, after jurors marched back with a verdict eighty minutes after starting deliberations.

The school year had certainly had its distractions. But underneath the troubled veneer, the College continued to prosper. Its endowment was growing; it was getting stronger and stronger. A major con-

Fig. 76 Colonel Oliver North

vocation to honor Vietnam Veterans was held, and a capacity crowd (almost 4,000) was addressed by Colonel Oliver North (Fig. 76). In his emotional remarks, North quoted from the Bible, Isaiah 40:31: "But they that wait upon the Lord shall renew their strength; they shall mount up with wings as eagles; they shall run, and not be weary; and they shall walk and not faint." Those words were an inspiration to many who needed the encouragement. This convocation was the forerunner of community convocations (later endowed by Leonard and Edith Gittinger) that would make the famous commonplace at *Hard Work U.* Former First Lady Barbara Bush, Mrs. Elizabeth Dole, General Norman Schwarzkopf, General Colin Powell, Dr. Franklin Graham, Lady Margaret Thatcher, President Gerald Ford, and many others would soon follow.

As the 1994 school year drew to a close, the Trustees of College of the Ozarks took another step forward when Trustee Alice Edwards "recommended that the College discontinue the GSL (Guaranteed Student Loan) Program..." The rationale for this was simple: Debt is bad, especially for young people; federal loans are too easy to get, and much harder to pay back (with interest). A first step needed to be taken to assure the College's independence, especially with respect to honoring its Christian commitment, which many of us thought might be jeopardized in the future.

Such a "controversial move" was another change that some didn't like. But it was yet another right decision. An editorial in the *Rolla Daily News* weighed in, "I think Davis's action is laudatory. I think so highly of it that as soon as I quit writing the editorial, I am going to send a check to College of the Ozarks. I want to do what I can...."

No one really doubted the College could attract more private support. This was clear in Sara Hansen's *News-Leader* article entitled, "C of O Brings Home $53 Million in Five Years. People who have never seen the place are giving big bucks to support a private school." She quoted me as to why this was so important.

> The future of this college is tied directly to growth of this endowment. One of the goals of the Trustees is to remove the College from the dependency of government money. Doing that is tied to the successful growth of the endowment.

An even more significant event occurred during such a tumultuous period. A review of one of the College's premier academic programs by the DESE (Department of Elementary and Secondary Education) brought an accolade that surpassed anyone's expectations. The evaluation team gave the College's program the highest rating possible ("Exemplary") for commitment to mission. The Director of Teacher Education for the state of Missouri subsequently commented, "I feel that this is a significant endeavor, because College of the Ozarks is the first, and so far the only college to have received an 'Exemplary' rating for this standard." It was yet another reflection of the quality of education being made possible by the College, its faculty, and staff.

This recognition in 1994 was in addition to the incredibly good work by Public Relations Director Camille Howell, which resulted in the College being recognized concurrently by *U.S. News*, America's Best Colleges--Ranked #1 for Best Buy in the Midwest; *U.S. News*, America's Best Colleges--Top Tier in America's Best Liberal Arts

Colleges in the Midwest and *Money Guide,* Best College Buys Now.

Clearly, much good was being accomplished at *Hard Work U.*--apparently too much for some. In mid-1994, shortly after school was out, a handful of former students gathered signatures asking for my removal. The number one grievance of this group was "abolition of faculty tenure." Other grievances cited included the College's refusal to accept a donation from a show that didn't promote family values, cancellation of federal loans, and even a complaint about the prohibition of long hair and earrings on men. Indeed, the College had come through many dangers, toils, and snares--financial restructuring, layoffs, calendar change, governance revision, and tenure policy change, just to name a few. Yet the College was thriving, gifts were pouring in, recognitions were stacking up, ten students were vying for each place in the freshman class, and renowned speakers were coming to campus one right after another.

The unhappy vocal minority had attributed every policy change to me. Such was not the case, although I was the willing instrument of change. The Board of Trustees of the College of the Ozarks, unlike many weaker college boards, had a strong sense of direction and was devoted to doing what was right for the school in assuring its future. In the mid-'90s, the College was caught up in the culture wars, as well as an ideological struggle for the direction of the College. After the Chairman of the Board of Trustees responded to the dissidents, a letter came to me indicating some enlightenment had occurred. It offered to "extend a qualified apology," saying the group originally "believed your efforts to be at the heart of many of the changes... but now we know better..." and that the group "no longer seeks your resignation as a matter of course...." Unbelievably, the writer concludes that his group "is not hostile in any way to college authorities...." After conducting what appeared to many to have been a hate campaign, the adversaries now only wanted "dialogue."

While all of this was going on, the national AAUP announced it was going to send a two-person team to investigate the happenings at College of the Ozarks. The press anticipated an imminent confrontation:

> Davis has often shot back with force, even now hinting that AAUP investigators--both are from colleges of similar size to C of O--may not be allowed on campus. Consider the final words in a letter he sent to the AAUP, dated April 7: 1) This college will not cooperate with your 'investigation.' We think you need to be investigated... 2) No member of your team is to be on our property without the written consent of the College... 3) The College of the Ozarks intends to hold your organization, its agents, chapters, or affiliates accountable.

The writer added, "In a written statement to the *News-Leader* about the issue, Davis said, 'In my opinion, the AAUP is a left-wing, Washington, D.C.-based organization that doesn't practice what it preaches.'"

In yet another letter to the AAUP in Washington, I tried to explain what was believed to be a bigger problem: "In my opinion, the AAUP should change its name to the American Association for Unaccountable Professors. In my view, it's special interest groups such as the AAUP that pose the greatest threats to accountability in education by using self-serving, big union tactics." In closing, I gave them some advice with respect to their so-called "censure list": "Go ahead and add us to your list. I will consider it a badge of honor to be on your list...."

In such a tension-filled environment, the Board of Trustees gathered for its spring meeting (1995). The demands for resignation and the impending AAUP "investigation" were just the latest in a string of controversies brought on by decisions some deemed unpopular. There was concern the Trustees might blink. I knew the Board pretty well, and I knew I was doing the best I could to carry out board policies and willingly taking the heat. I did not believe they would waiver. But even I was surprised at the resolve and strength this group showed. They were not about to walk away from doing what was right for the College or its future.

After discussing everything (petitions, malcontents, AAUP), the Chairman recommended the Board adopt a lengthy resolution to condemn the AAUP and "to extend the employment contract of Dr. Jerry C. Davis to six years"--the maximum allowed. In its May 12, 1995, issue of *The Chronicle of Higher Education* under "College Turns Tables on AAUP," a report of trustee action was clear: "The College's Board charged the AAUP with 'inappropriately intervening in the internal affairs of the College, violating its own published standards, and compromising its investigation of the College through its own misconduct.' Then, for good measure, the Board extended the contract of the President...."

No wonder the local headlines read, "AAUP Visit Deemed 'Futile'" when the so-called visit did take place. But it did not take place on campus; very few people even talked to the "investigators" who holed up in a Hollister motel. The AAUP investigation was insignificant; only the media got much out of it. The College has yet to be censured for abolishing tenure.

After the AAUP left town, some thought that major controversy would end. Unfortunately, this was not the case.

Though the critics of the College had indicated they no longer sought my removal from office, their new strategy had become crystal clear: discredit the College in any way possible. The approach sank to its lowest point when the College was notified by the accrediting agency that serious complaints had been made against the institution.

In responding to the charges, I characterized them as "a stack of material which includes serious misrepresentations, personal attacks, and outright dishonest statements which have been part of a massive campaign to discredit the College and me in particular. It has been going on since a jury found in favor of the College in a controversial lawsuit." The College invited the agency to send a representative to the College, speak with whomever they wished, ask whatever they wished, and then go from there.

In fact, that is what occurred. The agency representative made such a visit, and the verdict became a turning point in a bitter struggle. The published report read in part:

> At your invitation, I made a fact-finding visit to the College on September 18 and 19. While there, I met in discrete groups with the Board of Trustees; some off-campus persons; a representation of about forty students drawn from all disciplines and classes; faculty division heads; the Evaluation Committee; and, in separate meetings,

with most of the full-time faculty, professional staff, and support staff. These meetings were held without either you, the President, or the Dean being present. My last two meetings were with the President's Cabinet, again without you, and with the Board of Trustees to summarize my findings. As a result of these many meetings, I found nothing that negatively affects the continued accreditation of the College of the Ozarks. In fact, there is much to support that accreditation and your leadership. I wish you and your colleagues the best as you deal forthrightly, yet creatively, with the negative publicity that you and the College have unfortunately received.

Unwilling to accept defeat, a spokesman for the dissident group wrote in the local paper, "At those meetings, I heard the College of the Ozarks administrators chastised to the limit...." Apparently, this sort of misrepresentation was too much for one of the College's most distinguished professors to take. Also writing in the local paper, Dr. Bradford Crain, himself a product of a work college and holder of a Ph.D. from Harvard University, set the public record straight:

No doubt he heard criticism; after all he talked...In my view, the words of support were the most convincing. Maybe that is because I was forced to dismiss much of what [the former faculty member] said at the meeting I attended, since so much of it seemed a strange mix of nonsense, personal complaint, misstatement of fact, and misunderstanding of much of what is happening today in higher education. [He] appears more anxious to dictate the terms for leading the College he claims to love than he is to learn the truth about challenges facing the College of the Ozarks. It is easy to criticize college leaders who are accountable when one himself is unaccountable.

Fittingly, during the same week, the school paper reported that "C of O Ranks High with the Best of the Nation's Colleges" and that the College had again "been named to the John Templeton *Honor Roll for Character-Building Colleges* (Fig. 77)." Under the heading "Character Counts," the Honor Roll recognized colleges and universities that promote high integrity as well as education.

So as *Hard Work U.* gained fame across the country, one thing was clear. It was at a turning point as it moved toward the end of the century. Caught up in the culture wars and in the midst of a bitter ideological struggle for the future, the College was on course and flourishing. The Trustees were standing firm. There would be no turning back.

Fig. 77
Honor Roll for Character-Building Colleges

Chapter XI
"An Oasis of Character-building"

"Today, the College of the Ozarks is a nationally-recognized school that provides the opportunity for an education to any student willing to work hard enough to earn it." So said former First Lady Barbara Bush, speaking on campus in April of 1996. Her words reflected the observations of many who had watched the College over the years. The College had indeed become nationally recognized, had kept the "Gates of Opportunity" open wide, and had reminded everyone of why it was called *Hard Work U.*

Barbara Bush was invited to speak to students at the Community Convocation honoring teachers. Her visit was widely covered in the press as well as by the ever present Secret Service! Kathryn Buckstaff, writing for the *Springfield News-Leader* reported on the exciting event. "At a dinner before her speech, Bush presented appreciation

awards to teachers or administrators representing the fourteen schools

Fig. 78 Mrs. Bush (left) joins in recognizing Miss Lamar Louise Curry.

in Stone and Taney counties...." Buckstaff also reported on presentations made at the Convocation: "She was there to present plaques of appreciation to six area colleges that offer teacher training...." Finally, Mrs. Bush joined the College in paying tribute to Lamar Louise Curry, long-time trustee, benefactor, and educator (Fig. 78). It was a very successful event for College of the Ozarks and provided high visibility for its own outstanding teacher education program.

The occasion was yet another well-earned recognition for the College, in addition to the *Number One* rating on commitment to mission its education program had received from the Missouri Department of Elementary and Secondary Education. One of the activities (Teacher Appreciation Banquet) surrounding the visit of Barbara Bush was held in the newly completed Youngman Agricultural Center, a campus addition built by staff and students.

During this period of time, alumni were being recognized for their achievements. One young alumna and ABC News correspondent, Erin Hayes (Fig. 79), received the Edward R. Murrow Award for her coverage of the Oklahoma City bombing. Clearly, the College was basking in a welcomed aura of positive momentum.

The College's excellent music

Fig. 79
Alumna Erin Hayes being interviewed on campus

Fig. 80
Students singing in
Russian cathedral

programs also enjoyed high public visibility and recognition during this time. Founder James Forsythe would probably have had a hard time believing that one day a group of students from the Ozarks would travel halfway around the world to Russia. Such was the case in May of 1996, when the College's Chorale and Handbell Choir (Fig. 80) made a trip which was widely viewed as "the chance of a lifetime" by students like Kerry Lenk. The fact that friends of the College would underwrite this opportunity was special enough, but the impact such a tour had on students was even more special. Kerry tried to express this by writing in the *Ozark Visitor:*

> It is virtually impossible to sum up the entire experience in one single word. Too many come to mind: wonderful, educational, eye-opening, mind-boggling, thrilling, and the list could go on and on...It is really amazing how this experience made me appreciate what I have. It also strengthened my love for College of the Ozarks. The dorms may not be the Ritz-Carlton and the cafeteria may not always serve exquisite cuisine; but I know that I have a chance to express my faith, I have a clean bathroom, toilet paper, clean water, and food always on the table. It was a wonderful reality check....

Although the Russian tour was special, it was not the first such trip. Such opportunities had started a few years earlier and were financed by unsolicited gifts. Chorale Conductor Lynda Jesse recalls how the tours originated and the meaningfulness of these opportunities.

"The first tour was in 1991. Students were selected from the Chapel Choir, which then evolved into the Chorale. The Handbell Choir was also included in the tour, and it was the first chance for a group of students to go overseas on a music tour. Many of these kids had never been on an airplane before, let alone out of the country. It was a real challenge planning the music and selecting pieces which would represent our Christian faith, as well as our feelings of patriotism; then, to connect with audiences in Germany and The Netherlands was quite an undertaking."

Those of us who went on that first tour were fortunate. We had an exchange student, Tineke (Willering) Scheppers, with us on the trip. Lynda Jesse fondly recalls her help: "Tineke was our first exchange student from The Netherlands. She was an education major, but she fit in well with the music department because she came from a musical family. Looking back on the experience, I think her participation in the Chapel Choir and Handbells really helped make the connection with C of O students that many international students don't achieve. She really helped us on the tour because she could translate our program into both German and Dutch."

Early experiences made the Russian tour less intimidating, but the tour itself originated with the encouragement of Lynda Jesse who had received a sabbatical in 1995--"a chance to go teach at our sister school in Leeuwarden [The Netherlands]...." While there, she stayed in a boarding house and made friends with three other visiting professors--from Russia. It was an unusual experience. "We really got to know each other very well. From my generation of coming from the Cold War--the mentality of not knowing what Russian people were really like, how they think, or how they think about us--it really gave me a chance to sit down with them...They were always saying, 'You must come see Moscow. Come. Come. Come!'...So I did." After the sabbatical was over, Lynda Jesse went to Russia and reported, "just an amazing experience!" She returned to the College with a plea for a Russian tour. "And, lo and behold, it happened in 1996!" she remembers.

All who went on that tour will likely never forget it. It was more than educational. "It was freezing," Lynda remembers about the weather at the start of the tour in St. Petersburg. It was so cold, in fact, that the boat got stuck in ice and was a few days late. The tour group was temporarily housed in an old hotel. She continues, "It was scary, because the rooms were so dark...On every other floor at the end of the hall was some stern-looking woman."

The group was fortunate that one of the tour guides (Nadya) became a special friend to College of the Ozarks students. "She had kids of her own and was very personable. She was so helpful...She was just great," Lynda explains. "The tour was a great success." And she is grateful for what such experiences mean to the College's students.

"You don't know what you have sometimes until you leave it; we take things for granted." Lynda Jesse (Fig. 81) knows more than most how important such activities are. Having come from the tiny Ozarks town of Galena,

Fig. 81 Lynda Jesse, as a student

217

Missouri, and then having graduated from The School of the Ozarks, she is a testimony to the mission of College of the Ozarks and a local girl made good.

Barely a month after the group returned to campus from Moscow, they were again reminded of the blessings of living in America. Many in the group were on campus for what has become one of the College's most enjoyable traditions. Dawn Peterson described it in a major article which appeared in the *Springfield News-Leader,* shortly after the Fourth of July in 1996. In this article, "C of O Celebrates Patriotism," she reports: "About 1,200 people attended the free Fourth of July event at Lake Honor on the College campus...The event is one of the ways in which the ninety-year-old college fulfills part of its purpose...." This community event, known as Honor America Day (Fig. 82), is an old-fashioned family-styled occasion--complete with a military band, and even a visit from 'Uncle Sam' for the children. Games, food, fellowship, and fireworks follow the presentation of colors by the local Boy Scouts and the

Fig. 82 Honor America celebration on campus

playing of the National Anthem. Those of us in the crowd that still had fresh memories of Russian onion domes in our heads were especially moved that day by the playing of the National Anthem.

During the Fall 1996 Board Meeting, the Trustees received yet another report with encouraging news about gift income to the College. "The College is having another good year with gift income. Annuity income was significantly higher...." They also were introduced to two students (Reneé Hughes and Aaron Little), members of the College's outstanding SIFE (Students in Free Enterprise) program. They explained to the Trustees that the SIFE organization had been asked to help plan for the upcoming visit of Lady Margaret Thatcher. They excitedly told the Trustees of an anticipated banquet before the Community Convocation, and suggested that this be a "Business Leadership Banquet" since the theme for the Convocation was free enterprise. They went on to suggest that prominent business leaders be recognized at the Convocation, as well as at the banquet. And, finally, they wanted to recognize the Trustees (certainly distinguished business leaders) at the banquet. Such an ambitious plan was enthusiastically accepted by the Board.

As with any major undertaking, the College marshaled all its resources to stage the event. It wasn't the first such event, but it was the most complex to date. The Dean of Administration, Larry Cockrum, had to oversee everything from music, food, color guards, and ticket arrangements, to elaborate protocol expected for a foreign head of state. We all went over our responsibilities--over and over and over again. Student (SIFE) planners, workers, and supervisors helped mobilize the College. It was a team effort. I was especially concerned when, a month before the event, I found myself recovering from neck surgery wondering if I could meet my responsibilities to serve as host, preside over the event, and then introduce eleven dignitaries and a number of trustees. Two weeks before the (February, 1997) event, movement returned to my neck, bringing a sigh of relief from my wife. She knew that I would find a way to go through with the event even if I had to crawl down the aisle beside the former Prime Minister of Great Britain. Fortunately, that wasn't necessary, and most in the vast audience didn't know anything about the anxiety preceding the occasion.

Eagerly, everyone at the College of the Ozarks stepped up to the occasion, which will long be remembered as a highlight of the College's first one hundred years. Lady Thatcher showed up on campus early, along with agents from Scotland Yard and our own Secret Service. She was easy to greet and conversation flowed smoothly. She requested a tour of the campus and wanted to see everything. So, together we did. No dignitary before and none since has taken as much time to visit the student industries on campus.

When we showed up at the Fruitcake and Jelly Kitchen (Fig. 83), Lady Thatcher inquired about how the famous fruit- cakes were made. We all stood around her in awe as she matter-of-factly

Fig. 83 Lady Margaret Thatcher observes a student preparing the famous C of O fruitcake.

discussed the ingredients of fruitcakes. She was just as inquisitive at Edwards Mill, Williams Chapel, and Ralph Foster Museum. She was especially fascinated with a 1931 Rolls Royce car in the Ralph Foster Museum. She even looked under the hood and asked questions about the engine; I conveniently referred her to the museum director, as I did not know much about it. But she walked unquestioningly past the original Beverly Hillbillies car--probably not viewed as a cultural icon by the British.

Prior to a banquet which honored Lady Thatcher, the handbell choir played several musical selections. Lady Thatcher took note of the bell ringers and asked to speak with them, saying how pleased she was because the bells were of English tradition. With 1,000 people watching, she shook hands with (and thanked) each student, a master touch for a politician and the thrill of a lifetime for these students and their capable director, Marilyn Droke.

After the meal, Lady Thatcher joined in presenting plaques to our distinguished trustees. She seemed very comfortable doing this. There was a graceful air about her, a dignity that is hard to describe. When we finally made our way to the field house, we were surprised at just how many people could crowd into the arena--over 4,000 and beyond the normal limit! Amidst much pomp and circumstance the occasion unfolded, complete with Marine color guard, processional, and singing of the National Anthem, led by United States Senator John Ashcroft (a native of the Ozarks). Lady Thatcher sang right along, and she nodded approval when we next sang the British National Anthem. I had memorized the words, knowing it would be obvious to her and everybody else if I led by example!

Fig. 84

Fig. 84
Lady Margaret Thatcher joins in recognizing J. B. Hunt.

The event was heavily covered by the press. Before Lady Thatcher's speech, she joined in giving special recognition to some prominent business entrepreneurs. A few of the business leaders recognized are well known, not just in the Ozarks, but around the nation. One example is J. B. Hunt (Fig. 84). I briefly told the audience something about Mr. Hunt's remarkable career--rising from working in his sawmill to Chairman of J. B. Hunt Transportation, with revenues of over a billion dollars. Jack and Peter Herschend, co-founders of Silver Dollar City, were recognized. From humble roots to national theme park operators, they are known in the Ozarks for their leadership and philanthropy. James P. Keeter, Chairman of Royal Oak Enterprises, was recognized. From the tiny Ozarks community of Bradleyville to the top of one of the world's largest charcoal production companies, Mr. Keeter is likewise known for his business success. John L. Morris, Founder of Bass Pro Shops, was recognized. Few companies are as successful or as well-known as Bass Pro, a company Mr. Morris founded with the idea of offering specialized fishing tackle and other outdoor gear. Another business entrepreneur recognized was E. Stanley Kroenke, well-known in Missouri for part ownership of the Rams National Football League team, development of shopping centers, and many other businesses. Mr. Kroenke rose from the small Missouri town of Cole Camp to become one of the nation's most successful business leaders. Lady Thatcher seemed genuinely interested (and impressed) with our effort to recognize these and a number of other business entrepreneurs and leaders.

In addition to joining the College in recognizing successful business leaders to accentuate the theme of free enterprise, Lady Margaret Thatcher gave a speech that focused on the distinctive character of *Hard Work U.* Her remarks were reflected in positive press accounts, but those who heard the address were most inspired--by what she said about an education at *Hard Work U.,* our place in the world, and the importance of traditional values which have stood the test of time. The headlines in the local paper, the B*ranson Daily News,* captured this: "Thatcher Calls for Return to Values." The event was a momentous occasion. "Lady Thatcher Visit a Success," said *The Outlook* (campus paper). The *Springfield News-Leader* reported "4,500 Hear 'Iron Lady' Thatcher Speak." But more meaningful than all of the publicity was the substance of her remarks. Some of her remarks are unforgettable. "I've read of the work and ideas of this unique college. And now that I have seen it, I'm not only tremendously impressed, I'm very enthusiastic about it...The education that you get here is not only an education or a qualification for a degree; it is an education for life...." She went on to say, "Now, my friends, what we learn is that the most important thing of all, wherever you are, is the values in which you believe and the values by which you live...Values are extremely important and matter more than anything else--the values and the traditional family." Lady Thatcher went on to cite a concern, "We have a problem. You are taught your values in a traditional family...What happens if you don't have a traditional family...?"

We all knew what she was talking about. She had put her finger on one of the world's (and certainly America's) biggest problems--the family unit and how youngsters are brought up. In finishing her remarks, Lady Thatcher cited C. S. Lewis, "If we fail to pass on specific standards of right and wrong, of what is worthwhile or worthless, or what's admirable or ignoble, then we must share the blame for the consequent failings of character."

After Lady Thatcher's moving address, prior to going to a photo reception, she and I retreated to a small room behind the stage for a respite. Her escort closed the door. We had coffee, tea, and cookies and a conversation forever stamped in my memory. I thanked her for her thoughtful address, especially for her comments on values and the importance of the family. I had read about Lady Thatcher's family and how she grew up. But I was startled when she asked about my own. I stammered in telling her a little something about my youth and home--how my two brothers and I were raised by godly grandparents and how I understood what happens to children from broken homes. She observed how unfortunately common such situations are nowadays and asked about the background of our students. I related to her that some, no doubt, were confronting the same issues that I did. She shook her head in understanding. Before we left the privacy of the little room, I tried again to express our appreciation for her effort and interest in speaking to so many students--how important that was.

The afterglow of the visit of Lady Margaret Thatcher

was significant. Her visit not only dramatically raised the College's visibility, but it also inspired us to build on such events. The growing financial strength, prominence, and success of the College suggested that it could (and should) take a national leadership role in speaking not only to its students but to the nation at large regarding what Lady Margaret Thatcher had focused on--values, or more specifically, character. We thought that *Hard Work U.,* as a unique institution of "the head, heart, and hands," had something to say.

It was with such a background that College of the Ozarks joined the budding character education movement in a most unusual way. At the Fall 1997 Board Meeting, with Lady Thatcher's words still fresh on our minds, and with the belief that we could play a bigger role by placing into perpetuity these existing programs and creating new ones, I presented a new vision to the Trustees. The plan was summarized in the minutes of the Board under "Proposed Center for Character Education and Citizenship." With diagrams and what I thought was a good rationale, a plan was presented "to bring national visibility to the College and to institutionalize its character education and citizenship...to be accomplished through an endowed 'Center.' Under the Center will be endowments for a special convocation series, character and citizenship forums, publications, community service programs, an international program, our 'Honor America' program...." My concluding point got right to the heart of the matter as I "challenged the Board to make a special effort to raise funds for the individual segments of the program." In other words, someone should take a leadership role in putting "wings" on my dream. But not much response was received, other than all thought it to be a worthwhile idea. Later in the day my wife asked how the meeting had gone. "Not good," I said. "What happened at the meeting?" she continued, puzzled. "Nothing. That's the problem. I wanted something to happen about the big character center idea. But not a single bite. Just kind words--not what I was looking for. Maybe I scared them with the numbers!" "Well, don't give up," she said. "Don't worry, I won't. I'll find the funds," I vowed.

What became known as The Keeter Center for Character Education materialized a lot quicker than I thought. My

Fig. 85
Vester and Ruby
Keeter

impatience turned out to be unjustified. The Center and its programs were named in honor of Vester and Ruby Keeter (Fig. 85), parents of Trustee James P. Keeter, who was present at the Board meeting when the concept was presented.

Mr. Keeter recalls the occasion and reflects why he and his family identified with the character center idea and wanted to honor his parents. He, in fact, called the next morning after the meeting and asked if I had somebody to get the program started. When I told him, no, not yet, he said he and his family wanted to do it and told me why. "I had always wanted to do something that I thought was appropriate in memory and in honor of my dad and mother. When that came up I thought, 'That's the perfect thing to honor them and for them to be remembered by...' it has turned out to be better than anything that we had dreamed of."

Mr. Keeter was profoundly influenced by his mother

and dad. He reflects their work ethic and entrepreneurial spirit and to this day remains grateful for their influence on his life. "No one in this county had more respect or character than my dad. His word was his bond. He believed everyone should be that way, and there shouldn't be any deviation from it."

Mr. Keeter's parents overcame many obstacles and had humble roots. And Mr. Keeter has never forgotten, "My dad and mother both came from very large families, and they were very poor families. My dad came from a family of twelve; he had four brothers and eight sisters... My mother just the opposite; there were four girls and eight boys." Mr. Keeter's father had to grow up in a hurry, and he developed a strong work ethic early. "My dad felt responsible for his brothers and sisters, especially his sisters." Mr. Keeter remembers, "He would farm and raise cotton; he would hire his sisters to help pick the cotton so they could earn money to buy shoes and clothes to go to school. Otherwise, he said, they wouldn't have anything. So, as I grew up, every time we would visit with family, they were always telling me how good my dad was to them and how they would have had a tough time even getting by if he hadn't helped them. So, that always made me proud of him."

The parents of Mr. Keeter were frugal, and, as he recalls, they took their various family responsibilities seriously. "They worked from daylight to dark. This was a way of life for both of them." Mr. Keeter saw in his father some of the roots of his own success in the business world. "Even back then he was an entrepreneur. He was always looking ahead to do something more than just working for someone else or working by the hour." And when a profit was made, Vester Keeter gave it to his wife to keep. "She was the bank," as Mr. Keeter recalls. "When he would make a profit, he would give it to her, and she would save the money...when he needed money for a project in the future, he would have to talk to her for weeks and weeks before she would let him have any money. She controlled the spending."

Their business model was certainly successful. Vester Keeter had many business interests; he became a timber buyer and then got into the charcoal business. It was the forerunner of what became one of the most successful manufacturing companies in the world--Royal Oak. As Mr. Keeter recalls, "We started from the smallest in the U.S. and became the second largest in the world."

Mr. Keeter remembers that his parents wanted him to get an education and were big supporters of what became known as the College of the Ozarks. "He knew of the College and what it stood for. He and my mother bought a lot of property...several hundred lots. Then he gave all those to the College. Then, my mother gave what was left to the College after he passed away. He knew what the College stood for and talked about it quite often."

The naming of the character education center for Vester and Ruby Keeter affirms much of what the College represents. The Keeters provide many examples of the values Lady Margaret Thatcher was talking about, and they still remind Mr. Keeter of how to live. Mr. Keeter reflects on his father's leadership role, "He expected you to do what was right. He would reprimand my sister and me if we did something that he didn't think was right. No one could make him deter from what was right. He was known as a man of his word throughout the whole area." That Mr. Keeter and his family wanted to endow a program to honor such people as Vester and Ruby Keeter is admirable, for their lives reflect old-fashioned, basic American values--a mirror image of an education of the "head, heart, and hands."

Shortly after this big boost, the Fall Convocation (1997) was held featuring Elizabeth Dole, then President of the American Red Cross and later U.S. Senator from the state of North Carolina. Although this event was very different from the Thatcher occasion, nevertheless, it was meaningful and captured the spirit of the emerging Keeter Center for Character Education. A theme of community service could not have been more timely or appropriate. In her remarks, Mrs. Dole said, "We have to trust ourselves and our values and not the government and its intentions. We are a good and noble people, but we've forgotten that the strength of our rights depends on their limits." She went on to say, "I feel a different spirit on this college campus...." Mrs. Dole sensed pretty quickly the uniqueness and worth of College of the Ozarks.

At a banquet honoring eighteen local community service organizations, Mrs. Dole privately informed us she would take no speaking fee, choosing instead to donate it to the College. Such an act of goodwill enabled us to build two new cabins at Camp Lookout, a summer camp operated by the College to serve local kids who couldn't afford such an opportunity. No charge is made to these youngsters, and College of the Ozarks students serve as camp counselors. Mrs. Dole was touched by the fact the

College was doing something for deserving youngsters of the Ozarks.

At the Convocation, Mrs. Dole joined us in recognizing Mrs. Bertram F. Bonner who, along with her husband, founded the Bonner Community Service organization which supports students (in various colleges) working in community service areas. The Bonner Community Service Program at College of the Ozarks was one of the first funded by the Bonner Foundation.

Fig. 86 Mrs. Dole joins in recognizing S. Truett Cathy (center).

Also honored and equally as deserving of recognition was Mr. S. Truett Cathy (Fig. 86), Founder and Chairman of Chick-fil-A Corporation which operates WinShape Centre Foundation--to help young people succeed in life through scholarships and other youth support programs. It was Truett Cathy who provided the inspiration to me for developing our Camp Lookout. I had gotten to know this remarkable man in an unusual way; we had some common bonds--faith and an interest in helping deserving kids.

Some years earlier I had become acquainted with Mr. Cathy through a camp in North Carolina, Camp Ridgecrest. My son attended the camp. Many youngsters came from Georgia because Mr. Cathy provided them scholarships. My son, Jeff, was a cabinmate with one of Mr. Cathy's foster children. Jeff arranged for our meeting the Cathys, well-known figures in the South. When Mr. Cathy founded his own camp (girls and boys) on the campus of the old Mount Berry School for Boys (on the Berry College campus), he hired one of my longtime friends to run it.

As a youngster trying to find my way in life, I had shown up at the Mount Berry School for Boys. This was a work school of the "head, heart, and hands" and turned out to be the gateway to my future. Although it had been closed by Berry College, Mr. Cathy breathed new life into it by creating WinShape Centre and Camps. It was his leadership of the camps that so impressed me, and I went down one summer and worked a few days at Camp Win-Shape. Upon my return, Camp Lookout became a reality at College of the Ozarks. Mr. Cathy's interest in helping youngsters from broken homes was especially inspiring to me, since I had experienced the same thing and struggled with the consequences. So when Mrs. Dole and I gave public recognition to Truett Cathy, it was more than a ceremony to me, because I knew personally the good wrought by Camp WinShape and Camp Lookout.

The compelling purpose of the College of the Ozarks unfailingly cast its spell on all who visited the campus. Whether rich and famous or unassuming, people of varying material means continued to support the College with their gifts, their presence, and their prayers. Some friends of the College needed me to come to them.

Before the end of the year (1997) I made my usual December trip to California to visit with now longtime donor and friend Dr. Joe T. McKibben. Year after year he had faithfully continued his giving. After what turned out to be my last visit with him, my field notes reminded me of the bond that had formed with the stranger who had walked off the street and into my life some ten years earlier:

> ...Kind of sad, health is obviously deteriorating. He's concerned about his health...Took down three certificates/plaques to take with me. Said I could get the other three on the next trip and he hoped to be alive then. This is very sad...now the end may be near, and I think he senses this....

The year 1997 had been a significant and historical year, and the College was on the move. Buoyed by the Thatcher and Dole visits and the establishment of The Keeter Center for Character Education, the College geared up to raise funds for the new programs and a facility to house them. Before 1998 faded, not only had the College obtained a matching grant from The Mabee Foundation for its building project, but many parts of The Keeter Center for Character Education program were endowed. Almost overnight Dr. and Mrs. Leonard Gittinger endowed the Community Convocation Series; Mr. and Mrs. Willard Walker endowed the Character Forum; Mrs. Thelma Stanley provided for the Citizenship Forum; the Rollins Work Ethic Forum was endowed, as was the Berger Citizens Abroad Program; the Sherry Herschend Focus on the Family Exchange Scholarship and the Gittinger Focus on the Family Exchange Scholarship were added.

On top of this tremendous fund-raising success was national publicity that far exceeded what anyone could have envisioned. Although it was Public Relations Director Camille Howell's work that resulted in the College being listed in the rankings in *U.S. News* and numerous other national publications, it was her work with Associated Press writer John Rogers that resulted in the College of the Ozarks being featured throughout the United States, cities and small communities alike. Mr. Rogers' well-written article focused on the unique character of the College as a demanding work school with high expectations. He wrote:

> New buildings spring up on college campuses all the time. Except elsewhere, the students don't usually build them. Here they do, and that's not the half of it. Students also run the College's fire department, airport and restaurant, and raise cattle and pigs, some of which wind up, in one form or another, on the menu...'This is *Hard Work U.*'...anyone who came to the College to have fun picked the wrong place. The School has no social fraternities and says its mission is to provide [a] Christian education. That means, among other things, being polite to teachers and offering prayer before meals..."[They] don't want to be like everybody else."

The Associated Press (AP) story must have hit a national nerve, for Rogers' article ricocheted all over America with each paper describing the College in ways we could not have imagined. "College Tuition: Backbreaking Work" according to *The Valley Press,* Lancaster, California; "Hard Labor Isn't So Bad," declared the *Florida News-Press,* Fort Myers; "At College of the Ozarks, Hard Work Is the Rule," said *The Arizona Daily Star;* "Ozarks Students Really Work Their Way Through College," reported *The Denver Post;* "Really Working Their Way Through College--Ozarks Students Don't Pay, They Toil," concluded the *Richmond Times-Dispatch;* "Admission to the College Is Paid in Labor," exhorted the *Hawaii Tribune-Herald;* "This Is Hard Work U.," described *The Post-Standard,* Fulton, New York; "College in the Ozarks: the Price of Admission Is Back-breaking Labor," extolled the

Potomac News; "At 'Hard Work U.' Jobs Required in Lieu of Tuition," wrote the *San Francisco Chronicle;* "College Promotes Work, Discourages Debt," advised *The San Juan Star;* "No Tuition at 'Hard Work U.'" exclaimed *The Times* (Bay Area, California) carrying a picture and the caption, "President said, 'I think this is the only college today that promotes work and discourages debt'"; "This College's Tuition Is Free, but It Doesn't Come Without Cost," said the *Maine Sunday Telegram.* And, there were many more.

Clearly, the country had been served notice that out in the heartland was America's most unusual college promoting the core values of America herself. This was affirmed in July of 1998 by Paul Harvey on *The Rest of the Story:* "There is another oasis of character-building education at Point Lookout in Missouri, College of the Ozarks. *Hard Work U.* They call it *Hard Work U.*"

Chapter XII
"An Education for Life"

With the College's success in starting The Keeter Center for Character Education as well as a major building project, a public expression of appreciation was made for the leadership role taken by Trustee James P. Keeter and his family. General H. Norman Schwarzkopf was the featured speaker at the Fall 1998 Community Convocation. Associated Press (AP) reports of General Schwarzkopf's remarks appropriately cited, "Leadership Focus of Missouri Speech." This was very much in evidence throughout the evening before a capacity audience.

General Schwarzkopf joined in recognizing some of the College's prominent friends: Dr. Arthur Schwartz, President of the John Templeton Foundation; Mr. Ron Robinson, President of Young America's Foundation; Dr. Edwin

Feulner, President of the Heritage Foundation; Dr. Kenneth Ogden, Vice President of the Focus on the Family Institute; and General Terrence R. Dake (Fig. 87), Assistant Com-

Fig. 87
General Norman Schwarzkopf and General Terrence R. Dake (right)

235

Fig. 88
General Schwarzkopf joins in tribute to Mrs. Ruby Keeter (center).

mandant of the United States Marine Corps and a distinguished graduate of the College.

Culminating the presentations was a tribute to Mr. James Keeter's parents for whom The Keeter Center for Character Education was named. Although Vester Keeter had passed away, Mrs. Ruby Keeter (Fig. 88) came to the stage with her son and family for a standing ovation and touching tribute.

As the College entered the last year of the decade, it was riding a tide of support and recognition from far and near. At home, the Branson community was energized when, in March of 1999, the *Branson Daily News* reported that the NAIA Division II Men's National Basketball Tournament was coming to the College in the year 2000. "March Madness is coming to the Tri-Lakes Area, and with it will come a multitude of opportunities and national exposure," wrote *Branson Daily News* Editor Wiley Hendrix.

Two months after this publicity, a major story ran nationwide in *The Wall Street Journal* entitled, "Promises from a Stranger." The remarkable story of this great benefactor (who had passed away) had come to the attention of *The Journal* because of Public Relations Director Camille Howell's work with staff reporter Ellen Graham who wrote the article. Graham's article was revealing:

Odd Visitor's Talk of Big Bequest Stunned College... When Joe T. McKibben walked into the President's Office at College of the Ozarks, looking sheepish and unkempt, he said he was considering making a big bequest. The President, Jerry C. Davis, began a long and bizarre courtship of a potential benefactor.

Graham, reporting from our interview continued:

'He was either a fraud or angel,' Dr. Davis says. But the timing seemed downright providential. Dr. Davis had been named President the previous year, and his tenure had been stormy. A plainspoken disciplinarian with an almost military bearing, Davis had come in with a mandate to put The School on a firmer financial footing....

The article went on to tell the inspiring story of how Joe T. McKibben became one of the greatest benefactors of the College *The Wall Street Journal* had dubbed earlier as *Hard Work U.*

As the story of Joe T. McKibben came to the attention of the nation in 1999, so did a major project by The John Templeton Foundation--in a major resource publication entitled *Colleges that Encourage Character Development.*

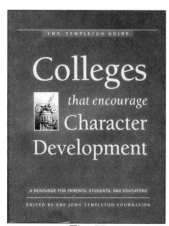

Fig. 89
The Templeton Guide

The Templeton Guide (Fig. 89), as it became known around the country, was distributed nationwide as "a resource for parents, students, and educators." And, as *The Outlook* student newspaper exclaimed: "College of the Ozarks Named to Unprecedented Five Categories in Templeton Honor Roll." The five categories included First-Year Programs (Character Camp), Academic

Honesty (Honor Code), Civic Education (Keeter Center), Presidential Leadership, and Character-building Colleges Honor Roll. The College was profiled at length as "unique among higher education in that it charges no tuition, requires all students to work on campus, and discourages debt." Quotations from surveyed students were included; for example:

> As a College of the Ozarks student, I have learned that the classroom offers only the beginning of education. College of the Ozarks has strengthened my character, taught me the value of work, and allowed me to graduate debt free.

Following this publicity which focused on the character of the College, it indeed seemed appropriate that The Keeter Center for Character Education presented Franklin Graham as keynote speaker for its Fall 1999 Convocation. As reported in *The Keeter Report,* a publication of The Keeter Center, "Franklin Graham, the President of Samaritan's Purse, addressed a capacity crowd at College of the Ozarks Monday, October 25. His message 'Christianity on Campus' was the first program of the series endowed by Leonard B. and Edith Gittinger (Fig. 90). The

Fig. 90
Franklin Graham joins in recognizing Leonard and Edith Gittinger.

Community Convocation Series is a part of The Keeter Center...." Dr. Graham described many problems of the world and then asked our students, "What are you going to do about it?" Hearing such a question reaffirmed for many the slogan above the stage in the College's auditorium: "Why Come Ye Here?" Dr. Graham focused on the answer to his question. "It doesn't matter where you are, God can use you, as long as you're willing to put your faith and trust in Him." As the century was ending for a school once called "The School that Runs on Faith," Franklin Graham had put things in perspective. Before he left campus, he told us that he would donate his fee to the College to be used as we best needed. I told him we would use it to fund a student mission trip--which we did a few months later.

What was known as Y2K dawned to find the College of the Ozarks geared up for the first national basketball tournament ever held in this part of the Ozarks. To say that people were excited seems an understatement. But expectations were modest for our team. I wanted very badly at least to win the first round, which we did. But then we won the second one, and the third one, too. All of a sudden the College was faced off against an outstanding team from Huntington, Indiana, in the semi-finals. The game seemed lost until a last second shot, at the buzzer by a player who had no three-pointers all year, banked in. The crowd of almost 4,000 exploded as the College of the Ozarks catapulted into the final game. Although we lost the final game, the tournament was a needed boost to the entire campus, for a cloud of despair had hung over the campus since a plane accident had tragically taken the lives of six members of the College family.

Fig. 91
President
Gerald Ford
chats with
students.

The spring of 2000 saw The Keeter Center present its first endowed Citizenship Forum (named for John N. and Ella C. Marsh), which featured the 38th President of the United States. President Gerald R. Ford (Fig. 91) followed a growing list of distinguished guests to campus. The forums (Character, Citizenship, Work Ethic) of The Keeter Center involve more than just a speech. Students must sign up for a semester and obligate themselves to attend meetings or classes prior to the Citizenship Forum activities. On this occasion, President Ford addressed the student participants and was especially good at informally chatting with them in a classroom setting.

This very educational concept has gone beyond the College's own students, as other schools annually send participants. Attending the Forum with President Ford were cadets from the United States Air Force Academy in Colorado Springs and a few other invited colleges. The Air Force Academy was the first participant, with the eventual attendance of students from the United States Naval Academy at Annapolis; United States Military Academy at West Point; United States Coast Guard Academy in New London, Connecticut; United States Merchant Marine Academy in Kings Point, New York; and even the Marine Military Academy cadets from Harlingen, Texas.

It is ironic that President Ford, while speaking to students at The Keeter Center's Citizenship Forum, foresaw what would later become a serious concern in post 9/11 America. Pat Nolan, staff reporter for the *Branson Daily News* reported on the President's remarks, "What worries me is--as we are reducing our active duty readiness, we are increasing our responsibilities. I think we are putting our military security in danger, and The White House and Congress should do something about it." This insight, discussed at the Forum by President Ford, was validated some eighteen months later with terrorist attacks on American soil and with ensuing wars in Afghanistan and Iraq stimulating broad debate about our active duty readiness.

Fig. 92
Dr. Beulah
Winfrey

The fall semester of the first full academic year of the new century at College of the Ozarks brought the College sadness and excitement. Sadness, with the passing of longtime professor Beulah Winfrey (Fig. 92) and excitement with the visit of General Colin Powell.

The outstanding teaching faculty of today is a reflection of the life of Beulah Winfrey, a life of dedication, faith, and a love of young people. Beulah Winfrey served fifty-two years at the College and was a yardstick against which service and excellence could be measured. During her years at the College, she received many awards which reflected her own values, as well as those of the faculty and the College in general. She was one of the first recipients of the Governor's Teaching Award for Excellence in Teaching. During the 2000-2001 year, another of the College's outstanding teachers, Dr. David Dalton, received this recognition; others preceded and followed him. Dr. Beulah Winfrey, and many like her, form the heart of the excellent academic program which has evolved at College of the Ozarks.

Excitement engulfed College of the Ozarks with the coming of General Colin Powell. At the time (2000), General Powell had retired from the military as the Chairman of the Joint Chiefs of Staff; he was a much sought-after speaker and served as the Chairman of America's Promise--an organization supporting opportunities for youth around the United States. At a banquet prior to the Fall Community Convocation, General Powell recognized the College as a "College of Promise" for its Camp Lookout program (Fig. 93) and Bonner Community Service Program. Although General Powell made an outstanding speech and received an honorary doctorate, along with three others (alumnus and Marine General Terrence R. Dake, United States Air Force Academy Superintendent Lieutenant General Tad J. Oelstrom, Army Major Gener-

Fig. 93
General Colin Powell with Camp Lookout youngsters

Fig. 94
Private First Class Roy
Hopper recognized by
General Colin Powell and
General Terrence R. Dake,
alumnus

al Stewart W. Wallace), it was his participation in honoring alumnus Roy Hopper that tugged at the heartstrings of the capacity crowd.

A hush swept over the audience as Private First Class Roy Hopper's story was told, starting from the time he left Point Lookout. Private Hopper (Fig. 94) had experienced the beaches of Normandy, fierce fighting in the hedgerows of France, capture and imprisonment by the Germans, and ultimately his escape to freedom. An Associated Press (AP) article reporting on the occasion spoke of Hopper's medals and sacrifice, adding, "But the greatest achievement for him came on October 2 [2000] when he returned to The School [College] of the Ozarks campus to receive his high school diploma. 'His service was greater than all of ours put together,' retired General Colin Powell said of Roy during a ceremony attended by several high-ranking military leaders." That seems an understatement, though he was on stage with officers who had a total of thirteen stars among them! Staging such an event was certainly one of the most meaningful things we had ever organized. As the *Christian Observer* said in its October (2000) issue, "Hard Work U. The incredible College of the Ozarks." Indeed, what we had witnessed was recognition of incredible sacrifice, an example of one of many alumni who have served our country. No one could have imagined that twelve months after recognizing such sacrifice for America, more was going to be required.

As the College entered the year 2001, The Keeter Center hosted the first Left-Right Debate between Alan Keyes (Fig. 95) and Joseph P. Kennedy (Fig. 96) amidst anticipation of a visit by a team from the North Central Association. The faculty and staff had worked hard to prepare for the typical ten-year self-study for re-accreditation. It was a time of introspection and planning. Dr. Eric Bolger, another of the College's outstanding teachers, served as chair of the Accreditation Steering Committee. The Self-Study Report was presented to a visiting team of evaluators in January (2001) who then spent three days on campus. This well-done report was important,

Fig. 95
Dr. Alan Keyes

Fig. 96
Joseph P.
Kennedy, II

and the College was pleased with a renewal of its ten-year regional accreditation. The issues (including tenure) that had stirred up so much attention outside our gates were not issues at all. The College had moved ahead.

The day after the evaluation team departed, those of us who live on campus awakened to the sound of fire alarms and sirens. From my home, I could see smoke billowing from the construction area of campus. The College's maintenance facility had gone up in smoke--burned to the ground, the fifth major building lost by fire in the College's history. The College lost the building and equipment but, thankfully, no one was seriously hurt. The building was replaced rather quickly and the fire served as the basis for some laughter; some joked that the accreditors had burned it down on the way out of town so we could get a new facility!

Shortly after the NAIA Tourney (the second one held at the College), the College family had to say goodbye to

Fig. 97
Dr. and Mrs.
M. Graham Clark

the veritable "Wizard of the Ozarks," as Dr. M. Graham Clark (Fig. 97) passed away at age ninety-two in his apartment on campus. Although he had been in declining health, he had enthusiastically thrown out the basketball at the NAIA opening two weeks prior to his death. Kathy Buckstaff, in the *Springfield News-Leader,* wrote, "Beneath the stained glass windows of the Chapel at College of the Ozarks, friends, former students, and colleagues said farewell to the man credited with creating the nationally-recognized college. 'He was usually going full speed when the rest of us were weary,' said College President Jerry Davis. 'It's easy to look around and see the dividends of the investments he made of his time. He had an influence on several generations... scattered across the whole world.'" Like Dr. R. M. Good, Dr. Clark had given his life to the College through a long tenure and a lot of hard work. Meeting in the spring of 2001, the Trustees passed a resolution, "expressing appreciation...for a lifetime of dedicated service given by Dr. M. Graham Clark to the institution which he led for many years." They also stood for a moment of silence in memory and tribute.

The College's program for the 2001-2002 school year started in typical fashion--with Character Camp. The camp is a ten-day orientation program unique to the College in which students become acquainted with the expectations and character of the College. But shortly after Character Camp and the starting of school, terrorists struck in New York, Washington, and in the sky over Pennsylvania, testing the character of the whole country and ushering in a new era of anxiety. The College family pulled together as the nation geared for war--and sacrifice. The Keeter Center's Gittinger Community Convocation Series brought former Secretary of State James Baker, III, (Fig. 98) to campus for its fall presentation. It was timely. And his remarks were widely reported in the press. Kathy Buckstaff, *News-Leader* reporter, wrote in her article entitled, "'War Unlike Any Before,' Baker says":

Fig. 98 James S. Baker, III, welcomed to campus by Trustee Chairman Larry Walther and Mrs. Walther

...Former Secretary of State James Baker III gave a riveting speech about the roots of terrorism and the outlook for the coming war against it...Defeating that enemy will take an all-out sustained war. It is necessary and right and a just war...The course will require sacrifices, he said--perhaps rising energy costs and some wavering by our allies as casualties and costs mount.

She then quoted Baker as saying, "We may not be rich enough to do everything we want to do, but we are rich enough to do what we have to do." All in attendance got the idea of what our nation must do. In the meantime, the College had to get on with its future.

At the Fall 2001 Board Meeting, the Trustees heard discussion for the first time about the prospect of adding a school of nursing. They also approved a vision statement for the College: "To develop citizens of Christ-like character who are well-educated, hardworking, and patriotic." This lofty statement resulted from a strategic planning effort which the Board approved. The Strategic Plan charted the course for the College (short-term and long-term) for the foreseeable future.

Results were obvious in early 2002 when Leonard and Mrs. Gittinger underwrote the cost of two major academic facilities, a music center and a campus ministries center. "The kids needed these buildings," said Dr. Gittinger to

the *Springfield News-Leader.* This was a big boost for the academic program which, too, was gaining prominence.

Shortly after this good news, one of the College's outstanding students, Shelly Compton (Fig. 99), was notified that she

Fig. 99 Fulbright Scholar Shelly Compton

was a recipient of the Fulbright Scholar Award. This very prestigious award spoke volumes about the College and its learning environment.

Dr. Courtney Furman, who mentored Shelly Compton, recalls with pride how it all came about. "I was asked by Dr. Camille Howell if I would serve as campus advisor for this particular award--the Fulbright...they are competitive across the country and across the world...It's a fine honor." Dr. Furman took a personal interest in Shelly, "I met with her a number of times. Any time anything came in and had to be filled out, she normally did it...but I always read over it." Shelly Compton did her Fulbright work in Kuopio, Finland, after completing her baccalaureate in dietetics at the College. Dr. Furman beams while saying, "Something to be proud of. It's a fine honor."

Such an honor is a reflection on Shelly, the many fine faculty members at College of the Ozarks, and the breadth of Shelly's education. The shadow of the College's education program was lengthening. Almost every semester the College sent classes overseas with their professors. At home, The Keeter Center and its programs were regularly attracting figures any campus would have been privileged to host.

Former Secretary of Defense Caspar Weinberger conducted the 2002 Spring Forum, and in the fall The Keeter Center featured former Israeli Prime Minister Benjamin Netanyahu. Given the tension of the times, no one was really surprised at the security that came with him. "Security 'Tightest Ever' for Netanyahu Address" wrote *Branson Daily News* staff writer Bruce W. Bowlin. "Agents of the Israeli Secret Service have been on campus a number of days...."

The College had to change some of its protocol for receiving dignitaries. Instead of greeting the Prime Minister in my office, we did our welcome in the guest house, next to my house--an area literally turned into an armed camp. Nevertheless, I found Mr. Netanyahu to be a very warm and personable visitor. At our banquet, he and Shirley conversed throughout most of the meal about Christian sites in Israel. I just listened in, as Shirley had visited Israel, but I had not.

Few speakers have delivered the message that character is related to leadership as did Benjamin Netanyahu. He was direct about what needed to take place in the Middle East. "Sadam and Arafat must go" was the headline of Kathy Buckstaff's *News-Leader* article concerning the event. She went on to say of the response, "Netanyahu's hard-line anti-terrorism rhetoric [was greeted] with standing ovations, rousing applause, and shouts of 'Amen' that sometimes drowned out parts of his forty-minute speech." He certainly picked up on *Hard Work U.'s* uniqueness by telling the students, "I think this place builds character, and you should be commended for it."

The program was not without some very unusual moments. The Prime Minister seemed to be genuinely pleased when the choir sang the Israeli National Anthem in Yiddish after performing our National Anthem. Mr. Netanyahu also appeared deeply moved when student Kimberly Bess presented him with a portrait she had done of the Prime Minister and his brothers.

Mr. Netanyahu graciously joined in helping the College recognize two very fine individuals of strong char-

Fig. 100
Mr. Netanyahu
and Mrs. Laurie
(McDonald) Bouchard

Fig. 101 Mr.
Netanyahu with
alumnus Lt. General
Gary Hughey

acter and leadership. Mrs. Laurie (McDonald) Bouchard
(Fig. 100) accepted a Leadership and Service Award on behalf of the J. M. McDonald, Sr., family. Also, Lieutenant
General Gary Hughey (Fig. 101) was presented a Leadership and Service Award as a distinguished Marine and
alumnus of the College.

The years of 2002-2003 were times of tremendous
achievement at the College. Its alumni were distinguish-
ing themselves--as a Fulbright Scholar, teachers, service
members, and in all walks of life. The story of this "incredible" college was heard all over the nation by way of
Paul Harvey and on a National Public Radio (NPR) special. During the year of 2002 alone, nine different national
recognitions were received--featured in the *Washington
Times, Kansas City Ingram's Magazine, U.S. News, Newsweek, Barron's,* and many others. The Public Relations Office continued its efforts to promote the College from coast
to coast, and it showed.

The NAIA and College of the Ozarks had settled in with
the National Tournament, and the community support
for this undertaking did not waver. Also in 2003 the proposed new nursing school was authorized with the Trust-

ees passing a resolution, "to name the School of Nursing the Josephine Armstrong McDonald School of Nursing." Josephine Armstrong McDonald was the beloved wife of Mr. J. M. McDonald, Sr., one of the College's greatest benefactors.

In 2004 The Keeter Center brought to campus former congressman and Oklahoma athlete J. C. Watts who told students, "If we [America] are to maintain our greatness, we can never think that character doesn't matter." A most unusual fall convocation was held which was shared with hundreds of coaches from throughout the Ozarks. Few visiting speakers have attracted as much interest as did Duke Coach Mike Krzyzewski (Coach K). And no other speaker chose to wear a *Hard Work U.* shirt during a speech. "It's truly a great school and a great concept," he said, obviously carried away with the reception he received. The Coach K Forum was the first program to utilize the magnificent new Keeter Center, a state-of-the-art conference center (including lodge, dining, and meeting facilities) at the entrance to the campus. Coach K told us, in private, that if he had known what a great facility he would be occupying, he would have brought his wife and stayed longer!

Although the College opened The Keeter Center in the fall of 2004, it was not officially dedicated until the spring semester of 2005. Keynote speaker General Tommy Franks (Fig. 102) came a day early to join with Air Force hero Captain Scott O'Grady in conducting a forum (The Willard and Pat Walker Character Forum). Krystal Carman, staff writer for the *Branson Daily News* wrote, "Cadets from military academies across the nation converged

Fig. 102
General Tommy Franks accepts student-made gifts from ROTC cadets Justin (right) and Jason Copley.

at College of the Ozarks Thursday to hear a four-star general described as a 'soldier's soldier' speak of his love for America and the military." General Franks' speech was inspiring. "I don't care what your politics are. You are blessed to live in this country," he told the audience.

That night we honored many who had paid the price for our freedom. Recognized in the audience were members of Missouri Guard Unit 1107, just returned from Iraq and under the command of Colonel (Dr.) Don McMahon, longtime faculty member, who also received special recognition. General Franks also joined in paying tribute to Captain Scott O'Grady, the American pilot shot down over Bosnia whose harrowing story was made into a movie, *Behind Enemy Lines*. Even more inspiring was a posthumous memorial led by General Franks for two service members. Kathryn Buckstaff cited this in her *Springfield News-Leader* article:

> Retired Army 1st Sergeant Michael Jay Copley, 50, was killed while working as a civilian contractor in Iraq. His sons, Justin and Jason Copley--two of seven brothers--attend College of the Ozarks...Also recognized was Marine Corporal Nathaniel Hammond of Springfield...a flight in-

Fig. 103 Amy Leaming (third from left) presents stained glass rendition of The Keeter Center to Mr. and Mrs. James P. Keeter.

structor at College of the Ozarks.

The formal dedication of the College's new Keeter Center facility was held the day after the Spring Forum, and General Tommy Franks gave the keynote address. "Head, heart, hands; family, faith, flag; values, leadership, and the American dream--all that is right here today," said General Franks in moving remarks at the dedication. Present were Mr. and Mrs. James P. Keeter who had taken a leadership role in making the vision of The Keeter Center a reality. Student Amy Leaming (Fig. 103) presented the Keeters with a beautiful stained glass rendition of The Keeter Center. Mr. Keeter's subsequent remarks reminded everyone of his parents and character and the importance of influence by example.

As the College approached its centennial, it was timely that respect be paid to the generation that sacrificed so greatly for the country. In the fall of 2005, journalist Tom Brokaw was a guest of the College and the featured speaker for the Gittinger Community Convocation Series of The Keeter Center. The purpose of his visit was to recognize the "Greatest Generation" with some examples from this generation who were a part of the College's family. "Shaping the Future, Honoring the Past" was appropriately picked as a theme for the occasion. At the banquet prior to the Convocation, Brokaw joined in presenting special recognition to leaders of the character education movement of which the College is a part. Also singled out were youngsters from area schools who were recognized by their schools for their good character--youngsters who will shape our future.

In his address, Brokaw said writing *The Greatest Generation* was the single most fulfilling achievement in his career. This was very much in evidence as Brokaw joined the College in making some very special recognitions, not to be forgotten by those fortunate enough to witness the occasion. Alumni Harry Basore (Fig. 104) and Bonita Bailey (Fig. 104), along with former employee John T. Brown (Fig. 104), were called to the stage. Writing in the *Ozark Visitor*, student Katherine Aguayo discussed the unusual event:

> College of the Ozarks honored alumnus Harry Basore first...who graduated seventy years ago, for his courage in combat and extreme modesty in his heroism. Basore flew for the United States Navy during World War II after several years as a flight instructor...The second honoree was Bonita Bailey, who graduated...sixty-one years ago. She was recruited to work at the Pentagon for the United States Casualty Branch (Civil Service) at the age of eighteen and was responsible for notifying families of losses during duty, including the destructive Battle of the Bulge. She worked sixteen hours per day, seven days per week...John T. Brown was the third special example. Brown managed the College's dairy operation and served as a student work supervisor...He told students

Fig. 104 Tom Brokaw with Harry Basore (upper), Bonita (Orr) Bailey, and John T. Brown, members of the *Greatest Generation*

that his 'middle initial T is for trouble, and that's what you're going to have if you don't get to work!'...the story of Brown's role in World War II...a squad leader in a small platoon of twenty-four men. Seventeen of his men were killed by Germans, and he was taken as a POW...in a vehicle with some other POWs, a British soldier asked Brown if he could take the German driver. He declared that he could and did take (kill) the driver as the British soldier took the guard. Although they all escaped, they were soon taken again, and all were killed except Brown. Altogether, he endured three enemy captures...Brown once said he wouldn't take a million dollars to go through again what he went through, but he would pay a million

Fig. 105 Members of the East Florida Chapter of American Ex-POWs with Tom Brokaw (center)

dollars to keep from going back.

This very moving ceremony was captured by Katherine's explanation of another special part. "The College of the Ozarks Community Band, Chapel Choir, and Chorale performed 'Battle Hymn of the Republic' and invited the fifteen Ex-POWs (Fig. 105) [from the crowd] on stage to help sing the final chorus...The audience responded with tears, and many veterans presented them with salutes." It was an emotional occasion and served as a stark reminder of the price paid for freedom. And it was a proud moment for reflection on the patriotic goal of the College.

The centennial year for the College (2006) brought with it great excitement and accomplishment. This special year represented the seventh year the College had been host to the Men's Division II National Basketball Tournament. But it was the fifth year in a row that both men's and women's teams had made it to the national tournament--a remarkable accomplishment for student athletes at a demanding work college. Both teams made it to the national finals, and how they got there will long be remembered.

First of all, the women's team (Lady Cats) won the conference championship and entered the national tournament in Sioux City, Iowa. The team got into the semi-finals (and eventually the finals) in a miraculous fashion. During the third round, playing against a strong Benedictine College team, the Lady Cats averted a loss by tieing the game at the buzzer with a three-pointer by sophomore Rebekah Howard. Winning the game in overtime granted

Fig. 106 NAIA National Tournament Runner-up Lady Bobcats and coaches with Missouri Governor Matt Blunt (center)

a reprieve, and the Lady Cats won the next round and then came up short in the final game. Led by Kodak All-American Cara Painter, the team was a great reflection of the work ethic, skill, coaching, and fans. They also turned in top academic honors, having the highest grade point average of any athletic team in the College. The Lady Cats (Fig. 106) were named by the Women's Basketball Coaches Association (WBCA) to the Nation's NAIA Academic Top 25 Team Honor Roll. This was quite an achievement.

While the women's team competed in Sioux City, the men's team entered the national tournament held at Keeter Gymnasium on the College's campus. Perhaps the turning point of the tournament was the second round with the Bobcats of College of the Ozarks paired against traditional rival William Jewell College from Kansas City. It was a hard fought seesaw affair. And with eight seconds left the College was down by one point. After a missed field goal attempt by William Jewell, MVP Michael Bonaparte rebounded and threw the ball to Andrew Boyce who raced

Fig. 107 NAIA National Champions and coaches with Missouri Governor Matt Blunt (center)

in for a lay-up. Unfortunately, he was fouled (some say "hammered") and went to the line. Most of the 4,000 fans held their breath as Boyce sank the first free throw. When he hit the second, the arena erupted; the Bobcats won by one. In its best showing ever, the Bobcats won the final game against Huntington University of Indiana and the College's first NAIA national title (Fig. 107).

As pandemonium broke out, I couldn't help but remember the first game I attended at the College. It was almost eighteen years earlier, a time when we had benches on one side of the court and no one had dreamed of a national tournament, let alone a championship. In many ways it reflected how far the College had progressed--overcoming challenges, "bumps" in the road, struggles, and hardships. But perseverance was a trait of the College from its beginnings and was on display. Watching the players receive the national pennant in mid-court was a moving experience; watching the expression on Dr. Howell Keeter's face was also rewarding. He sat just a few seats down from me. Such a win was a high point in the life of one who, when he came to the College, had helped install the floor of the gym himself. As Dr. Keeter transitioned through the

years from work coordinator to associate dean to chancellor and interim president, he had always found time to encourage athletics at *Hard Work U.* I was as happy for

Fig. 108
Former Senator Zell Miller displays his *Hard Work U.* sweatshirt.

him as for the team, coaches, and school.

So much of what had been accomplished on the court was reflected in the theme for the Spring Forum of 2006. Keynote speaker Senator Zell Miller (Fig. 108) delivered that message when he said, "Work Ethic Opens Gates of Opportunity" to the audience of students and visitors alike. So much of what Senator Miller said to our students and visiting military school students was associated with the achievements (academic as well as athletic) of College of the Ozarks students. He described a magic formula for success. "When followed," he said, "this formula should allow a person to climb to the top and be successful. The first step can allow you to beat out fifty percent of competitors simply by working hard. The second step, which would allow you to beat out an additional forty percent, is achieved merely by being a person of integrity and honesty. The final step," Miller said, "must be a dog fight, because the remaining ten percent want success just as bad as you. But the important thing to remember when competing with that remaining ten percent is not to give up." Finally, Senator Miller told students, *Hard Work U.* is preparing you to not only learn how to earn but how to live." Remarkably similar advice had been given to students at the College some years earlier by Lady Margaret Thatcher.

The centennial year revealed a beehive of activities far beyond athletic championships at the College. The academic SIFE (Students in Free Enterprise) team again won the regional competition in St. Louis; agricultural professor Tom Smith received the Meritorious Service Award by the Missouri Dairy Hall of Honors; the Chapel Choir went

Fig. 109

Mrs. Sue Head, Executive Director of The Keeter Center for Character Education, and former Missouri Senator John Danforth

on a mission tour to Alaska and Vancouver; faculty and students traveled abroad under the Citizens Abroad Program, studying in London, Ireland, Paris, Finland, and Brazil; and The Keeter Center for Character Education was nationally recognized for its FirstPLACE Character Initiative (Fig. 109). Construction on campus quickened with progress on the new McKibben Center, renovation of McDonald Hospital, the start of a new animal science

Fig. 110 Homecoming 2006

facility, and even a start on the long-needed student dining hall renovation project. Student summer missionaries traveled to Kenya while SIFE students and faculty alike went to Cameroon, Africa.

For one hundred years (Fig. 110) the College has kept the "Gates of Opportunity" wide open. No better evidence of this can be found than the remarkable story of a member of the centennial year graduating class. This student's story, told in her own words, reflects much about the character of College of the Ozarks and what its founders envisioned:

> My mother and father were married at a very young age and had three children by the time my mother was twenty-two. My dad divorced my mother when I was two, leaving her to raise three babies under the age of four. Mom did the best she could to provide for us, with little or no support from her family. Fortunately, she leaned on God to get her through and provide for us three children.
>
> We lived in Northwest Arkansas and remained there until my freshman year in high school. When I was six, my mother remarried. She married a man with three children of his own. We always had food and necessary items, but my siblings and I also went without because there wasn't a lot of extra money. My parents kept their foundation in church and relied on God. They taught me that little in life is free and that it is well worth it to work hard. When I was thirteen, I got my first job working ten hours a week in the church nursery. It wasn't a lot, but it allowed me to be involved with extracurricular activities at school.
>
> At the beginning of ninth grade, my mother was diagnosed with a mental illness. She became unable to provide for her family of six kids. She filed for divorce and was very sick for several months. Because she was unable to care for us, we moved in with our father. My siblings and I lived with him for six months and returned to live

262

with our mother once she was stable. My mother married for a third time and both were disabled, only receiving income from disability. I immediately began working at a small retail shop, and for the next three years, I supported myself and my younger brother through high school. My income went to help my family pay bills and provide necessities, such as groceries.

Late in my senior year of high school, my family and I were hit with a terrible tragedy. Our home burned to the ground. We lost almost everything we owned. Fortunately, God provided for us once again. Our church family pulled together to help us find a new home. With this happening late in my senior year, it made it difficult for me to think of preparing for college, but college had been a goal of mine since I could remember. So I made myself take time to focus on finding a college.

No one in my family has ever graduated from college. As long as I can remember, my goal has been to graduate from college with a degree in elementary education. I wanted to attend a small Christian college, but I knew money would be a factor. I spent a lot of time in prayer and God brought College of the Ozarks to my attention through my youth pastor. I read the literature and knew College of the Ozarks was the one for me.

Being accepted to C of O is proof that God is in control and that He does answer prayers. I am currently a junior and have only one more semester of classes before I start student teaching. I will graduate in May 2007 with a degree in elementary education. I enjoy being involved and giving something back to this fabulous school. I am so fortunate to have been given the gift of graduating debt free and with a great education.

People say that hard work will eventually pay off. I have found that working hard is not supposed to be done so that you receive something in return, but so that you can be a strong, well-rounded individual. This is what *Hard Work U.* has done for me. C of O has helped me fulfill my dreams academically, financially, and spiritually.

Though I cannot tell you what my future holds, I can tell you that because of College of the Ozarks, I know that my future will be great. I hope to be a great elementary education teacher and have a family of my own some day in the future. I want to establish myself financially so that one day, I will have the opportunity to give to my family in a way that my parents were not able. Whatever God has in store for me, I know that it is bright because of the character, principles, and work ethic that have been instilled in me from this school.

Much of this student's story of hardship, struggle, and character-building is reflected in the history of the unique institution which educated her. Values such as faith, hope, and hard work have made the difference.

As Lady Margaret Thatcher so eloquently stated, "The education that you get here is not only an education or a qualification for a degree; it is an education for life and will stand you in good stead throughout the years, whatsoever you do."

An education of the "head, the heart, and the hands" is what a young missionary envisioned one hundred years ago. May God grant that it be so for the next one hundred years and beyond.

The journey--and the *Miracle in the Ozarks*--continues unabated, enthusiastically endorsed by all who believe in faith, hope, and hard work.

Timeline

1906 The School of the Ozarks begins at Forsyth, Missouri, after pleadings and the work of a young Presbyterian missionary to the Ozarks, James F. Forsythe; opening for students in September, 1907.

1915 Early January fire destroys Mitchell Hall and The School with it; campus moved to Point Lookout in fall as classes resumed in newly acquired hunting lodge (formerly State of Maine building, St. Louis World's Fair of 1904).

1921 Longtime Board Chairman W. R. Dobyns leaves as R. M. Good assumes presidency, signaling a long period of growth and accomplishments.

1930 Fire again devastates school as Dobyns Hall (formerly State of Maine building) destroyed. Despite this, R. M. Good leads school ahead through times of Great Depression and World War II.

1946 M. Graham Clark joins Dr. Good as vice president and energizes effort to transition a self-help boarding high school to junior college status. Clark becomes president in 1952 as construction on Williams Chapel commences.

1956 First junior college students enroll, graduating two

years later. Williams Chapel dedicated in 1958 after loss of two longtime trustee leaders and benefactors, Lewis Wilkins Hyer and J. M. McDonald, Sr.

1965 Transition to senior college status begins; college struggles to overcome third major fire (A. P. Green Building); first four-year students graduate in 1967 along with last high school graduates.

1970 First Lady Pat Nixon visits campus in March. *Wall Street Journal* article (1973) forever brands The School as *Hard Work U.*

1975 As school struggles financially, M. Graham Clark shares leadership of school with Dr. Howell Keeter, who becomes chancellor and chief operating officer. Dr. Clark continues as chief executive officer but focuses on fund-raising and retires in 1981.

1983 Dr. Stephen G. Jennings enters presidency. Financial operation of college improves, major building projects undertaken, strategic planning occurs before Jennings leaves in 1987.

1988 Dr. Jerry C. Davis assumes presidency; major restructuring occurs; *Promises to Keep* Campaign begins; *U.S. News & World Report* recognizes institution as one of America's best.

1990 Operating name changes from The School of the Ozarks to College of the Ozarks. As decade progresses, college experiences a growing endowment, successful campaign, increasing national exposure in *Money* magazine, *USA Today,* Templeton Foundation guide, and others. Bonner Community Service Program established, as is Camp Lookout. International travel program started.

1997 Keeter Center for Character Education endowed. Major building project continues. Prominent speakers, such as Elizabeth Dole and others, continue as Keeter Center Programs expand. Keeter family honored at General Schwarzkopf Convocation in 1998.

2000 As college enters 21st Century, NAIA National Men's Basketball Tournament comes to campus; national acclaim continues as first Fulbright Scholar named from C of O; yet another professor receives Governor's Award for Teaching Excellence.

2006 Centennial Year begins with two alumni serving on The White House staff. College wins (men) NAIA National Tournament, women runner-up; SIFE (Students in Free Enterprise) Team excels nationally; student named to *The Wall Street Journal* Academic Achievement list. Keeter Center Program receives national recognition for CHARACTER*plus* initiative. McDonald School of Nursing begins. College named as one of the top fifty *All American Colleges.*

Reference Notes

Cover

Harvey, Paul. "The Rest of the Story." July 1998.

Hasday, Lisa and Samson, Sarah. "Schools that March to the Beat of a Different Drummer." *U.S. News & World Report. 1997 America's Best Colleges:* 78.

Hohl, Paul. "Elbow Grease and Academics Blended at 'Hardwork U.'" *The Kansas City Star.* 10 August 1980.

Martin, Richard. "Hard Work U. At School of Ozarks, the Students Flunk Out if They Shirk Chores." *The Wall Street Journal.* 15 March 1973: 1.

Photos courtesy of Larry Plumlee, Kevin White.

Chapter 1

"About The School of the Ozarks." *Taney County Republican.* 16 August 1906.

Beatie, A. Y. "Speech to local citizens." *Taney County Republican.* 9 August 1906.

"Bible Study." *Our Visitor.* September 1909: 2.

Board of Trustees Minutes, 1906 through 1915. The School of the Ozarks. Board Records. College of the Ozarks.

College Catalog 2006-2007, College of the Ozarks. Point Lookout, MO: 3.

Dobyns, William R. "The Best Education." *Our Visitor.* September 1909: 1.

Forsythe, Mrs. James F. Notes (handwritten research work) circa 1967. Ozarkiana Room, College of the Ozarks.

"Founder's Place Secure in S of O History." *Ozark Visitor.* September/October 1969: 6, 8.

Godsey, Townsend and Helen. *Flight of the Phoenix.* Point Lookout: The School of the Ozarks, 1984. p. 129.

Gordon, Dr. E. C. "What The School of the Ozarks Stands For." *Taney County Republican* 26 Sept. 1907.

Head, Dr. Hayden. Provided translation information. August 2006.

Jackson, York. Personal Interview. 29 March 1993.

King, Willa (Coulter). Personal Interview. 23 April 1993.

"Opening of The School of the Ozarks." *Taney County Republican.* 26 September 1907: 1.

Prather, Colonel A. S. "Address of Welcome." Opening Day, The School of the Ozarks, Forsyth, Missouri. 24 September 1907.

"Salutatory." *Our Visitor.* September 1909: 1.

"School of the Ozarks, The; Synopsis of the Addresses at the Laying of the Corner Stone." *Taney County Republican.* 25 October 1906: 1.

Chapter 2

Board of Trustees Minutes, 1915 through 1921. The School of the Ozarks. Board Records. College of the Ozarks.

Mahnkey, Douglas. Personal Interview. 9 July 1994.

Southard, Roy W. Personal Interview. 25 May 1993.

Chapter 3

Board of Trustees Minutes, 1922 through 1930. The School of the Ozarks. Board Records. College of the Ozarks.

Good, Dr. R. M. President. *Ozarka*. 1923. The School of the Ozarks.

Harp, Lucille (Knight). "Reflections." Notes received October 2003 regarding Dobyns Hall 1930.

Moore, June (Keener). Telephone Interview. 15 December 2001.

Shipman, Eula (Shelton). Personal Interview. 8 November 2000

Simkins, Ray and Delphia (Phillips). Personal Interview. 27 June 2000.

Ozarka 1923. The School of the Ozarks.

Chapter 4

Basore, Harry H. Personal Interview. 11 September 1995.

Board of Trustees Minutes, 1930 through 1935. The School of the Ozarks. Board Records. College of the Ozarks.

McMaster, Annabelle. Personal Interview. 13 May 1993.

Wise, J. Hugh. Personal Interview. 7 April 1997.

Chapter 5

"Another Loss Is Ours." *Our Visitor.* March 1944: 3.

Applegate, Margaret (Willbanks). Letter to the Provost Marshal General. 4 March 1943. Collection of Margaret (Willbanks) Applegate.

Applegate, Margaret (Willbanks). Personal Interview. 13 May 1995.

"Private Hopper, Private Leigh Home From German Prison Camps." *Our Visitor*. July 1945: 3.

Board of Trustees Minutes, 1936 through 1945. The School of the Ozarks. Board Records. College of the Ozarks.

Good, Dr. R. M. Letter to Mrs. Carl Hopper. 12 May 1945. Collection of Roy Hopper.

Good, Dr. R. M. "I Will." *Our Visitor.* June 1942: 4.

Hopper, Mrs. Carl. Letter to Dr. R. M. Good. 2 May 1940. Collection of Roy Hopper.

Hopper, Roy F. Personal Interview. 28 July 2000.

Hopper, Mrs. Carl. Letter to Dr. R. M. Good. 21 August 1944. Collection of Roy Hopper.

"Lieutenant Earl Woodard Missing." *Our Visitor.* July 1944: 1.

"PVT. Roy Hopper Prisoner of Germans." *Our Visitor.* September 1944: 1.

"SGT. Kenneth C. Collier Killed in Action in France." *Our Visitor.* September 1944: 1.

"The War Close to Us." *Our Visitor.* December 1941: 2.

Ulio, J. A. Adjutant General. Letter to Margaret (Willbanks) Applegate. 22 May 1942. Collection of Margaret (Willbanks) Applegate.

Ulio, J. A. Major General. Letter to Margaret (Willbanks) Applegate. 18 June 1945. Printed in *Our Visitor.* August 1945: 3.

Waters, Beatrice (Patton). Letter to all relatives of POWs. Undated. Copy from Collection of Margaret (Willbanks) Applegate.

Willbanks, Elkanah. Postcard to Margaret (Willbanks) Applegate. 5 May 1944. Collection of Margaret (Willbanks) Applegate.

Willbanks, Elkanah. Postcard to Margaret (Willbanks) Applegate. Undated. Received 13 September 1943. Collection of Margaret (Willbanks) Applegate.

Woodard, Earl. *The B-17 of LaGoulafriere.* Unpublished story. 83 pages. Used with permission.

Chapter 6

Board of Trustees Minutes, 1946 through 1956. The School of the Ozarks. Board Records. College of the Ozarks.

Clark, Dr. M. Graham. Personal Interview. May 1994.

Dixon, Stanley. Personal Interview. 13 June 1995.

Good, Dr. R. M. Letter to Beulah Winfrey. 26 March 1948. Winfrey Collection, College of the Ozarks.

Good, Dr. R. M. Letter to John Swift. 8 April 1946. Board Records. College of the Ozarks.

Good, Dr. R. M. Letter to Lewis Wilkins Hyer. 6 October 1952. College of the Ozarks.

269

McDonald, J. M., Sr., *The Story of a School*. The School of the Ozarks. Undated.

Moreno, Frank. Letter and Notes to Jerry C. Davis. 27 September 2003. Unpublished.

Price, Richard G. and Bohling, Beth. *The J. M. McDonald Story.* Undated: 33.

Program of Dedication, Josephine Armstrong McDonald Hospital. 3 May 1951. College of the Ozarks archives.

"Report on Junior College Interview." April 13, 1953. Board of Trustees Minutes. College of the Ozarks.

Winfrey, Beulah (Gutridge). Personal Interview. 20 June 1995.

Chapter 7

Arbaugh, George B. "Report on College of The School of the Ozarks." 26 February 1965. College archives.

Board of Trustees Minutes, 1956 through 1967. The School of the Ozarks. Board Records. College of the Ozarks.

Evers, N. H. "Consultant's Report: School of the Ozarks." November 1965.

"Fiftieth Commencement Brought Many 'Firsts.'" *Ozark Visitor.* June 1958: 3.

"First College Graduates of The School of the Ozarks." *Ozark Visitor.* June 1958: 4.

Fry, G. Stanley. Personal Interview. 13 January 2006.

Hughey, Gary H. Letter to G. Stanley Fry. 14 May 1993. Collection of Stanley Fry.

Hyer, L. W. "Let's Help 'Em." *The Ozark Visitor.* November 1958: 8.

Lashly, Jacob M. "The Control of Power." Address for dedication of Williams Memorial Chapel. The School of the Ozarks, Point Lookout, Missouri. 1 May 1958.

Ledford, Joseph B. Letter to Board of Trustees, The School of the Ozarks. 10 December 1964.

Morisset, Judy (Mackey). Letter to Jerry C. Davis. 25 October 2005.

"Our Golden Anniversary...1906-1956" *Ozark Visitor.* January 1956:8-9.

Program of Dedication, The Williams Chapel and Hyer Bell Tower. 1 May 1958. The School of the Ozarks.

"Projection for the College of The School of the Ozarks, A Report." 1964-1970. Board Records. College of the Ozarks.

"Time of Beginning Again, The." *Ozark Visitor.* September 1956: 2.

Chapter 8

Alumni News. The School of the Ozarks. Summer 1975.

Blunt, Roy D. Certificate of Incorporating a General Not for Profit Corporation. Registered Name Change. 29 May 1986.

Board of Trustees Minutes, 1968 through 1987. The School of the Ozarks. Board Records. College of the Ozarks.

Brannan, Jerry D. Personal Interview. 26 February 1995.

Clark, M. Graham. "Statement of Dr. M. Graham Clark." *Ozark Visitor.* July 1975 Special Edition: 2.

Davidson, Mayburn. Personal Interview. February 2006.

Keeter, Howell W. Personal Interview. February 2006.

Ledford, Joseph B. *Religion on the Campus.* Point Lookout, Missouri. 8 October 1974.

Martin, Richard. "Hard Work U. At School of Ozarks, The Students Flunk Out If They Shirk Chores." *The Wall Street Journal.* 15 March 1973: 1.

Parnell, Ben A., Jr. Memo to Executive Committee of Board of Trustees. 27 May 1968. Board Records. College of the Ozarks.

"Proposal for Strengthening the Spiritual Growth Objectives of The School of the Ozarks." September 1973. Written by Campus Minister to Students.

Wortman, Gary L. Personal Interview. 6 June 1994.

Chapter 9

Basore, Harry H. "Charge to Dr. Jerry Davis." Matriculation Convocation. 25 August 1988.

Basore, Harry H. "Matriculation Convocation Welcome." Matriculation Convocation. 25 August 1988.

Berger, Frances C. Letter to Jerry C. Davis, 15 December 1989. College of the Ozarks.

Board of Trustees Minutes, 1988-1992 College of the Ozarks. Board Records.

Clark, Christopher. "College of Ozarks Simmers Over President's Power." *Springfield News-Leader.* 19 April 1992: 1A, 8A.

Clark, Christopher. "Storm Gathers Over College As Discontent Goes to Court." *Springfield News-Leader.* 19 April 1992: 8A.

Clark, Christopher. "Work Schools Made Him, Davis Says. Education, Career Began at Similar Institution." *Springfield News-Leader.* 19 April 1992: 8A.

Crockett, Dan. "Administration to 'Reinterpret' Dress Code." *The Outlook.* 25 April 1991: 1.

Davis, Jerry C. Notes/Recollections during President George H. W. Bush's visit. August 1992.

Davis, Jerry C. Personal Statement. 14 December 1987.

Hoy, Martha. "C of O Appearance Policy to Remain." *Branson Beacon.* 15 May 1991: 1-2.

John Templeton Foundation *Honor Roll for Character Building Colleges 1990.* 24-25.

John Templeton Foundation *Honor Roll for Free Enterprise Teaching for 1990.* 8, 10.

Katzenell, Michelle B. "S of O Chief Trims Budget $2.5 Million." *Springfield News-Leader.* 26 April 1989: 1B, 2B.

Katzenell, Michelle B. "S of O President Appears Casual, Sets High Goals." *Springfield News-Leader.* 9 October 1988: 1B, 2B.

Keeter, Howell W. Personal Interview. February 2006.

Matriculation Convocation Program. Nettie Marie Jones Auditorium. College of the Ozarks. 25 August 1988.

Morgan, Linda. "C of O Commuting Students File Lawsuit." *Branson Daily News.* 8 February 1992: 1-2.

Olson, Kenton C. Personal Interview. 16 June 2006.

Price, Karla. "Californian Gives $10 Million in Trust to College of Ozarks." *Springfield News-Leader.* 26 October 1990: 1A, 10A.

Raley, Ruth. Personal Interview. 13 June 2006.

Secretary of State Document "Registration of Fictitious Name: College of the Ozarks" for The School of the Ozarks. 30 April 1990.

"S of O Reports Record Enrollment." *Branson Beacon.* 14 September 1989: 5A.

U.S. News & World Report. America's Best Colleges. 1990 College Guide (Revised). 16 October 1989: 77, 81.

U.S. News & World Report. America's Best Colleges 1990 (Revised): 23, 49, 69.

Chapter 10

AAPL. "A List of Decisions Under Jerry Davis, President of College of the Ozarks Since 1988, and Other Events." November 1994.

AAPL Officer. Letter to Dr. Jerry C. Davis. 28 March 1995.

AAUP Associate Secretary. Letter to Dr. Jerry C. Davis. 29 March 1995.

Associate Director, the College's accrediting agency. Letter to President of College of the Ozarks. 27 September 1995.

Board of Trustees Minutes, 1993 through 1996. Board Records. College of the Ozarks.

Cage, Mary Crystal. "AAUP Dispute." *The Chronicle of Higher Education.* 17 November 1995: A23, A24.

Clark, Christopher. "Professors' Group to Investigate C of O." *Springfield News-Leader.* 15 April 1995: 1A, 6A.

Clark, Christopher. "C of O Alumni Join Others in Call for Davis' Resignation." *Springfield News-Leader.* 20 July 1994: 1A.

Clark, Christopher. "C of O Dropping Federal Student Loans." *Springfield News-Leader.* 16 June 1994: 1B, 3B.

Clark, Christopher. "Reason for Nonrenewal Still Hidden." *Springfield News-Leader.* 24 February 1994: 1B, 4B.

Clark, Christopher. "Teacher Didn't Fit, Was Devious, Say School Officials." *Springfield News-Leader.* 25 February 1994.

Clark, Christopher. "Former Professor Loses Suit Against C of O." *Springfield News-Leader.* 26 February 1994.

Davis, Jerry C. Letter to Associate Director of College's accrediting agency. 20 June 1995.

Davis, Jerry C. Letter to Association Secretary AAUP. 22 March 1995.

Davis, Jerry C. Letter to Association Secretary AAUP. 7 April 1995.

Distinguished Visiting Professor. "...only got two things right in letter." Letter to editor. *Branson Daily News.* 18 October 1995.

Department of Elementary and Secondary Education (DESE) letter to Dr. Ray Gibson. 17 March 1995.

Department of Elementary and Secondary Education (DESE) letter to President Jerry C. Davis. 11 July 1994. College of the Ozarks files.

Drury College Chairman of Faculty Affairs Committee. Letter to Dr. Jerry C. Davis. 15 February 1994.

Hansen, Sara B. "C of O Brings Home $53 Million in 5 Years." *Springfield News-Leader.* 30 May 1994: 1A, 8A.

Hendrix, Wiley. "North Central Likes C of O." *The Outlook.* 13 October 1995: 1.

Hohenfeldt, R. D. "College President Thumbs His Nose at Big Brother." Editorial. *Rolla Daily News.* 17 June 1994: 4A.

Hohenfeldt, R. D. "Three Cheers for College of the Ozarks." Editorial. *Rolla Daily News.* 27 May 1993: 4A.

Hopper, John. "On the Dark Side: College of the Ozarks." *Missouri Academe.* Spring 1994: 3-4.

Hoy, Martha. "Market Will Determine Desirability of Entertainers' Material." *Branson Beacon.* 28 May 1993.

John Templeton Foundation *1995-1996 Honor Roll for Character Building Colleges.* "College of the Ozarks." pp. 183-185.

Leatherman, Courtney. "Abolition of Tenure Rattles Faculty at College of the Ozarks." *The Chronicle of Higher Education.* 26 January 1994: A18.

Letters (writer names not disclosed) 5 August 1993 (FL); 29 May 1993 (AR); 9 June 1993 (NE); 30 May 1993 (WI); 28 May 1993 (TX); 28 May 1993 (MO); 27 May 1993 (MO); 4 June 1993 (IL).

Letters to the Editor (writer undisclosed, CA, MT) 9 June 1993. *Branson Daily News.*

Letters to the Editor (writer undisclosed, Springfield, Cabool, Springfield, and Hollister, MO) 29 May 1993 and 1 June 1993. *Springfield News-Leader.*

Letter to the Editor (writer undisclosed). "Second Wayne Newton Show Full of Garbage, Offensive Language." *Branson Daily News.* 21 May 1993: 4.

Letter to the Editor (writer undisclosed). "C of O Needs to Make Some Changes in Modus Operandi." *Branson Daily News.* 8 October 1995.

McGee, Mike. "AAUP Visit Deemed 'Futile.'" *Branson Daily News.* 2 May 1995: 1A, 2A.

McMahon, Donald P. "College of Ozarks:...doesn't speak for all faculty." Letter to the Editor. *Springfield News-Leader.* 7 February 1994.

Money Guide, Best College Buys Now. 1994 Edition. 73.

North, Oliver. "Commitment, Trust and Family." Public Address. Patriotic Convocation. College of the Ozarks. 25 October 1993.

North, Oliver. Program, Patriotic Convocation. College of the Ozarks. 25 October 1993.

Oeschsle, Kathy. "'No Thanks,' C of O Head Tells Newton." *Springfield News-Leader.* 27 May 1993: 1.

(Southwest) Missouri State University Faculty Senate. Letter to Dr. Jerry C. Davis. 17 February 1994.

"Tit for Tat." *The Chronicle of Higher Education.* 12 May 1995: A19.

U.S. News & World Report. America's Best Colleges 1994: 67.

U.S. News & World Report. 3 October 1994: 80.

"Wayne's World." *USA Today.* 28 May 1993: 1D.

Winkler, Alicia. "College Discontinues Teacher Tenure." *The Outlook.* 9 December 1993: 1.

Winkler, Alicia. "Colonel Oliver North Speaks for College Convocation; Stresses Heritage of Nation and His Vision for America." *Ozark Visitor.* Winter 1993: 6-7.

Chapter 11

Associated Press, John Rogers. "College's Tuition: Backbreaking Work." *The Valley Press,* Lancaster, California. February 1998: B1, B6.

Associated Press, John Rogers. "Hard Labor Isn't So Bad." Florida *Fort Myers News-Press.* 12 February 1998: 8A.

Associated Press, John Rogers. "At College of Ozarks, Hard Work Is the Rule." *The Arizona Daily Star.* 16 February 1998: 1A, 12A.

Associated Press, John Rogers. "Ozark Students Really Work Their Way Through College." *The Denver Post.* 14 February 1998: 33A.

Associated Press, John Rogers. "Really Working Way Through College. Ozarks Students Don't Pay, They Toil." *Richmond Times-Dispatch.* Richmond, Virginia. February 1998.

Associated Press, John Rogers. "This Is Hard Work U." *The Post-Standard.* Fulton, New York. 12 February 1998: A9.

Associated Press, John Rogers. "Admission to College Paid in Labor." *Hawaii Tribune-Herald.* 13 February 1998: 7.

Associated Press, John Rogers. "College in the Ozarks: the Price of Admission Is Backbreaking Labor." *Potomac News,* Woodbridge, Virginia.

Associated Press, John Rogers. "College Promotes Work, Discourages Debt." *The San Juan Star.* 12 February 1998: 31.

Associated Press, John Rogers. "No Tuition at 'Hard Work U'". *The Times* (Bay Area, CA). 12 February 1998: A19.

Associated Press, John Rogers. "At 'Hard Work U,' Jobs Required in Lieu of Tuition." *San Francisco Chronicle.* 24 February 1998.

Associated Press, John Rogers. "This College's Tuition Is Free, but It Doesn't Come Without Cost." *Maine Sunday Telegram.* 15 February 1998: 2.

Board of Trustees Minutes, 1996-1998. College of the Ozarks. Board Records.

Buckstaff, Kathryn. "'Teacher's Can't Educate Alone,' Bush says" "Bush/Former First Lady Presents Teacher Awards." *Springfield News-Leader.* 12 April 1996, 1A, 5A.

Buckstaff, Kathryn. "4,500 hear 'Iron Lady' Thatcher speak." *Springfield News-Leader.* 22 February 1997:1.

Bush, Barbara. "Honor Teachers" Public Address. Convocation. College of the Ozarks. Point Lookout, Missouri. 11 April 1996.

Bush, Barbara. Program, "Honor Teachers" Convocation. College of the Ozarks. Point Lookout, Missouri. 11 April 1996.

Bush, Barbara. Program, "Honor Teachers" Banquet. College of the Ozarks. Point Lookout, Missouri. 11 April 1996.

Davis, Jerry C. Notes from McKibben visit. 9 December 1997.

Department of Elementary and Secondary Education (DESE) letter to President Jerry C. Davis. 11 July 1994.

Dole, Mrs. Elizabeth. "An America We Can Be" Public Address. Community Service Community Convocation. College of the Ozarks. Point Lookout, Missouri. 1 November 1997.

Dole, Mrs. Elizabeth. Program, Community Service Community Convocation. College of the Ozarks. Point Lookout, Missouri. 1 November 1997.

Dole, Mrs. Elizabeth. Program, Community Service Banquet. College of the Ozarks. Point Lookout, Missouri. 1 November 1997.

Figzgerald, Pat. "Elizabeth Dole Visits College of the Ozarks." *Ozark Visitor.* Winter 1998: 5.

Halverson, Pat. "Thatcher Calls for Return to Values." *Branson Daily News.* 22 February 1997: 1A, 2A.

Harvey, Paul. "The Rest of the Story." July 1998.

Jesse, Lynda. Personal Interview. 11 June 2006.

Kaplan Newsweek How to Get Into College. "College of the Ozarks." 1998 edition. p. 150.

Keeter, James P. Personal Interview. 22 April 2006.

Keeter Center (The) for Character Education. Publication booklet. College of the Ozarks, Point Lookout, MO.

Lenk, Kerry. "C of O on the Road: My Russian Experience--The Chance of a Lifetime." *Ozark Visitor.* Summer 1996: 6, 7.

Peterson, Dawn. "C of O Celebrates Patriotism." *Springfield News-Leader.* 7 July 1996.

Sturdivan, Jenifer. "Lady Thatcher Visit a Success." *The Outlook.* 28 February 1997: 1.

Thatcher, Lady Margaret. "Challenges Facing the 21st Century." Public Address. Free Enterprise and the Work Ethic Community Convocation. College of the Ozarks, Point Lookout, Missouri. 21 February 1997.

Thatcher, Lady Margaret. Program, Free Enterprise and the Work Ethic Community Convocation. College of the Ozarks. Point Lookout, Missouri. 21 February 1997.

Thatcher, Lady Margaret. Program, Leadership Banquet. College of the Ozarks. Point Lookout, Missouri. 21 February 1997.

U.S. News & World Report. America's Best Colleges 1998: 64, 83, 96.

U.S. News & World Report. Special Report. 7 September 1998: 81.

Chapter 12

Aguayo, Katherine. "Tom Brokaw Honors the Greatest Generation: Shaping the Future...by Honoring the Past." *Ozark Vistior.* Winter 2006: 8-9.

Aguayo, Katherine and Andrews, Elizabeth. "Zell Miller: The Gates of Opportunity." *Ozark Visitor.* Summer 2006: 6-7.

"All Things Considered." National Public Radio. 10 November 2003.

"America's Real Defense Is the Character of its Citizenry." *The Keeter Report.* Summer 2004: 1-2.

Associated Press. "Schwarzkopf Exhorts Crowd to 'Take Charge.'" "Leadership Focus of Missouri Speech." 14 October 1998.

Associated Press. "Soldier Gets Diploma 57 Years Late." *Southeast Missourian.* Cape Girardeau, Missouri. 9 October 2000.

Bailey, Eric. "Bank on It: C of O in Title Game." *Springfield News-Leader.* 14 March 2000: 2C.

Baker, James. "America's Role in the World After the Terrorist Attack." Public Address. Leadership: Leonard B. and Edith Gittinger Community Convocation. College of the Ozarks. Point Lookout, Missouri. 4 October 2001.

Baker, James. Leadership: Leonard B. and Edith Gittinger Community Convocation Program. College of the Ozarks. Point Lookout, Missouri. 4 October 2001.

Baker, James. Leadership Banquet Program. College of the Ozarks, Point Lookout, Missouri. 4 October 2001.

Barron's Best Buys in College Education, fourth edition. 2002. pp. 308-310.

Board of Trustees Minutes, 1996-2006. College of the Ozarks. Board Records.

"Bobcat Title Run: Championship U." DVD. College of the Ozarks. 2006.

Bowlin, Bruce W. "Security 'Tightest Ever' for Netanyahu Address." *Branson Daily Independent.* 4-5 October 2002: 1, 2.

Brokaw, Tom. "The Greatest Generation." Public Address. The Leonard B. and Edith Gittinger Community Convocation: Shaping the Future by Honoring the Past. College of the Ozarks, Point Lookout, Missouri. 10 November 2005.

Brokaw, Tom. Program, The Leonard B. and Edith Gittinger Community Convocation: Shaping the Future by Honoring the Past. College of the Ozarks, Point Lookout, Missouri. 10 November 2005.

Brokaw, Tom. Program, Character Banquet. College of the Ozarks, Point Lookout, Missouri. 10 November 2005.

Buckstaff, Kathryn. "C of O Tells Its Leader Goodbye." *Springfield News-Leader.* 20 March 2001.

Buckstaff, Kathryn. "'War Unlike Any Before,' Baker says." *Springfield News-Leader.* 5 October 2001: 1B.

Buckstaff, Kathryn. "The Kids Needed These Buildings." *Springfield News-Leader.* 7 February 2002: 1B, 3B

Buckstaff, Kathryn. "Saddam and Arafat Must Go." *Springfield News-Leader.* 4 October 2002.

Buckstaff, Kathryn. "Tough Talk and Humor from Army General," "Two Men Who Died in Iraq Honored." *Springfield News-Leader.* 15 April 2005: 1B, 8B.

Carman, Krystal. "'Soldier's Soldier' Shares Experience." *Branson Daily News.* April 2005.

"Character, Convictions You Will Fight For--Even Die For." *The Keeter Report.* December 2002: 1-2.

"Coach K: With Hard Work Comes Dignity." *The Keeter Report.* Winter 2004: 1-3.

"College of the Ozarks Has First Fulbright Scholar." *The Republic Monitor* (Missouri). 2 May 2002.

"College of the Ozarks Named One of Best Buys in the Nation." *Ozark Visitor.* Winter 1997: 5.

Colleges That Encourage Character Development. Philadelphia: John Templeton Foundation, 1999: 38, 299.

"Everybody Visits College of the Ozarks." *Insight on the News.* October 29-November 11, 2002. Inside cover.

Ford, Gerald. "Remarks by President Gerald R. Ford." Public Address. Citizenship Forum. College of the Ozarks, Point Lookout, Missouri. 11 April 2000.

Ford, Gerald. Program, Citizenship Forum. College of the Ozarks. Point Lookout, Missouri. 11 April 2000.

Ford, Gerald. Program, Citizenship Forum Banquet. College of the Ozarks. Point Lookout, Missouri. 11 April 2000.

"Franklin Graham Speaks at College of the Ozarks." *The Keeter Report.* December 1999: 1.

Franks, Tommy. "Character, Citizenship, Values and the American Dream." Public Address. The Willard and Pat Walker Character Forum. College of the Ozarks, Point Lookout, Missouri. 14 April 2005.

Franks, Tommy. Program, The Willard and Pat Walker Character Forum. College of the Ozarks, Point Lookout, Missouri. 14 April 2005.

Franks, Tommy. Program, Character Banquet. College of the Ozarks, Point Lookout, Missouri. 14 April 2005.

Furman, Courtney. Personal Interview. 16 June 2006.

"General Colin Powell Speaks at C of O: Emphasizes Patriotism, Character to Packed House," "Colin Powell Honors Three Distinguished Generals for Military Careers in Marines, Air Force, Army," "One Man's Heroism," "General Colin Powell Visits C of O in October: An Inspiring Evening with an Inspiring Man." *Ozark Visitor.* Winter 2001: 3, 5, 6-9, 15.

"General Colin L. Powell Visits College of the Ozarks." *The Keeter Report.* December 2000.

"General Tommy Franks Visits College of the Ozarks," "An American Hero, Scott O'Grady, Speaks to Forum Participants." *The Keeter Report.* Summer 2005: 1-5.

"Gerald R. Ford Urges Responsible Citizenship." *The Keeter Report.* June 2000.

Graham, Ellen. "Promises from a Stranger." *The Wall Street Journal.* 19 May 1999: B1, B6.

Graham, Franklin. "Christianity on Campus." Public Address. Leonard B. and Edith Gittinger Community Convocation. College of the Ozarks. Point Lookout, Missouri. 25 October 1999.

Graham, Franklin. Program, Christianity on Campus: Leonard B. and Edith Gittinger Community Convocation. College of the Ozarks. Point Lookout, Missouri. 25 October 1999.

Graham, Franklin. Program, Christian Missions Banquet. College of the Ozarks. Point Lookout, Missouri. 25 October 1999.

"Hard Work U: The Incredible College of the Ozarks." *Christian Observer.* October 2000: 1, 11, 12.

Harvey, Paul. Noon radio address. 17 March 2003.

Hendrix, Wiley. "Economic Impact of Tourney to Be in Millions." *Branson Daily News.* 26 March 1999.

Howell, Camille. "C of O Named to Unprecedented Five Categories in Templeton Honor Roll." *The Outlook.* 12 November 1999.

Insight on the News. The Washington Times. "Insight's Top 15 Colleges." 9 September 2002: 11.

John Templeton Foundation 1995-1996 Honor Roll For Character-Building Colleges. pp.183-185.

Kaplan Newsweek, How to Get Into College. "College of the Ozarks." 2002 edition. p. 194.

Keeter Center (The). Program of Dedication. College of the Ozarks. 15 April 2005.

Krzyzewski, Mike. "Victory Through Teamwork and Leadership." Public Address. Leadership: Leonard B. and Edith Gittinger Community Convocation. College of the Ozarks, Point Lookout, Missouri. 21 September 2004.

Krzyzewski, Mike. Program, Leadership: Leonard B. and Edith Gittinger Community Convocation. College of the Ozarks, Point Lookout, Missouri. 21 September 2004.

Krzyzewski, Mike. Program, Leadership Banquet. College of the Ozarks, Point Lookout, Missouri. 21 September 2004.

Letter from student in Centennial Graduating Class "Janelle." 2006. College of the Ozarks.

Kipp, Samuel M., III, Price, Derek V., and Wohlford, Jill K. "Affordability Ratings for Missouri's Admissible Institutions by Type and Control." Lumina Foundation for Education New Agenda Series. January 2002.

McNelis, Raven. "Character Camp: Getting the Recipe Right for Higher Education from the Very Start." *Ozark Visitor.* Fall 2001: 8-9.

Miller, Zell. "The American Work Ethic: The Gates of Opportunity." Public Address. The O. Wayne Rollins Work Ethic Forum. College of the Ozarks, Point Lookout, Missouri. 6 April 2006.

Miller, Zell. Program, The O. Wayne Rollins Work Ethic Forum. College of the Ozarks, Point Lookout, Missouri. 6 April 2006.

Miller, Zell. Program, Forum Banquet. College of the Ozarks, Point Lookout, Missouri. 6 April 2006.

Morgan, Linda. "Blaze Destroys Building." *Taney County Times.* 31 January 2001.

Netanyahu, Benjamin. "Terrorism: How the Constitutional Democracies Can Win." Public Address. Leadership & Service: Leonard B. and Edith Gittinger Community Convocation. College of the Ozarks. Point Lookout, Missouri. 3 October 2002.

Netanyahu, Benjamin. Program, Leadership and Service: Leonard B. and Edith Gittinger Community Convocation. College of the Ozarks. Point Lookout, Missouri. 3 October 2002.

Netanyahu, Benjamin. Program, Leadership and Service Banquet. College of the Ozarks. Point Lookout, Missouri. 3 October 2002.

Nolan, Pat. "Ford Speaks to Students." *Branson Daily News.* 13 April 2000: 1A, 2A.

Powell, Colin. "Management in Crisis and Change" Public Address. Patriotism: Leonard B. and Edith Gittinger Community Convocation. College of the Ozarks. Point Lookout, Missouri. 2 October 2000.

Powell, Colin. Program, Patriotism: Leonard B. and Edith Gittinger Community Convocation. College of the Ozarks. Point Lookout, Missouri. 2 October 2000.

Powell, Colin. Program, Patriotic Convocation Banquet. College of the Ozarks. Point Lookout, Missouri. 2 October 2000.

Schwarzkopf, Norman. "Leadership: From the War Room to the Board Room" Public Address. Character and Leadership Community Convocation. College of the Ozarks. Point Lookout, Missouri. 13 October 1998.

Schwarzkopf, Norman. Program, Character and Leadership Community Convocation. College of the Ozarks. Point Lookout, Missouri. 13 October 1998.

Schwarzkopf, Norman. Program, Character and Leadership Banquet. College of the Ozarks. Point Lookout, Missouri. 13 October 1998.

Sevier, Robert. "Get Ink." *University Business.* December 2002: 16.

Strategic Plan 2003-2013. College of the Ozarks.

"Tom Brokaw Visits College of the Ozarks." *The Keeter Report.* Winter 2006: 2-5.

"Top Private Colleges & Universities" (MO-KS). *Ingram's Kansas City's Business Magazine.* June 2002:46.

U.S. News & World Report. America's Best Colleges 2002: 58, 96, 102.

U.S. News & World Report. 30 September 2002: 104, 106.

Watts, J. C. "Citizens Across the Country." Public Address. The John N. and Ella C. Marsh Citizenship Forum. College of the Ozarks, Point Lookout, Missouri. 8 April 2004.

Watts, J. C. Program, The John N. and Ella C. Marsh Citizenship Forum. College of the Ozarks, Point Lookout, Missouri. 8 April 2004.

Watts, J. C. Program, The John N. and Ella C. Marsh Citizenship Banquet. College of the Ozarks, Point Lookout, Missouri. 8 April 2004.

Winfrey, Beulah. Memorial Service Program. College of the Ozarks. 21 September 2000.

Wood, Cody. "Bobcat 'Glory Road.'" *Ozark Visitor.* Spring 2006: 8-10.

"Work Is Love Made Visible." *Kansas City Ingram's Magazine.* September 2002.